Praise for Dana Stabenow's acclaimed
Liam Campbell mysteries

Better to Rest

"A taut, pleasingly complicated idyll."   —*Kirkus Reviews*

"Campbell makes an engaging hero, one who bids fair to become as popular as Kate Shugak, the heroine of Stabenow's other, long-running series."—*Publishers Weekly*

Nothing Gold Can Stay

"Brisk [and] satisfying . . . lively."   *Houston Chronicle*

"Exciting . . . [Stabenow] improves with each outing and is in ever-more control of her characters and stories."
—*The Dallas Morning News*

So Sure of Death

"As good as it gets—among the best of the year."—*Booklist*

"Has the vivid descriptions, rich characterization, and compelling plot that distinguish her Kate Shugak books. . . . Colorful characters abound."   —*Publishers Weekly*

Fire and Ice

"Every time I think Dana Stabenow has gotten as good as she can get, she comes up with something better. Campbell is a delightful character, already fully formed in the skilled, inventive mind of Miss Stabenow, and meeting him is a pleasure. Please, Miss Stabenow, give us more."   —*The Washington Times*

"Exciting . . . a mystery that's still thickening when most authors would be calling it a day."   —*Kirkus Reviews*

Also by Dana Stabenow

The Liam Campbell series

FIRE AND ICE
SO SURE OF DEATH
NOTHING GOLD CAN STAY

The Kate Shuqak series

A COLD DAY FOR MURDER
A FATAL THAW
DEAD IN THE WATER
A COLD-BLOODED BUSINESS
PLAY WITH FIRE
BLOOD WILL TELL
BREAKUP
KILLING GROUNDS
HUNTER'S MOON
MIDNIGHT COME AGAIN
THE SINGING OF THE DEAD
A FINE AND BITTER SNOW
A GRAVE DENIED

The Star Svensdotter series

SECOND STAR
A HANDFUL OF STARS
RED PLANET RUN

DANA STABENOW

BETTER TO REST

A LIAM CAMPBELL MYSTERY

A SIGNET BOOK

SIGNET
Published by New American Library, a division of
Penguin Group (USA) Inc., 375 Hudson
Street, New York, New York 10014, U.S.A.
Penguin Books Ltd, 80 Strand,
London WC2R 0RL, England
Penguin Books Australia Ltd, 250 Camberwell Road,
Camberwell, Victoria 3124, Australia
Penguin Books Canada Ltd, 10 Alcorn Avenue,
Toronto, Ontario, Canada M4V 3B2
Penguin Books (N.Z.) Ltd, Cnr Rosedale and Airborne Roads,
Albany, Auckland 1310, New Zealand

Penguin Books Ltd, Registered Offices:
80 Strand, London WC2R 0RL, England

Published by Signet, an imprint of New American Library,
a division of Penguin Group (USA) Inc. Previously published in a
New American Library hardcover edition.

First Signet Printing, September 2003
10 9 8 7 6 5 4 3 2 1

For Susan B. English,
my first and still my favorite librarian

ACKNOWLEDGMENTS

My thanks to the Literary Ladies of Anchorage, Alaska, for their (until now) unwitting loan of their name to the book club described herein, which is at best only a pale imitation of the magnificent original.

During World War II, 8,094 American-built aircraft were ferried up through Canada to Nome and Krasnoyarsk, many of them the ubiquitous and much-beloved Gooney Bird flown by Amerian crews. The story about the medevac comes from an account by Lt. Alta Mae Thompson, 805th Medical Air Evacuation Squadron, of a trip she made in September 1943 from Elmendorf to Dutch Harbor and back. They were heroes all.

Thanksgiving, 1941

Turkey and stuffing in the mess. It was awful. The cook runs a laundry in Memphis Tennessee in civilian life. He says he told them that when he signed up and doesnt know how he got assigned to be a cook. Typical army situation normal all fucked up.

It never gets this cold in Birmingham. There arnt any hangars so the mechanics are working on the aircraft right out in the snow. There arent any quarters either just tents and theyve got these heaters like big bunsen burners that keep catching the tents on fire. Ive only been here two weeks and in that time three tents have burnt down. A guy on one of the other crews got burnt pretty bad and everybodys scared of the tents and the heaters but theres nowheres else to go. Were all glad to get in the air. Its cold in the cockpit of a Gooney Bird but it aint as cold as it is on the ground.

I got a letter from Helen. Shes pregnant. We were so careful I dont know what happened. I dont know what Im going to do my pay isnt enough to pay for a kid. I could get promoted pretty soon though if Roepke doesnt get us kilt first. That would mean more pay not much but some. Ive got to figure out a way to get more money home. I joined up so I could provide for us and they send me to Alaska. I still cant believe it.

I better hide this log I dont want anybody else reading it. But I have to tell someone what Im thinking even if its only my own self and I cant write the truth to Helen because of the censers. Ill keep it in my flightsuit. I never take it off its too cold.

ONE

"I'm a vampire."

"Of course you are," Diana Prince said.

"I suck blood."

"Of course you do."

The young woman sitting on the other side of Diana Prince's desk was thin to the point of emaciation, with sharp cheekbones emphasized by fine, black, almost certainly dyed hair sleeked into a severe knot at the back of her head. Her eyebrows, eyelids and lips were painted black, and she wore a high-necked, long-sleeved, ankle-length dress of some dense fabric that seemed to suck up all the available light, which, considering that the ceiling of the post was wall-to-wall fluorescent tubing, was quite a trick. Maybe she really was a vampire.

Then again, Diana was well into overtime, after a day of duty that had had its moments, highlighted by the disarming of an enraged father bent on avenging the defloration of his seventeen-year-old daughter by her fisherman boyfriend, who was a little less than six months older than she was. It was also the last day of what had proven to be a labor-intensive week. Maybe it was just that she was tired, and about to fall face-forward into the now cold bean burrito sitting on her desk.

"Officer Prince," the vampire said, leaning forward in her chair, every line of her gaunt body taut with earnest sincerity, "I don't want to hurt anyone else. So if you will . . ." She proffered the items in her lap in mute appeal.

Diana eyed what looked like a leathercrafter's rubber mallet and a wooden stake that appeared to have been carved from the limb of a very dead spruce, and gave an inward sigh.

From what she could hear, her boss was doing a lot better than she was, and he looked like he was in love.

"So there I was, arms around four bags full of groceries, and coming out of the store I see this guy breaking into my car."

"And that was when you hit him with the jar of tomatoes," Alaska state trooper Sgt. Liam Campbell said, his gaze rapt.

"Sun-dried tomatoes," the woman sitting next to his desk said. She uncrossed and crossed her legs, rearranged the skirt of her blue-flowered housedress, fussed with a short, smooth cap of still-black hair, and smiled at Liam. "And no, or at least not then. I was going to hit him with the two-pound loaf of Tillamook sharp, but it just didn't seem hard enough to stop him. He is a pretty big guy."

They both turned to look at the six feet, five inches and two hundred twenty pounds of Guamanian male, by way of Chicago and Anchorage, handcuffed to the chair on the opposite side of the desk. He was bent over, his free hand cupping the left side of his face. His left eye was swollen shut with the beginnings of what looked to become a shiner of truly fabulous hue. The left shoulder of his blue T-shirt was stained a dark brown. He pulled his hand away from his face and looked at his bloody palm. "Fuck, man, how come you ain't arresting her? How come she ain't in the cuffs? She assaulted me! I'm wounded here, man! I'm bleeding!"

Liam opened a drawer and handed him a Wash'n Dri. "Here, Harvey, see if you can't clean yourself up a little. You look disgusting." He turned back to Mrs. Lydia Tompkins, a seventy-four-year-old housewife, mother of four, grandmother of two, who topped out at four-foot-eight and couldn't have weighed a hundred pounds wringing wet with six-pound lead weights strapped to each ankle. "So," he said, radiating a quiet joy, "instead of hitting him with the cheese, you hit him with the tomatoes—excuse me, the sundried tomatoes."

"Well, yes," said Mrs. Tompkins, "but not yet. I was going to hit him with the artichoke hearts, but it's an awfully big jar—did you want to see?"

"Absolutely," Liam said.

"Oh, fuck me, man, do I have to sit here and listen to this?"

"Shut up, Harvey," Liam said.

Harvey shut up. He was the bouncer at the Bay View Inn and he and Liam had already met professionally.

Mrs. Tompkins dove headfirst into one of the four paper shopping bags clustered at her feet. She upset her purse on the way down and a couple of coir rolled out. She pounced on them, holding them up to the light and squinting at them. She frowned. "No good," she said, and caught Liam's eye. "Except to spend."

She dove back into the shopping bag and emerged flushed and triumphant, jar of artichokes in hand. It was a big jar, Liam noted with respect, forty-eight ounces, and always assuming it hit its target, would have put a hell of a dent in Harvey's head. Funny how Harvey didn't look grateful for the reprieve.

"It was too big, I thought," Mrs. Tompkins said with the air of a woman who had right on her side and who knew it. "I mean, I didn't want to kill him; I just wanted to protect my property."

"Of course."

"There he was, breaking into my car, and that car's my property."

"Certainly."

"And I really didn't know how else to stop him."

"Perfectly understandable," Liam said. "So that was when you hit him with the sun-dried tomatoes."

"Yes," said Mrs. Tompkins, and fluttered her eyelashes. She was as taken with Liam as he was with her. "I was going to use the olive oil, but it was a plastic bottle. I figured it'd just bounce off, and then he'd probably hit me."

"Oh, man!" Harvey said, unable to resist. "You see how she's dissing me, man! Did I lift a finger to hurt this woman? Did I?" He appealed to the room at large. There was only Diana Prince and the vampire at the other desk, so the appeal failed. "No! Alls I'm doing is going to the store to buy some smokes and this . . . this feminazi comes along and brains me with a jar of love apples! I want a lawyer!"

"So," Liam said, entering a note in the case file, "*that* was when you hit him with the sun-dried tomatoes."

The jar in question was smaller than the jar of artichokes but larger than the loaf of Tillamook, all three lined up on Liam's desk. Liam liked the look of them. Mrs. Tompkins' arsenal.

"Yes." Mrs. Tompkins sat back in her chair, eyes bright with militant satisfaction. She crossed her legs again. For legs with that many miles on them, they still looked pretty good. Liam allowed himself an admiring glance. Mrs. Tompkins smiled at him again.

The phone on Diana's desk rang. "Excuse me a minute," she said to Dracula's bride, who gave the rubber mallet a dismissive wave, and raised the receiver. The steady voice of the dispatcher spoke without haste and to the point. "Okay, we'll be right there." She hung up and tried not to sound jubilant when she told Liam, "Sir, somebody tried to rip off the ATM machine down at Last Frontier."

"Again?" Liam was sorry to end the interview but duty called. "Mrs. Tompkins, we've got to go, but I want to say that it's been a real pleasure. We'll be in touch."

"Will I have to testify?" Mrs. Tompkins looked eager to do her civic duty.

The fierce, diminutive woman glowed with family values and middle-class morality and the Boy Scout oath, for crissake, a woman who was every prosecuting attorney's dream and every defense lawyer's nightmare. A slow smile spread across Liam's face. He would love to have her sworn in in front of Bill Billington. It was with real regret that he said, "I doubt it. I have a feeling the public defender will recommend a guilty plea. But I will certainly keep you informed on the progress of the case."

"Thank you." Mrs. Tompkins fluttered her eyelashes at him, gathered up her bags of groceries and marched out of the post on her first-class legs. Liam thought there ought to be a trumpet playing somewhere in the background, or at the very least, a round of applause.

"Come on, Harvey," Liam said, "we'll drop you off at the cop shop on our way."

"Oh, man, you can't put me back there! What are the rest of the guys going to say! Knocked on my ass by a little old lady with a bag of groceries! Campbell, come on, man, have some heart!" Then, when Liam uncuffed him from the chair and steered him toward the back door with a determined hand, he shouted, "I want to talk to my lawyer, goddamn it! I'm constitutionally entitled to a phone call!"

In the meantime, Dracula's bride waited with the calm certainty of one who knew she had eternity at her disposal for someone to put an end to her reign of terror.

TWO

"Poor bastard."

"Yeah, I guess."

"Whaddya mean, you guess? He just lost his wife of fifty years a year ago. He's allowed."

"Accent on the year ago. He was getting better there for a while; I don't know why he had to go off the deep end again." Bill used the bar towel to mop up the vomit around Eric Mollberg's head where it lay sleeping peacefully on the bar. "I oughta call Liam."

"Cut him some slack, woman. He's been picked up on D-and-D twice already this month."

"Yeah, well. He sits on the city council, for crying out loud."

"Guys on the city council can't get blind drunk when their wives die on them? You wouldn't get blind drunk if I died?"

Bill didn't have an answer for that, but the fact remained that Eric Mollberg had gone from city father to public nuisance in a downward spiral that had been dizzying to watch. Still, it was something else they could fight about, not that they had lacked for bones of contention to growl over in the past month. The events at Old Man Creek had taken a toll on both of them, Bill because Moses had been shot and Moses because he had lived. Amelia Gearhart had died. Young, wounded Amelia, scarred by neglectful parents, abused by her husband. Moses had been on a fair way to rescuing her, to breaking the cycle of abuse and setting her feet however shakily on the path to a different life, and then she was dead, shot to death by the same man who had tried to kill him, just when she had begun to learn how to live. Bill and Moses had been snapping and snarling at each other ever since they got back.

As testified to by Evan Gray, one of Bill's regular customers currently seated three stools down. He was also Newenham's main connection for dope. If you rolled your own, you went to the Moccasin Man (so called because he wore beaded buckskin from head to toe) for the best grade of Thunderfoot from Wasilla or Kona Gold from Hawaii. "Gets kind of tiresome, cleaning puke off the bar," he said. Evan was also a serious rounder, and he smiled at Bill Billington, happy to give her aid and comfort in her argument with Moses.

Moses Alakuyak, certified Alaskan old fart, only smiled, albeit his nastiest, dirtiest, most spawn-of-Satan smile. "Playing out of your league, sonny. She'd eat you alive."

Bill's spine stiffened and she glared at Moses. Never mind that they'd been lovers from the night of the day they had met. When he got proprietary she got her back up.

And even when he didn't. "I beg your pardon?" she said, her tone frosty.

"You can make your apology horizontally," Moses said. "Later."

The other patrons sitting at the bar roared their approval, including the women.

Bill slapped the bar towel down. "That's it, Alakuyak. Out. Out!"

He repeated his evil grin, only it was a lot more personal this time. He didn't leave, either, instead swaggering over to the jukebox. Moments later, Jimmy Buffett was singing about a smart woman in a real short skirt. Bill, her eagle's mane of white hair considerably ruffled, ignored him, and called Liam to come pry Eric Mollberg off her bar.

There was no answer. She left a message that should have melted down the voice-mail circuitry and slammed the phone into its cradle.

"Bad day?"

She looked up to see Wyanet Chouinard regarding her with a sympathetic eye. "Bad month," she said, casting a sidelong look at Moses, now regaling a tableful of other old farts with some yarn about a duel to the death with a king salmon the size of Moby Dick.

Wy followed her gaze. "I hate men," she said in agreement.

"Liam?"

"And Tim."

"What's wrong with Tim?"

Wy sat on a stool. "Nothing caning wouldn't cure."

Bill, startled out of her irritation, laughed. "Ship him off to Singapore, then." She pulled Wy an Alaskan Amber and set it on the bar in front of the pilot.

Wy took a long pull and said, "I can't do that. He'd

probably start a war, and then I'd have the State Department all over my ass."

They laughed together this time. "But seriously, folks," Bill said. "What's wrong with Tim? Usual teenage stuff?"

"That, too."

"What else?"

"I'm letting his mom see him. He hates her. And he hates me for making him see her." Wy took another long, soothing draft of beer, and regarded the mug with a weary kind of satisfaction. "The great thing about winter is that daylight decreases by five minutes and forty-four seconds a day and I can drink earlier every time I come in here."

"Yeah, you're such a heavy drinker, Chouinard."

"Sometimes I wish I were."

Bill looked at Moses over her head. "No, you don't."

Wy sighed. "No, I don't."

"How is Natalie behaving?"

"She's still sober," Wy said. "She's staying in town, renting a room from Tatiana Anayuk. Got herself a job bagging groceries at Eagle."

"She's living with Tasha?"

"Yeah, I know, the oldest established permanent floating party in Newenham. But they're cousins, and Natalie's pretty much broke. And like I said, she's still sober."

"She must go straight into her room and lock the door." Bill made Moccasin Man another margarita and sent a pitcher of beer over to Moses' table. The place was in its usual lull between the people-getting-off-work crowd and the people-coming-in-for-their-after-dinner-drink crowd, and she was able to return to Wy in a few moments. "Why did you do it?"

"Do what?" Wy said, startled out of her absorption with beer suds.

"Let Natalie see Tim."

Wy made a face. "I didn't really have a choice. The judge ordered visitation. Limited, supervised, but still."

"Bullshit," Bill said, speaking with all the authority of the magistrate she was. "You could have run her off. You still could. Why haven't you, if it's making the boy so miserable, and you miserable with it?"

Wy drank beer. Bill waited.

"She's his mother, Bill," Wy said at last. "She's got rights."

"Just because you didn't give birth to him doesn't make him any less your son. Crying out loud, Wy, I could tell you stories from now until next year about cases I've had before my court, parents aren't fit to keep a dog, much less a child. She's one of them."

"She is when she's drunk," Wy agreed. "Maybe if she stays here . . ."

"What? You going to give him back?"

Wy's head snapped up, her eyes narrowing.

"I didn't think so," Bill said, her voice very dry.

"It was right to let her see him. It was right for him to see her, so that he doesn't always remember her as the drunken monster who beat him. Damn it, Bill, it was the right thing to do!"

Bill sipped her Coke. "Want another beer?"

Wy looked at the bottom of her now empty glass. "No. I'm just trying to put off going home."

"Want some takeout?"

Wy brightened. Tim was notoriously susceptible to Bill's fatburgers and greasy fries. "Make it two, and a double order of fries for Tim."

Bill raised an eyebrow.

"Oh, all right," Wy said. "Three." Not that Liam Campbell deserved any special consideration in the way of meals. Or a roof. A roof it looked like he wouldn't be under for longer than it took to pack for a move back to Anchorage.

"Hey, big spender."

Wy looked around and a smile broke out across her face. It was a good smile; it displayed white teeth saved from perfection by overlapping incisors, crinkled the corners of her brown eyes, and seemed somehow to make her bronze-streaked brown hair curl out of its long braid even more than it already did. "Jo!"

The two women hugged. "What are you doing in Newenham?" Wy said. "I can't believe your editor let you come down again so soon. Is there some story going on around here I don't know about that the *Anchorage News* is crying out for copy on?"

"No, I just grabbed a couple of vacation days 'cause I could," Jo said. She was a chunky blonde with intense green eyes and a short cap of curls. A newspaper reporter with the wit of Dorothy L. Parker and none of the nastiness, she'd been Wy's closest friend since college and, for a few months, her sister-in-law. "Gary's back in Anchorage."

"Is he?"

"Yeah, he came down with me." Jo didn't look at Wy when she said this, thanking Bill for the draft beer instead. "Don't worry; we're not going to land our-selves on you—we've got a room at the Bay View. But we were hoping you'd have time for us."

"Sure," Wy said, and managed a smile. "Always time for you, Jo. And you wouldn't be landing your-selves on me, either one of you. So long as one of you doesn't mind sleeping on the floor."

Jo laughed. "Thanks, but no thanks."

"How about I order up a couple more hamburgers?"

"How about we eat right here and have a steak?"

Wy cocked an eyebrow at Bill, who shouted a can-cellation through the pass-through to the kitchen. Dot-tie, her fry cook, growled an acknowledgment and slammed the burger patties back into the fridge.

"Let me call Tim." Wy went to the pay phone in the corner and dialed her home number.

"Yeah?"

"Hey, Tim."

"Hi, Wy."

He had been calling her Mom right up until the first time she'd admitted Natalie to their home. "Jo's here, and her brother, Gary. We're going to have dinner at Bill's. I'll be there in ten."

She hung up and turned to Jo, standing just behind her. "Don't worry; he'll come. The combination of his favorite auntie and one of Bill's steaks will offset hav-ing to sit next to me."

Jo followed Wy out to her truck. "What's the prob-lem with Tim?"

Wy sighed. "It's not just Tim."

Jo went very still. "Liam?"

Wy nodded.

Jo bristled. "What's that prick up to now?"

Wy turned. "Why do you always automatically assume the worst about Liam, Jo?"

"Let's just say I stand on his record. He's always beating up on my best friend."

"He doesn't beat up on me."

"Emotionally he sure as hell does."

Wy was silent. Jo's fierce loyalty to the people she loved was one of her best qualities. It could also be one of her worst.

"What's wrong this time? His wife is still dead, isn't she?" Jo said in sudden suspicion. "He didn't go and get married again just so the two of you could have another hopeless love affair?"

"No, no, no," Wy said. "Cut him some slack, Jo, Jesus."

"He hurt you," Jo said. "What hurts you, hurts me. When I get hurt, I get pissed off. When I get pissed off, I get even. I'm not square with Liam yet."

"That why you brought Gary to Newenham with you?"

Jo ignored the question with a dignity that didn't look quite natural on her pugnacious face. "What's up, Wy? What's going on?"

Wy leaned back against the door of the truck. "You know this last case, the serial killer?"

"Hairy Man? Sure. He's still in jail, so far as I know. It's been a month. Got to be some kind of record."

Jo Dunaway's ideal Supreme Court would have had all the justices named Scalia, but then she was a reporter and had seen firsthand the evil that men do far too often. Had she but known it, Liam's ideal Supremes would all have been named Rehnquist. Wy thought about making the obvious comment but her courage failed her.

"Anyway," Jo said, "what's that got to do with anything?"

"John Barton, Liam's boss, called. Said Liam had done so well in Newenham that John was promoting him back to sergeant."

Jo digested this. "Wow. That was quick."

"It's partly your fault. You wrote that story with all those quotes making Liam sound like a hero."

Jo looked at her. "So you're not just pissed at Liam, you're pissed at me, too."

"Shit." Wy smoothed back the curls that had escaped the braid falling down her back. "I'm not, Jo. Really, I'm not. It's just that things were . . . It's not like we don't have other issues to deal with, you know? And now we've got to deal with this, too."

"Liam must feel like a yo-yo," Jo said.

"Yeah, well, apparently you're only disgraced in the Alaska state troopers so long as you're not clearing cases. When you are . . ."

"You're undisgraced. Back in favor. Back on the fast track," Jo said in sudden realization. "Okay. Got that. What else?"

"John offered him his old job back."

"His old job?"

"Uh-huh."

"His old job, as in, his old job in Anchorage?"

"Uh-huh."

"Oh."

"So you see."

"I sure do. Where can I buy a gun?"

"Jo."

"If he dumps you again, Wy, I swear I'll—"

"He didn't dump me last time; I dumped him."

"He could have left his wife, and he didn't."

"He had a baby son at the time. He couldn't leave both of them."

"He could if he'd loved you enough."

"He could if he was a total slimeball, Jo, and that wasn't the guy I fell for. Now knock it off. I'm done with that, and you should be, too."

A brief silence while Jo battled her baser self. "So what's he going to do?"

"I don't know."

Jo raised an eyebrow.

"What?" Wy said. She knew that eyebrow.

"You haven't asked him."

"He hasn't said."

"You haven't asked him?" Jo said, making it a question this time.

"I don't think he knows."

"You haven't asked him!"

Wy gave a quick glance around to see who was listening. "Stop yelling. He hasn't given John an answer, okay? And John asked almost a month ago."

"Ahuh. Well." Jo put her hands on her hips and surveyed Wy from head to toe. "Things must be pretty tense around the Chouinard household. You let Liam move in yet?"

Wy hunched a shoulder.

"Right. Why not?"

Wy didn't answer.

"Yeah," Jo said. "So, getting so much in the way of solid commitment from you, naturally he would leap at the chance to blow off his boss' offer of promotion and spend the rest of his life in Newenham."

Wy was as affronted at this turnabout on the part of her first, best friend as she had been annoyed at Jo's attack on Liam. "So now you're on his side?"

"Somebody has to be, poor bastard."

"Up yours, Dunaway."

"Backatcha times two," Jo said promptly. "Okay, enough with this. You go get Tim, I'll go get Gary, and don't worry, all will be well." She waved all-inclusive hands. "Leave it to me; Auntie Jo will fix everything."

"That's what I'm afraid of," Wy said, but she was saying it to Jo's back going away.

November 30, 1941

A C-47 came in today with the heat exchanger out. One of the passengers kept his feet warm with a blowtorch all the way from Watson Lake. Man Im glad I wasnt on board that flight.

The airstrip isnt even paved and everytime we land we kick dirt and ice up against the fuselage. I hope none of that stuff is making it up into the props or the engines.

To cold today to snow. Gray overcast about ten thousand feet. Saw a dozen moose laying next to a frozen river southwest of Anchorage. They looked like theyd laid down to die and I dint blame them but theres an old Eskimo guy who hangs around the base doing odd jobs for cash who says the moose are conserving energy and that they dont move around much in the winter.

He says hes a gold miner and that he sells it to Russians because their money is no good and they pay more than Americans will. He has to be careful because its illegal anymore for private citizens to own gold. Im wondering what the Russians buy the gold with if their money is no good but thats what he says.

THREE

Liam and Diana were still recovering from the fit of giggles caused by the vampire-disposal kit when they pulled up in front of the small square building with the Last Frontier Bank sign over the door. A burly man waited for them on the steps. He had a belly like a beer barrel, a head like a rectangular bullet, hair that stood up all over it in stiff white bristles, and a scowl carving lines into his cheeks and forehead. He wore button-fly jeans and a blue cashmere sweater with a button-down collar peeking out from underneath the crew neck. Liam suspected that the laces on his boots were ironed. "Brewster," he said as he stepped out of the white Chevy Blazer with the badge of his service emblazoned on its door.

The burly man gave a curt nod. "Campbell. Took your time getting here."

Liam felt rather than saw Diana stiffen. "We had some things to take care of at the post." He hitched up his gun belt. "Molly says somebody tried to steal your ATM again."

Brewster Gibbons, manager of Newenham's only

bank and general pain in the civic ass, watched Liam's hand settle on the butt of the nine-millimeter Smith & Wesson strapped to his right hip. "Yes."

Liam ambled forward to inspect the machine secured to the wall of the bank. Its corners were dented. Further investigation found a length of heavy galvanized chain tossed in a careless heap beneath the porch, as well as a horizontal burn in the right-hand upright of the porch railing, and two deep ruts in the driveway. The last two links of the chain were bent open, as if the chain had been made from clay. "Looks like someone tried to haul it off, all right."

In spite of its wounds, the machine's screen continued to flash advertisements for credit cards and car loans and home mortgages. Liam got out his wallet and inserted his cash card. Obediently, the machine spit out fifty dollars. "Although it doesn't seem to have hurt it much." He stuffed the cash into his wallet and the wallet back into his pocket. "My turn to cook dinner," he told the bank manager. "I'm thinking takeout chicken from the deli counter at Eagle."

Prince made a face. "I don't know, sir, that burrito I got from there was pretty awful. You might want to reconsider."

"What I want to know," Brewster said, his face tight and his eyes angry, "is what you intend to do about it."

"I don't know," Liam said. "Probably pick up some Maalox on my way through the checkout counter."

Brewster Gibbons took a visible breath, looked again at the hand resting on the gun butt, and bit back what he had been about to say.

A raven's soft croak sounded from a nearby tree, followed by a series of *click-click-click*s and *craaaa-ack*s.

A stiff breeze blew on shore from Bristol Bay, dropping the already crisp chill factor to a temperature close to freezing. After a summer's absence the stars had returned to the Alaskan sky, and Liam looked up to let the Big Dipper show him the way to the North Star.

Brewster stood it for as long as he could. "Well? Somebody tried to rob my bank! I want to know what you're going to do about this! When Anchorage finds out, they're going to want some answers, and they're going to be talking to our friends in Juneau!"

Diana Prince hadn't been working with Liam Campbell for even four months, but it was long enough to look at Brewster Gibbons and think, You poor dumb bastard. Every two years Brewster Gibbons contributed five hundred dollars to the campaign of anyone of the Democratic, Republican or Libertarian persuasion running for state office from the Newenham district and thought that bought him influence. It was the maximum amount allowed by law, as anyone in Alaska could have told him, and was standard operating procedure for any businessman covering his political bets. It hardly rated a thank-you note. But then, she'd always been something of a cynic when it came to politics.

Without ceasing communion with the celestial beings overhead, Liam said, "Trooper Prince? How many times has someone attempted to kidnap Mr. Gibbons' cash machine?"

"I believe this makes it four times, sir."

"Uh-huh. And the first time was, when, exactly?"

"That would be June. June sixth, I believe."

"Hmmm. And the method used?"

"The first time they wrapped an electrical cord around the machine and pulled. The cord snapped."

"I see. And the second?"

"The second time was eight days later, the fourteenth. This time they tried to open it up with a saw."

"A saw. Refresh my memory. What happened?"

"The blade snapped in two. Mr. Gibbons found pieces of it on the porch when he came in in the morning." She added, "The night before, a Ferdinand Volinario called to say that his shop had been broken into, and that he was missing some tools, including an electric Skilsaw."

"I'd forgotten all about Nando," Liam said. "Well done, Trooper Prince. And the third time?"

She hesitated just long enough to make it interesting. "We think a sledgehammer, sir, but we're not absolutely sure. The machine was pretty severely dented. You can still see some of the dents." She pointed.

Liam lowered his eyes to peer at the machine. "So you can." He laid hands on the machine and tried to rock it loose. It wouldn't budge. "Pretty sturdy piece of equipment," he told Gibbons, his tone congratulatory. "You've got it fastened down pretty solid, too."

"We can only hope they ripped their axle out," Prince said.

"Your security camera working yet?" Liam said.

Gibbons' flush was easy to see from the light over the door. "I need to pull it and send it to Anchorage to get it fixed."

"Yeah. Camera on the machine itself working yet?"

"Not since June."

"Uh-huh. Did you see anything yourself?"

Gibbons lost patience. "I didn't have to! It was

Teddy Engebretsen or John Kvichak or Paul Urbano or Mac MacCormick or one of that worthless bunch, or maybe the whole boiling lot of them together! You know it as well as I do! I want you to go over there and arrest them!"

"Did you see Teddy Engebretsen this evening, Brewster?" A brief silence. "Brewster? Did you see Teddy Engebretsen trying to kidnap your ATM machine?"

"No," Gibbons said, his face sullen.

"How about John Kvichak? No? Then Paul Urbano? Again no? Brewster, I know you watch a lot of television, with that fancy new satellite dish and all, so I know you have at least a speaking acquaintance with probable cause. Absent witnesses, absent evidence, I have no reason to suspect Teddy or John or Paul of anything except smoking a little dope at Tasha Anayuk's Saturday-night party." Not lately, anyway, he thought. "In the meantime, in spite of someone's best efforts, it doesn't look like your machine is going anywhere. Get your security cameras fixed or hire a security guard or both, and maybe we'll catch them in the act next time."

"Next time! I don't want there to be a next time! And where the hell am I supposed to hire a security guard in Newenham?"

"Job Service in Anchorage always has clients looking for employment," Liam said, and tipped his flat-brimmed Mountie hat in grave salute on his way back to the Blazer.

"Job Service! Sure, if I wanted to hire a moron who—" The rest of Brewster Gibbons' words were cut off when Liam's door closed.

"All the same," Prince said when he put it in gear, "it probably was Teddy or John or Paul. Or Art Inga and Dave Iverson. Or—"

"Probably," Liam agreed. "Which is why we're going over to John's to say hi."

"Did I mention that I have a hot date tonight?" Prince wondered out loud. "And that I'm already late?"

"Did I mention that so do I, and so am I, and that I've got a better chance of getting laid at the end of it than you do?" Liam said, wondering if it was true.

"Just a passing comment," Prince said, and slumped in her seat with a sigh.

Liam pulled out onto the road and put the Blazer into a skid over the icy ruts. The road looked like his life. He hit the gas and powered out of the skid, the rear wheels missing the ditch by a hair. Next to him Prince let out a pent-up breath.

Things had cooled off considerably between Liam and Wy since John Barton's offer to bring Liam back to Anchorage. It was the difference between fire and ice, and ice, as the poet foretold, for destruction was also great and would suffice. He knew it was partly his fault; he was holding both Wy and Tim in limbo, which made him feel guilty. He was pissing off John Barton, too, who was calling on average once a day before breakfast to bellow down the line for Liam to shit or get off the pot in tones clearly audible all over Wy's house. The job wasn't helping much, either. He and Prince had been hard at it for a solid month, responding to a series of burglaries, robberies and assaults aggravated by the rapidly weakening economy. It was the first practical lesson Liam had learned in the practice of law enforcement: It was easy to obey the law when your kids had full bellies. He understood, but it was not comforting to watch the lives of the people under his protection fall apart. Especially while he seemed to be helpless to stop the deterioration of his own.

Newenham, population two thousand, was a fishing town and regional market hub sitting on the eastern edge of Bristol Bay. It was built on a thick deposit of silt and clay washed down by the Nushugak River, and its topography consisted mostly of rolling hills covered with stands of birch and alder and fireweed and spruce clustered around houses with vinyl siding and trailers and mobile homes and log cabins with sod roofs and Quonset huts left over from World War II. There wasn't a straight street downtown; a series of looping curves wound around that part of Newenham with delusions of grandeur, city and business buildings in all their prefabricated glory and even a town house condominium complex sitting at the edge of the river overlooking the small boat harbor. A forest of masts of varying heights crowded the slips like nursing piglets, their backs to the bay and another bad fishing season. By February only a quarter of their skippers would have filed for bankruptcy, if the town was lucky. Meanwhile, they were all drinking their misery away, and their good sense with it.

Wy could have offered some solace, some counsel, he thought, taking a corner too fast. Instead she had withdrawn behind a façade that was as cool as it was irritating. Anyone would think she didn't care if he went or stayed. Anyone would think that she was just waiting for him to screw up so she'd have the opportunity to kick him out.

Not that she'd ever asked him to move in in the first place. What was her problem with that, anyway? They were single, in love, in heat, had a boy who needed two parents, had jobs that gave them financial security; just what the hell *was* her problem? Was it him? Was it marriage?

He could have asked. He could win everything or lose it all, but he feared his fate too much. What was the name of that poem? After a moment's thought it came to him. "My Dear and Only Love." Figured. The author, as he recalled, had wound up with his head on a pike outside London, the only proper end for anyone who dared to put that much truth into rhyme. The road straightened out and he stepped on the gas, only to send the vehicle into a protesting fishtail.

"Did you say something, sir?" Diana Prince said, knuckles white on the door handle.

He let up on the gas. "No."

Sometimes he thought he read too much poetry.

John Kvichak's house sat on the river's bank, too, although too far upstream of Wy's house for Liam to see the lights. Liam hoped she wasn't pissed that he was late. He could have called before he left the office. But then she might have picked up instead of the answering machine, and he would have had to talk to her. Or Tim.

Tim hadn't exactly been a barrel of laughs lately, either. Seeing his first girlfriend shot in front of his eyes the month before had been traumatic enough. Now his adoptive mother Wy had invited his birth mother into the house. This was the same woman under whose porch Wy had discovered a broken and bleeding Tim a little over two years before. Tim's hatred of Natalie Gosuk was fierce and visceral; he openly resented being forced to spend time with her, and the house was, to say the least, unsettled after one of her visits. Wy was allowing one a week. Today had been the third. Liam and Tim had been forging a relationship one cautious step at a time, their mutual love for Wy the impetus behind the journey. Now Tim had barricaded himself behind a wall of resentment that even Wy was having trouble getting through. Not that she would stop trying. She'd die first.

Liam had met Wy three years before, when he'd had to fly into the Bush to investigate a murder. It hadn't been a memorable murder, a subsistence fisherman shooting a sports fisherman over some alleged trespassing of fishing territory. He couldn't even remember now if the investigation and subsequent arrest had resulted in a conviction.

But he could remember every single second of the flights out and back, and for once his memories had nothing to do with his fear of flying. He remembered Wy had her hair pulled back into a ponytail, the easier to wear the headset. He remembered hearing her laugh, loving the sound of it, and trying deliberately to provoke a repeat. He remembered the feeling of instant recognition when she introduced herself as his pilot, the brief feeling of incredulous dizziness when their hands clasped for the first time in greeting, the dismayed realization of instantaneous attraction, of sharp-edged, undeniable need.

A need that a four-day weekend in Anchorage had only whetted. A weekend that, due to Wy's uncomfortable conscience, constituted the main portion of

their affair, before she sent him back to his wife and
son. They had parted in grief and in anger, and the first
time they had seen each other again they had coupled
in the front seat of her truck like a pair of randy
teenagers.

Oh, yeah, the need was still there, as strong and as
certain as it had ever been. Need wasn't enough,
though. Sometimes even love wasn't enough. He used
to know what was, but he was no longer as sure of
himself as he had once been.

It was with relief that he pulled up in front of John's
house, where, to judge from the lack of parking spaces,
there appeared to be a monster truck rally in progress,
and consigned his personal life to a folder in the back
of his mind marked *Later*. Wy would be there when he
was ready to open it again.

John Kvichak's house had started life as a dugout, a
pit with sod walls and roof, and over the intervening
hundred and fifty years had migrated up and out. One
wall was log, another plywood with tar-paper shingles, the third and widest of round river rock that rose
into a chimney that, however unsteady in construction, appeared to be functional, if the smoke pouring
out of it was any indication. The fourth was a bright
blue vinyl siding Liam tried to convince himself
wasn't the same shade as the new siding Seafood
North sported across from the small boat harbor. On a
drive-through of the dock area the day before, Liam
had noticed that part of one wall of the cannery was
still bare except for the Tyvek house wrap. Probably,
he told himself, Seafood North had ordered short.
Probably.

"Don't look now; it's Delinquentville," Diana

Prince said. "That's Teddy's Ranchero, isn't it? And Kelley MacCormick's Dakota? And Paul Urbano's Cherokee Chief. What's with those tires, anyway? He could drive over a moose without grazing the rack, the body sits so high." She released her seat belt and looked at Liam. "The gang's almost all here. You think they're planning their next heist?"

"I hope not," Liam said, and he meant it. He didn't know Paul that well, but Teddy and John were the sole support of their families, and pretty good at it so long as they stayed sober. Mac MacCormick was fresh out of the hospital and was in no shape to do more time. "Might as well get it over with."

He got out of the Blazer just in time to see Brewster Gibbons haul his Eddie Bauer Ford Explorer to a halt and bounce out. Gibbons must have been behind them the whole way and Liam had been so preoccupied that he hadn't spotted him, which did not improve his temper. "Brewster," he said, his voice very different from the irritating drawl he had used before, "what are you doing here? We don't need you. Go home."

"I didn't think you were going to do anything." Gibbons panted up, full of righteous wrath. "I came to warn them to stay away from my bank."

"As you can see, it's not necessary. We're here, and we'll handle it. Now go home." To underscore his command, he stepped forward to take Gibbons' arm and escort him back to the SUV. He even went so far as to open the door. With bad grace, Gibbons climbed in.

Liam caught Diana as she reached the porch, which along with the stairs up to it and the overhang looked brand-new, the wooden planks neatly lined up and not yet gray from weathering. Liam wondered who next would be pounding on the trooper post's door to report a theft.

The door swung open.

"Hi, John," Diana Prince began.

She didn't have time to say anything else. The man standing in the door took one look at her uniform, another at Liam's blue-clad bulk looming up behind her, said, "Oh, shit," and vanished.

From behind him there was a panicked yell and some shouts and a lot of swearing and a rush of footsteps. Something crashed inside the room and the lights went out. There was a thump and a moan and some more swearing.

"Okay, guys, we're coming in," Diana Prince said, pushing the door wide and feeling for a wall switch. She found one. An overhead light revealed a terrified Teddy Engebretsen with something in his hand and that hand pulled back to throw. "What's— Teddy? Teddy, what the hell is that? Teddy, don't— Christ! Look out, sir!"

She ducked, and on instinct Liam followed suit. Something pale and elongated sailed over their heads.

There was a loud *smack!* followed by a howl of outrage and the thump of a butt hitting the ground, hard.

Still crouching, Liam turned to look.

Brewster Gibbons was sitting on his fanny in the snow at the foot of the stairs, staring at the thing lying half on the bottom step and half on his lap. As Liam watched, he let out a yell and scuttled backward on his hands and feet. The thing slid from his lap and skidded across the icy path to bounce off the berm on one side and back off the other. "Keep it away from me! Keep it away from me!"

"What the hell?" Liam said, and went to investigate.

On closer inspection, he didn't blame Brewster for yelling.

The object was a human arm, the left, severed above the elbow.

Its hand was clenched into a tight fist.

FOUR

They were having a great time until Liam walked in.

Tim was a math whiz, and Gary, a building contractor, was showing him how to calculate how many trusses were needed to hold up the roof of your average split-level house. Jo was not helping by telling the story of the time Gary had made the family of a burned-out home wait through three tries before he got the truss size right.

"It wasn't me; it was the fabricator," Gary said in protest. "And in the interest of full disclosure," he told Tim, "it took four tries for them to get it right. I was downtime thirteen days on that job." He shook his head and drained his beer. "Plus the granite for the kitchen counter kept breaking. Hard to get quality work done right and on time in this state."

"Unless they get you to do it," Jo said, regarding him with a sister's sapient eye.

Gary grinned and did not deny the accusation.

"So you build people's houses," Tim said.

"And remodel them."

"Remodel?"

"Yeah, rip 'em apart and start over."

"Like?"

Gary tucked into his New York strip. Wy had always appreciated an enthusiastic appetite, being a feeder herself. "I just finished up the remodel of a split-level home in Spenard. The owner has had the house for three years and she's just getting around to correcting everything the previous owners did to it."

"Like?"

Gary cut off another piece of steak and used it for punctuation. "Like, they put up teak paneling, and stained all the trim mahogany and took down the old kitchen shelves and put the new ones up wrong. In the bathroom, they walled off the window and put in a six-hundred-dollar wall-hung toilet, which leaked. Lucky there wasn't any insulation between the floors."

"Why lucky?"

"Man, I'm going to be able to hire you on as an apprentice, you keep this up. Lucky because instead of pooling near and rotting the floor joists—"

"What's a joist?"

"Same thing as a truss, only under the floor instead of the roof." Gary reflected. "Well. Sort of. Same principle, anyway, supporting the structure. So, the water from the leak migrated down and only ruined the Sheetrock in the downstairs bathroom."

"So what did you do?"

"I gutted it right down to the studs, renewed all the plumbing. I closed off the door to the hallway, made it a master bath. I put the window back in—I love glass brick—and took out the wall-hung toilet and replaced it with a floor-mounted one. I built new cabinets—

maple slab, looks great, if I sez it who shouldn't—and laid down new linoleum. Now it looks about twice as big and feels ten times as light as it did before, and everything's new and done right. That bathroom's good for thirty years." His grin was not modest. He cut another piece of steak and inserted it into his mouth as if he were receiving the Year's Best Contractor award.

"You like doing that?"

Gary chewed while he thought. "Yeah," he said, swallowing. "It's fun to take something that's messed up and straighten it out, make it right again. You should have seen this woman; you'd have thought I was some kind of magician. She acted like she hadn't had to pay for it, like I'd given her a gift. Like I said, it's fun. Except I'm allergic to mahogany," he added, shaking his head, "and I sneezed all the way through the remodel. But other than that. It was fun."

"What's your next project?"

Gary let his gaze drift ever so slowly toward Wy. "I'm between projects at the moment."

Wy felt heat rise up into her face. Tim looked from one to the other with a gathering frown. Jo grinned, and if she'd been part Yupik and forty years older you'd have sworn she was Moses Alakuyak's twin sister.

At this auspicious moment, Liam walked in.

He didn't see them at first, walking straight to the bar and pulling off the ball cap that seemed suddenly too tight for his head. "I need a warrant."

"I'll give you a warrant," Bill said, "if you'll move this lush out of my bar."

Liam craned his head. "Oh. Eric."

"Yes. Again."

"Poor old bastard."

"What is it with you guys," Bill said, disgusted.

"I'm sorry?"

"Never mind. Who's the warrant for?"

"I'm not sure, exactly."

"Arrest?"

"Yes. At least I think so."

"For what?"

"I'm not sure about that, either."

"You're not helping me much here, Liam."

"I know. I'm sorry. The damnedest thing."

"What?"

"I got something I need you to keep in your freezer until I can get it on a plane to the lab." Liam opened up the white plastic garbage bag he'd carried into the bar with him.

Bill peered inside. "Sweet Jesus!" she yelled, turning heads all over the bar, which was when Wy saw Liam for the first time. "What the Sam Hill hell is that!"

Since Bill didn't seem to be in any hurry to take custody of the bag, Liam, who was even less thrilled to be carrying it around, set it on the floor at his feet. "It's exactly what you think it is."

"Where the hell did you get it?"

"I first saw it coming out of John Kvichak's house on a pitch that nearly brained me." He shook his head. "At first I thought it was a prosthetic. That clenched fist looked like somebody'd forgotten to throw the switch on the circuits."

Bill's face began to regain some of its natural color.

"For crissake. Where the hell did he find that? I mean, I know John and Teddy are scavengers, but . . ." Her hands were shaking a little when she poured out two fingers of Glenmorangie, neat. She frowned down at them and they steadied as she put the glass on the bar. "Oh. I forgot. You on or off?"

Liam sat down next to Eric Mollberg, who stirred and moaned a little, and turned his face to Liam in a preliminary attempt to surface from the sea of alcohol in which he had been submersed for going on three months. "I," said Liam, "don't give a damn if I'm on duty or off at the moment." He drank and felt the heat and flavor of the single-malt seep straight into his bloodstream. Comfort food, he thought, and finished it. Bill held up the bottle. He shook his head. "No. That did it. Thank you. From the bottom of my heart, thank you. You wouldn't believe the day I've had."

Bill cast a surreptitious glance over her shoulder at the group in the booth, one of whom was staring back with an undeniably guilty look all over her face, and thought, And it's not over yet. Because she was a woman, too, and had her own men problems—for starters the Alaska old fart sitting in the corner knocking back enough beer to fell Paul Bunyon and whooping it up with his pals—she bought Wy some time. "Where'd it come from?"

"You'll love this."

Bill ran a couple more margaritas down to the end of the bar for Moccasin Man, who was putting the moves on Susie Akiachak. Susie was a smart girl and knew better, but her defenses had been weakened by a nasty breakup with Jimmy Koliganek, and Evan Gray was first and foremost an opportunist. On the way back up the bar Bill hooked her foot beneath the bottom rung of the bartender's stool and sent it sliding into place across from Liam. "Okay," she said, settling in for the duration, "let's hear it."

"John Kvichak and Teddy Engebretsen were hunting."

"They're always hunting when they get into trouble. When they're not in town and getting into trouble. Or out fishing and getting into trouble."

"All too true." Liam rolled the glass between his hands as if the heat of his palms would evaporate anything left of the scotch and he could inhale the fumes. "So they were hunting, up around Bear Glacier, and they found it."

"Found what?"

"A plane wreck."

"What? What plane wreck? Did somebody go down?"

"Evidently."

"I haven't heard a thing."

"Neither have I, and neither has anybody at the airport. I called Anchorage Flight Service to see if anybody had gone missing and they said not to their knowledge. I called Elmendorf, to see if the air force was missing a mission. Nope. They checked with Eilson. Still nothing. So then I ask Teddy and John what are they talking about a plane wreck. And they say it was a plane wreck they found, and they found that"—he jerked his head at the bag, on the floor between him and Eric—"in the wreckage. So I take another look at it."

Bill repressed a shudder. "And?"

"And it's old."

"Old? What do you mean, old? You mean like from an old man? How can you tell?"

"No, I mean like desiccated old. I mean like from an old plane wreck, years and years old."

"You can tell that just from looking?"

"Bill, I'm telling you, it's practically petrified, it's so old. You want another look?"

"No."

"You don't see how old it is when you first look at it; all you see is . . . well."

"Yeah." Bill took a deep breath. "Bear Glacier, huh?"

"Yeah."

"Ice is a great preservative."

"Yeah."

"No telling how long it's been up there."

"No."

"You're going to have to go look."

"Oh, yeah," Liam said, with no visible enthusiasm.

"So? Tell me more about Teddy and John."

"So I talked to Teddy and John, and John says it's an old plane, and it's painted army gray, and he knows that color because he slopped enough of it on anything that didn't move out of the way in time while he was in the army."

"He get the tail numbers?"

"Said they didn't see the tail. Said there wasn't much wreckage, if it came to that. They weren't real coherent about it."

"Probably weren't real sober, either."

"I think they were sober when they stumbled across

too. The back of Liam's neck prickled in an unpleasant sort of way, and he took a step forward to see who was sitting across from them.

"Hey there, Liam," Jo Dunaway said with a sunny smile that was all teeth. "You remember my brother, Gary."

December 3, 1941

The goddamn radio went out again. We were coming back from Attu and the ceiling came down and we were wandering all over hell and gone. I know the way Ive been over it enough times but even I cant see through clouds. It doesnt help that the frigging maps are all wrong. Half the rivers are missing and the lakes are fifty miles away from their actual locations and we almost ran into a mountain that was only supposed to be 3600 feet high and was really 4600 feet high. Jesus!

Another letter from Helen There's some kind of problem with the baby she dosnt say what. I wrote and told her to go see the doctor and tell him well find the money to pay. If old Doc Bailey was still alive this wouldnt be a problem he knew my father and he delivered me he would know I was good for it. I wrote to Mom to go over there. I know they dont like each other but Helen shouldnt be alone. God how I hate being this far away.

Peter the old Eskimo guy is quite a storyteller. He says he's not really an Eskimo hes from a little village on the coast southwest of here. Hes got a name for his tribe but I can't pronounce it let alone spell it. He was telling me the other day about how his people used to paddle big canoes from Alaska to Russia to fight each other. He showed me a vest he said was armor. It dint look real substantial to me but then I want to be bullet-proof and his folks probably only needed to be spear-proof.

FIVE

The next morning was clear and cold enough to generate a thin layer of frost, but the wing covers were quickly removed and the problem solved. She was sorry for that. She wanted to be very busy. Liam had the worst case of fear of flying she'd ever seen, and so long as she was doing things with the plane he wouldn't bother her. If she made it look too easy, they would have to talk about the night before.

They leveled off at a thousand feet and she drew a bead on Bear Glacier, which according to the map hung off the lip of Carryall Mountain. "Carryall," if the little Yupik she retained from her upbringing in Ik'ikika, a village on the shore of One Lake, was accurate, was an anglicized version of one of the many words her ancestors on the Yupik side of her family used for *bear*. She didn't know if it stood for black bear or brown bear or polar bear, or feeding bear or sleeping bear or running bear, for that matter. She ought to study up on her Yupik. Maybe she and Tim could take a class. Maybe she and Tim and Liam could take a class.

She gave a mental snort. Yeah, right, that'd happen. Liam was all but packed for his transfer back to Anchorage, where he would have no use for Yupik. Other language skills, perhaps. Bureaucratese, maybe. Brownnosing, definitely.

She pulled herself up short, ashamed for automatically assuming the worst. Just like Jo. Liam hasn't said if he's leaving or staying, she told herself. You could ask, instead of getting mad over nothing.

Then again, if she asked, he'd have to answer. And then he'd ask her to come with him, which would entail leaving her home, selling her air-taxi business, and pulling Tim out of school to start all over again in a city whose population thought *Bush* meant half an hour out of town.

And then she would be faced with her own decision: Go or stay.

It wasn't like she didn't have a choice. It hadn't killed her to break it off with Liam the first time.

It had only felt like it had.

She found herself getting angry all over again. She took a deep breath and let it out slowly, grateful the noise of the engine covered the sound. She cast a surreptitious glance over her shoulder at the man sitting behind her, rigidly upright, knuckles white on the edge of his seat, his breathing audible over the headset. Liam wasn't noticing anything except how he was personally holding the plane up in the air.

According to John and Teddy, the crash site wasn't far from an airstrip not too overgrown with brush and long enough for a Super Cub, which in turn was accessible by what had been a game trail just wide enough to take a four-wheeler in from Icky. It was quicker to fly, though, and Liam had wanted to inspect the site as soon as possible.

The Wood River Mountains grew on the horizon, four- and five- and six-thousand-foot peaks covered with the winter's first snowfall. A series of four long, deep, narrow landlocked fjords filled up four long, steep, narrow valleys between the mountains, lying before them like the fingers of a giant's spread hand. Not quite like the outspread hand of the night before, but close enough to bring it to both their minds.

Liam cleared his throat. "So. Where are we landing?" He tried not to let the fact that he didn't care where it was so long as he was on the ground, alive and whole and soon, show in his voice.

Wy made an unnecessary adjustment to the prop pitch. "It's a dirt strip, about three thousand feet. I think the Parks Service put it in during a survey of the Togiak Wildlife Refuge."

"And everybody's been using it to hunt from ever since."

"Pretty much. I know Charlene patrols up here pretty regular, and she sees planes down there a lot."

Charlene Taylor was the fish-and-game trooper for the Newenham district. "Poaching?"

"She thinks so, although she has yet to catch anyone in the act." Wy adjusted her headset and fussed with the arm extending the voice-activated mike to her mouth.

"You have any ideas about this wreck?"

She shook her head. "It's got to be old, before my time."

"Did you ask around the airport?"

"Didn't have time; you wanted to be in the air at first light."

"Right." He made a minute shift to ease the strain on his vertebrae. The plane hit an air pocket and bounced. He stiffened back into immobility, like that would help smooth out the flight. Wy's braid dangled over the back of the seat in front of him. It swayed gently with the motion of the Cub. He tried not to look directly at it.

They flew on for a few minutes more, until they took a sudden, hard right bank and nosed down. Liam sucked in a breath. "There," Wy said.

It seemed to Liam's fevered gaze that she was intent on their doing chin-ups on the peaks of the Wood River Mountains. "Right there, do you see it?" Wy said, and aimed 78 Zulu at a strip of snow that might have had a patch of gravel beneath it the size of a baby's diaper. The strip got bigger the nearer they got to it but not much. Wy circled once, taking a look at the surface and coming much too close to the sides of the encircling mountains, and brought them in on an approach that feathered the tops of the stand of slender birches surrounding the strip. She pulled so far back on the throttle that they were practically hanging stationary in the air when they touched down. They didn't use up much of the strip, either—a good thing, Liam thought when a bull moose wandered out of the trees at the other end of the runway. He stopped and regarded them with an expression of mild surprise for a moment, before wandering back into the woods, evidently unworried by the thought that they might be after his rack.

They set off, finding and following the track through the brush and snow left by John's and Teddy's four-wheelers without difficulty. It was late October and they were lucky. It had snowed twice already that year, but so far only enough to stick, and the good news was it wasn't over their boots.

"Did they get anything?" Wy said when, after twenty minutes, the silence got too oppressive to bear.

"What?"

"Teddy and John. Did they get anything?"

"Oh. Yeah. A moose. Big bull. It was skinned out and hanging in the shop."

"Good."

"Yeah. Isabella and Rose'll be happy."

She stood it for ten minutes more. "Liam—"

"Look," he said. "We're here."

They had emerged from the woods into an area of glacial moraine, pile after pile of gray gravel so uniform in size it looked graded.

"There's no snow on the gravel," Liam said, confused.

"That's why," Wy said, pointing.

In back of the moraine loomed the glacier, and even at that distance they could hear the sound of running water. "It's not cold enough yet to stop the meltoff. Won't be long, though. Teddy and John hit it just right. Another snow and they wouldn't have found a thing. How close did they say they were to the face when they found the arm?"

He pointed at the four-wheeler tracks, which continued straight to the mouth of the glacier. "I figure we follow those, we find what Teddy and John found."

Wy took another look at the glacier, which looked far too unstable for her tastes. "Right."

They followed the tracks, which ended short of the wall of ice. The bottom half of the face was rotten and riddled with holes that created gaping caves, too dark to see inside.

"You don't think it's inside one of those?" Liam said.

"Even John and Teddy aren't that dumb," Wy said. She felt a prickle at the base of her neck. It was nippy out this cold, clear morning. She should have exchanged her jacket for a parka.

They cast back and forth along the wall of ice, careful not to stray too close, the detritus from recent calving fresh on the ground in front of them. They'd almost given up when they found the blood and guts of the moose John and Teddy had shot. Wy unshouldered the .30-06 she had brought from the plane.

"You hear a bear?"

She shook her head, eyes watching the edge of the trees. "Not yet," she said, which didn't reassure him.

"I thought they were all asleep by now."

"Nope."

There were ravens gathered at the corpse, shredding intestine with strong, bloodied beaks. They were unalarmed by the arrival of the humans, and continued to feed.

"So I'm not seeing any plane wreckage," Liam said, almost relieved. "They might have been shining us on."

Wy felt the prickle at the back of her neck again and tried to zip up her jacket, but the zipper was as far up as it would go. The face of the glacier glittered in the cold, clear light, fractured and chasmed and impenetrable. Bushes and grasses had implanted themselves at the sides of the face wherever a handful of dirt had collected in a hollow of rock. Even—

"Hey," she said. "Blueberries."

They were large, as big as the first knuckle of her little finger, and frozen. They melted in her mouth like candy, sweet and tangy.

Blueberries. She'd loved them as a child, loved picking them, loved the rich blue stain they left on her hands and lips and tongue, loved the tart, tangy taste that exploded in her mouth when she bit down. She could hide herself away in the bushes taller then than she was, and sit with a pail in her lap and pick and eat and pick and eat, and not come out again until the strident voice of her foster mother called her out. And sometimes not even then; sometimes she thought that if she could just fall asleep in the blueberry patch, when she woke up her real mother and father would be there, all love and smiles and welcome home, Wyanet.

An eagle flew overhead, for a moment blocking the sun, aware of their presence but indifferent to them, and she started, staring down at the handful of berries. "Liam! Come have some berries! They're—" She stopped.

Hidden until she'd been drawn to the berries, hidden almost completely behind a pile of ice-encrusted gravel overgrown with diamond willow, was a large patch of gray. As she approached, it resolved itself into a fragment of airplane fuselage. The edges were ragged and worn, the gray paint streaked and faded.

"No tail numbers," Wy said out loud. It wasn't much more than a foot across and she lifted it easily. "I'll be go to hell."

His footsteps came to a halt behind her and she felt him look over her shoulder. "What is it?"

"World War Two," she said.

"What about it?" He caught on. "Oh, you think—"

"I could be wrong, Liam, but I think this is a piece off an old C-47."

"What's a C-47?"

"It's the cargo equivalent of a DC-3." When he continued to look blank, she said, "Liam, I can't believe how little you know about flying and still manage to live in Alaska. The DC-3 was the first economically successful commercial airliner. The C-47 was the military application, a cargo and troop transport. Parachuters bailed out of them during the invasion of Normandy, for crying out loud. Mudhole Smith built Cordova Airlines around them. At the end of World War Two, when we knew we had the war won, the plant in Georgia started converting the cargo plane into the passenger plane, and Alaska Airlines puddle-jumped one all the way across the continent to Anchorage in May 1945 and started flying passengers." She looked at him and said incredulously, "Do you mean to say you've never been in one?"

"I don't know," he said, trying hard not to sound defensive. "I never pay any attention to the plane I'm in, Wy; you know that. All I care about is that they stay up in the air long enough to get me where I'm going."

She shook her head. "Man."

"Besides, that's just a little piece. How can you be so sure it's—well, it was a DC-3?"

"A C-47," she said. "It was a military plane. The color alone tells us that."

"How long's it been here? When did it crash?"

"We need to find something with numbers on it." Wy began foraging, climbing over boulders, pulling brush to one side only to have it pull free and slap her in the face. "Ouch. Damn it."

"John said they found the arm next to a big chunk of quartz." He walked upslope, crunching through a surface trickle of water frozen into a thin, rapidly melting crust. It had spent the summer running off the end of a slab of ice the size of Wy's house, with man-high holes melted through it. "There." He clambered over the ice, pieces of it collapsing beneath his weight as he went.

"Be careful!" she said as a big chunk fell with a loud *thunk!* Liam disappeared and for a moment she thought he had fallen through. His voice came to her a moment later. "Here it is, Wy. Walk around, though; don't climb over —the ice is rotten right through."

"Imagine my surprise." She walked around the slab, a scramble of smallish boulders in her way, and found him standing between the slab of ice he had negotiated and the face of the glacier itself, a wall of prismed white with shadowed blue highlights creating narrow, unexpected windows into an inconsistent past. Another dark cave yawned at its base, curving high and large behind the ice. The ground here was a gray mixture of sand and gravel, more textbook moraine. Water was trickling down somewhere, but not much and not in a hurry about it. Winter was coming on fast.

"Kinda spooky." Liam's voice echoed hollowly back at him from the cave.

"Kinda," Wy said, her voice short.

Liam looked at her. "What's wrong?"

"I don't like being this close to the face of a glacier. Glaciers calve. Where do you think that slab you just hauled your butt over came from?"

He squinted up at the face. "Think one might fall on us?" he said, sounding interested.

Her shadow lengthened on the ice in front of her, and the sun, well up over the horizon by now, felt warm on her back. "That's what glaciers do. Where's that quartz?" She followed his pointing finger. "I don't see— Oh."

He followed her, watched as she extricated a piece of plastic from the sandy gravel. "What's that?"

She turned it between her hands. "Transparent, convex. Part of a window, probably, or the windshield."

He repressed a shudder, his all-too-active imagination actively pursuing a picture of what the last few moments in the air had been like. Had they known they were going in, those unknown men in the cockpit of this unknown aircraft? He hoped not. He hoped it with fervor.

Two hours later, their total was three shards of metal that had been twisted like corkscrews—proving to Liam once again just how insubstantial were the craft to which he trusted himself in the air—and Wy's piece of plastic. Other, more macabre findings included the cuff of a dark blue shirtsleeve, and a tattered dark blue sock containing what appeared to be some small bones held together by what appeared to be sinewy cartilage.

Liam bagged and tagged everything they found.

"Nothing with numbers on it, though," Wy said with a sigh.

"Is there enough here to tell you what kind of a plane it was?"

Wy shrugged. "Military, for sure, with that paint job."

"When?"

"Not lately." She stared up at the face of the glacier. "What?"

"It's just . . . you don't expect to see a glacier giving up an airplane when it calves. A T. Rex, yeah, but a plane? Glaciers have been around a lot longer than planes. Takes a long time, centuries, millennia for a glacier to give up a secret. The face of a glacier, man, it's thousands of years old. It's—" She cocked her head. The prickle at the back of her neck was back.

"What?" he said.

"Shhh." She held up a hand. "I thought I heard—"

There was a distant, cracking sound, and the next thing Liam knew Wy had him in a low tackle that rolled the both of them over the blueberry bushes and beneath the high-standing lip of the chunk of ice he had climbed over. There was a *BOOM!* that caused chunks of ice to fall from the roof of their shelter, one of which hit Wy's head and another of which struck Liam smack in the left eye. "Ouch! What the—"

There was an extended rending sound, deafening in decibel level, so that he couldn't hear himself think, let alone talk. The ground shook beneath them. Earthquake? Wy buried her face in his shoulder and he held on. There was a split second of pure, clear silence. The light outside their shelter altered, shifted somehow, and then there was a *CRASH!* as something immense fell heavily to the ground, and a lingering series of cracks and thumps and bumps as it splintered into pieces and slithered down the gravel moraine.

He didn't know how long it took for the ringing in his ears to stop. "Wy?" he croaked. She was unmoving against him. "Wy! Are you all right?"

He could feel the jolt that went through her. "What? Liam?"

"Are you all right?"

He felt her come alive all along the length of her body. "I . . . yes, I'm all right. You?"

"I think so. Can we get out?"

She raised her head and peered over her shoulder at the way they had come. "I think so." She eeled backward, just enough room for her to wriggle over onto her back. She kicked, and something shifted.

"Wy!"

"It's all right. I'm just clearing a path. Follow me out."

She didn't have to ask him twice. He barely remembered to hang on to the evidence bags.

When they were well clear of the ice and a safe distance from the face of the glacier, they stopped to take stock. Wy winced a little when she stretched. "Something got me in the shoulder." She looked at him. "You're going to have a shiner."

He touched the swelling surrounding his left eye. "Ouch."

Her lips twitched. "And your uniform's kind of changed color on you. Well, maybe not changed, exactly, but it's sure bluer than it was."

"What?" He looked down to find his dark blue jacket and pants embedded with multiple squashed blueberries. "Oh, hell." She was looking over his shoulder at the face of the glacier. He looked up and her expression made him straighten. "Wy?"

"Liam," Wy breathed, and raised one shaking forefinger.

The skeleton of the plane was impressed into the

face of the glacier like a gigantic fossil, the ribs of the fuselage curving up and around, one wing folded like paper, the tail miraculously upright. The nose was gone and the cockpit with it, but there was a barred white star on the side close to the tail, and small letters or numbers in the same white paint on the upright portion of the tail.

"Liam," Wy said again, closing her eyes and opening them again. "Do you see?"

"Of course I see," he said.

She swallowed. "Good. For a minute there, I—"

"What?" When she didn't answer he said, "Let's get the binoculars from the plane."

SIX

Diana Prince was waiting for them when they taxied up to Wy's tie-down. "Did you find it?"

"Yeah, we found it."

"Damn," she said. "I figured it was just another one of Teddy and John's big stories. A pretty good one, I admit, but still."

"Me, too," Liam said. "But it's there, all right."

"What is it?" She looked at Wy.

"A C-47," Wy said. "World War Two vintage, if I had to guess."

Prince whistled. "Wow. On its way to the Aleutians, maybe?"

"Maybe. That's how Elmendorf got built, because of the traffic between Anchorage and the Aleutians after the Japanese invaded."

"What kind of shape is it in?"

"We couldn't get close to it. It's sort of stuck in the face of the glacier."

"You're kidding."

"Although I'd say, from the looks of it, and from the most recent evidence of calving, that a big chunk is due off any time now." Wy remembered the sheer terror of those few moments when she had thought they were both about to be crushed in the fall of ice, and looked at Liam to see him reliving it, too. "All we can do is wait. We got the tail numbers, though."

"Great, we'll be able to trace it."

"What are you doing here, Prince?" Liam said. "I thought you were going to check on that shooting out in the road last night. The one old Abe called in."

"Yeah, I was." Prince looked uncomfortable.

"Something else come up?"

Only one answer to that. For a state trooper, something else always came up. "Yeah."

Suddenly Liam didn't like the look on her face. "I'm not going to like this, am I "

"No."

Prince looked at Wy, who could take a hint of official police business when her nose was rubbed in it. Curiosity was not a trait that was encouraged to flourish in the significant other of a state trooper. She finished tying down the Cub. "I've got to pick up the mail for Kagati Lake. See you later." She included them both in a vague salute and climbed into her truck. Liam saw her watching them in the rearview as she drove off.

He shook his head once, firmly, and turned to Prince. "What's up?"

She took a deep breath. "You're really not going to like it."

She was right.

Death was careless of dignity. Sometimes Liam thought that that was what he hated most about murder scenes, and this one was no exception. Her flowered housedress was above her knees, revealing the legs he had admired the night before all the way up to the thighs. Her right foot was twisted so that one perfectly polished brown loafer had fallen off. The neat, shining cap of black hair was matted with blood. Her bowels had emptied themselves and the stink of urine and excrement fouled the air.

Her big brown eyes were open, looking at the ceiling with an expression of vague astonishment, as if she had tried and failed to understand how she came to be there and in that position.

She never would, now.

"You got pictures?"

Prince nodded.

Liam stepped forward, avoiding the blood, and closed the staring eyes, and then pulled the skirt down to a more decorous level. He turned to Joe Gould, a thin, intense man in his early thirties with a face by Giotto and hair as long and as black as the deceased's. Gould, Newenham's sole physician's assistant, operator of the local ambulance and the nearest thing the town had to a medical examiner, stripped the plastic gloves from his hands. "My guess is death was caused by a blow to the head incurred during a fight. Bruising on the face, knuckles, defensive marks on both arms."

"Anything under her fingernails?"

Gould picked up the corpse's left hand and displayed it. "She kept her fingernails short and filed smooth. I did scrapings, but I doubt there will be much there."

The house was silent, except for the sound of soft

weeping and muted whispers coming from the living room. The three of them stared down at the body.

Mrs. Lydia Tompkins, a seventy-four-year-old housewife, mother of four, grandmother of two, would never again come to the defense of private property with a jar of sun-dried tomatoes.

"God damn it to hell," Liam said.

Prince tried not to flinch away from the rage in his voice and on his face. Gould, impassive as ever, picked up the chair that had been lying on its side and set it at the table. He nodded at the counter and, following his gaze, Liam saw two mugs, both bearing the KAKM Anchorage public television logo, sitting next to the stove. The kettle was full, and cold to the touch. The mugs were empty. A canister of tea bags stood next to them, along with a sugar bowl and a spoon.

Gould nodded when Liam looked back. "I'd say she was making tea for two and never got the chance."

"So she knew him."

Gould shrugged. "Doesn't narrow it down by much. Who doesn't know everyone else in this town?"

The kitchen, a large room with windows overlooking the river and a table big enough to seat eight, had last been remodeled before Alaska was a state. The refrigerator was small, round-shouldered and noisy, the stove a sea of white enamel surrounded the propane-fired burners, there was no microwave, and the coffeepot was a silver percolator with a black plastic lid. The overhead light was fluorescent behind a translucent, rectangular plastic lens. Yellow flowers bloomed on the wallpaper, matching the yellow and white squares of the shabby linoleum. The narrow cabinets were metal painted white, with chrome handles looked like they'd come off a '57 Chevy. The phone was an old black rotary dial, mounted on the wall with a bulletin board beside it. Among the usual kids' pictures, grocery lists and plumbers' phone numbers was a tattered Peanuts cartoon, a color one out of the Sunday paper, with Snoopy on his doghouse thinking about the time he'd tried to go over the fence of the Daisy Hill Puppy Farm. "No matter where you are, you're still in the world," was his conclusion.

Liam lowered his eyes and saw the jar of sun-dried tomatoes sitting on the counter, shreds of dark red packed into golden olive oil.

Snoopy was right.

The room shone with elbow grease, not a coffee ground or a speck of egg yolk or a Cheerio dried hard anywhere. If it hadn't been for the blood, it would have been spotless, but there was blood, a lot of it, splattered over the small, square porcelain sink, the dish drainer and the dishes in it, the face of the cupboard beneath, and the floor. Most of it had dried to a hard brown.

"Did you take prints?" Liam said to Prince.

She nodded, taking refuge in the minutiae of the job. "There were a lot of them."

"And you got pictures?"

"Three rolls."

"All right, then."

Prince brought out the body bag she had carried into the house. Liam didn't move.

After a moment, Prince said tentatively, "Sir?"

"God damn son of a *bitch*," Liam said, and bent to task.

*   *   *

Liam and Prince saw the ambulance off and went back inside, through the kitchen and into the large living room made much smaller by all the furniture in it. There were two couches, a recliner and a couple of easy chairs upholstered in three different fabrics in four different patterns, with end tables spaced between. A wicker basket held copies of the *Ladies' Home Journal*, *Reader's Digest*, Jo-Ann Fabrics flyers, *Coin World*, the Denali Seed catalog, and the *New York Times Book Review*. A jumble of toys spilled out of a toy box in the shape of a large hollow plastic frog with lime-green skin and yellow eyes. A television, big and black and brand-new, dominated one corner, but what drew the eye was the window that took up most of the east wall. Like the kitchen, this room faced the river. Lydia Tompkins must have enjoyed some spectacular sunrises.

The weeping sound was coming from two women who sat close together on one couch, and the whispers from two men on the opposite couch. They looked nothing alike, and yet it was evident at first glance that all four were the children of Lydia Tompkins.

Liam stepped forward. "I'm Liam Campbell of the Alaska state troopers. Who found her?"

Prince frowned a little at his blunt question, but after a surreptitious look at the expression on his face decided not to intervene.

One of the women blew her nose and rose to her feet. "I did."

"And you are?"

"Betsy Amakuk."

"You're her daughter?"

"We all are. I mean, this is my sister, Karen."

"Karen Tompkins," the other woman said, standing.

"And my brothers."

The brothers followed suit.

"Stan Tompkins."

"Jerry Tompkins."

Betsy was large and regal in clean blue jeans and a dark blue sweatshirt with the boat name *F/V Daisy Rose* on the front. She wore pearl studs in her ears, her dark hair was immaculate, and her eyes and nose were red. Karen was petite and kittenish in hip-hugger cords and a cropped T-shirt. Her hair was short and streaked with gold and spiked with gel. Thin silver bracelets jangled from both wrists, and silver earrings touched her shoulders. Her belly button was pierced, and her mascara had run.

Stan, burly, tanned and fit, looked at Liam out of assessing eyes. His haircut looked left over from the marines, and his Carhartt's, though worn, were clean and well-kept, as was the brown plaid shirt beneath them. Jerry, on the other hand, was thin and nervous, with eyes that couldn't seem to stay focused on any one object for very long. He wore a dark blue windbreaker over a T-shirt with a large hole showing and a pair of jeans worn through at both knees.

They all looked to be in their late forties or early fifties, Betsy the eldest and, if he had to guess, Karen the youngest. He said to Betsy, "What time did you find your mother?"

"I don't know." She blew her nose again and looked at Stan. "What time did I call you, Stan?"

"About two o'clock, I think."

"Did you call him the moment you found her?"

"You understand," Prince said, "we have to ask these questions, Ms. Amakuk. We're very sorry for your loss."

Liam glared at her and she shut up. He repeated, "Did you call your brother as soon as you found your mother?"

"Yes. No. Wait. I— No, I called the ambulance first." Her eyes filled again. "Even though I knew it was no use. She was cold when I touched her."

Rigor had begun to set in. The house was cool. A murder before breakfast, then, most likely. "Did you touch anything else?"

"What? I . . . no. No, I don't think so."

"The stove wasn't on?"

"No."

"Did you see anyone leaving the house as you arrived?"

"No."

To Stan, Liam said, "And you came as soon as Betsy called?"

"Yes. Well, my wife had to come down to the boat to tell me Betsy had called and wanted me up to Mom's."

To Betsy, Liam said, "So actually you called Stan's wife."

"No. Well, yes, she answered the phone at their house."

"You might want to ease up a little here, sir," Prince murmured from the background.

Liam, who knew he was being a jerk, didn't seem to be able to turn it off. "Why," he said to Betsy, "did you come to the house today?"

A spark of anger glowed briefly in her eyes but she kept her voice level. "I come by every afternoon for coffee."

Liam thought of the two mugs on the counter, the box of tea bags, the full kettle, the empty percolator. "Your mother lived here alone?"

"Yes. After Dad died, I wanted her to move in with us but she wouldn't. Said she'd lived here for fifty-eight years and if she had another fifty-eight in her she wanted to live them in the same place."

All four siblings gave the same involuntary smile as Betsy called up the memory.

"Now let me ask you something, Mr. Campbell," Betsy said, drawing herself up to a height that allowed her to meet Liam's eyes straight-on. "Who did this to my mother?"

"I don't know."

"But you'll find out." It was a statement, not a question.

"I'll need to ask you all a lot more questions. I need to know what she did with her days, who her friends were—"

"A friend wouldn't do this!"

Liam looked at Jerry, red-faced and teary-eyed. "Can you all come down to the post this afternoon? The sooner we interview you, the sooner we can move the investigation forward."

He waited for their nods. "Who were your mother's neighbors?"

"There weren't any close by," Stan said. "One of the reasons we wanted her to move in with Betsy. Jim Earl bought out old Eric the Red six years ago when Eric had to put his wife in the Pioneer Home. That's the place north of here. The next house down belongs to the Isaacsons." He gave a dismissive wave. "Outsiders, haven't been in the country long. Mom barely knew them."

"We'll talk to them all," Liam said. "In the meantime, please leave the house as it is so we can have a chance to go through it."

"Why?" Betsy said.

Liam, suddenly very tired, pulled off his cap and ran his hand through his hair. His scalp felt tight. "We might find something that will lead us to who did this thing."

"Like what?"

"I don't know, Ms. Amakuk."

"You'll leave everything as you found it?"

Liam's lips tightened. "Alaska state troopers are not thieves, Ms. Amakuk."

She had the grace to look uncomfortable. "No," she said quickly. "Of course not."

"If you have a key, I'll make sure we lock up behind ourselves."

"Of course." She went into the kitchen and they heard drawers and cupboards opening and closing. In Newenham, house keys were not normally ready to hand. Eventually Betsy returned with a brass house key on a ring bearing a Last Frontier Bank fob and handed it over. She gathered what remained of her family together with a glance and they followed her out, Karen hanging behind to cast a languishing glance Liam's way.

"You sure are tall," she said. "I like tall men a lot." She stepped in close to him and her voice dropped to a purr. "They make me feel all little and feminine."

Liam slapped his cap back on and said to Prince, "Let's start in the kitchen."

"Yes, sir," Prince said woodenly, and followed him from the room.

December 6, 1941

We lost one the other side of the Canadian border. The weather was shitty and it sounds like they might have flown into a mountain. Probably another one of those mountains thats ten thousand feet higher than the map says it is. Didn't know anyone on board.

Peter invited me to dinner. It was great to get off base. He lives in this little dugout kind of a place down on this creek that is so muddy that the mud soaks through the snow and ice. He says its full of salmon in the summertime. I dont see any self-respecting fish swimming up that but thats what he says. He says the salmon get really big, forty, fifty pounds but I reckon thats just one of his storys. He fried some moose steaks and boiled potatos from his garden. There was even butter I dont know where he got it. Pretty good better than what were eating on base. He showed me some gold nuggets one was the size of a radish I never see such a thing. I asked how does one go about finding more of those and he says you dont stroll out and pick them up off the ground its hard work. He says he might have a proposition for me later on if I can find him a flight to Russia.

A letter from Mom today saying that Aunt Victoria saw Helen down to the Powder House dancing. Im glad shes feeling better. I wonder who she was dancing with. Ira said hed look after her for me.

SEVEN

Kagati Lake was covered with a foot of crusty snow, but someone had plowed enough of the strip for Wy to put the Cessna down. Leonard Nunapitchuk was there to help her unload the supplies for the little sundries store his wife, Opal, had started in their living room when she got the bid for postmistress.

"Good to see you, Leonard. How you been?"

However hard she tried to make it sound like a casual question, it wasn't one and they both knew it. His wife had fallen victim to the serial killer Liam had apprehended the month before. Still, Leonard wasn't a whiner. "Oh, muddling along."

"And the kids?"

His expression lightened a little, and he nodded upslope, where his three remaining children had built their homes and brought their spouses. "Fine." His eyes, nearly hidden in the mass of wrinkles surrounding them, narrowed with what might have been a smile. "I'll be a grandfather come spring."

"That's great news, Leonard."

"Yeah. If it's a girl, Sarah says they're going to call her Opal."

"Opal would be happy to hear that."

"Yeah," he said again. "I just wish—" He stopped himself and said in a bright voice, "It's too cold to stand around out here jawing."

Wy followed his lead, emptying out the back of the plane and reinstalling the seats that she had folded and stored. "Dusty and his wife are making a Costco run into town," she said in answer to Leonard's inquiring look.

"Who's minding the kids?"

"They're bringing them."

Leonard looked at the plane, which seated six, and back at Wy.

"They're all under eight. She'll hold the baby and I'll buckle the two smallest kids in one seat. I just hope nobody throws up. I hate people puking in my planes."

"Can't say I blame you." He loaded his boxes onto a handcart and waved good-bye. She watched him push it up the trail and disappear into the brush that hid the rambling log house from the airstrip. It was a big house. It had to feel pretty lonely after his wife's death. She wished she had time to follow him up, accept a cup of coffee, play some cribbage.

But she had to get back to town, and Tim. And Liam.

Before she could go very far down that road the Moore gang arrived. She got them sandwiched in and they were in the air fifteen minutes later. The most she could do was circle Leonard's house and run up and back on the prop pitch. He'd hear the engine *wah-wah* and know she was saying good-bye.

On the way back to Newenham she took a short detour to fly low and as slow as the Cessna would allow over Ted Gustafson's place at Akamanuk. A tall, spare, grizzled Scandinavian bachelor homesteader, Ted was also diabetic and dependent on the regular supply of insulin Wy delivered at three-week intervals. He came outside when he heard the engine and waved a reassuring hand. Everything okay there. She waggled the wings and climbed back to five hundred feet.

They landed in Newenham a little before five, just in time for the Moores to catch the last Anchorage-bound flight of the day. Wy noticed a body bag being loaded into the cargo hold, and wondered who had died, and if it had been a death Liam had had to respond to, and if so, what time he would be home. It was her turn to cook, and Jo and Gary both had been invited. She decided on macaroni and cheese with onions and garlic, her mother's specialty and a dish that could easily be made larger by the addition of another vegetable on the side. She snugged down the Cessna, checked the Cub's tie-down lines, and headed for Eagle to lay in supplies.

Jo and Gary were already at her house, engaging Tim in a fierce battle of cutthroat pinochle. "I can't believe you shot the moon!" he was saying when she walked in.

Jo gathered up cards with a complacent air. "Yes, well, like I always say, cutthroat is not for the faint of heart."

"Only the hard of head," Gary chimed in, so opportunely that it could only have been something he had said and she had heard many times before.

Jo aimed a halfhearted cuff at the side of his head

and shuffled the cards in an alarmingly professional manner, fanning them, flipping them, and dealing them out again in a blur. Tim was trying hard not to look impressed and failing. "Could you, like, maybe, teach me how to do that?"

"Like, maybe, I could."

Gary looked up and saw Wy, and flashed a warm, intimate grin. "Hey, girl."

"Hey, Gary."

Tim observed this exchange through narrowed eyes.

"Back on the ground, fly girl?" Jo said. "Just in time to pour another round. You have your uses."

"You're welcome," Wy said dryly, and got three Coronas from the refrigerator.

"Did you get any Coke at the store?" Tim said.

"How many have you had already today?"

He looked annoyed. "I don't know."

"At school?"

"I don't know," he said.

"One at lunch, one every break, did you stop off at Eagle and pick one up after school?"

"I don't know!"

She kept her voice soft and even. "We talked about this, Tim. There's too much sugar in those things, more than six teaspoons a can. They'll rot your teeth, make you fat, give you diabetes like Ted."

"I don't care." At least he wasn't yelling anymore.

"I do. And what I say goes." She pulled a can out of one of the bags. "How about a Diet Coke?"

"They don't have the kick. And they're too sweet."

"I'll squeeze a lemon into it."

"Great."

"You in?" Jo said, giving his handful of cards a pointed look. "It's your bid."

He examined his cards, and eyed the kitty with a suspicious expression. "I guess I'll open."

"Pass," Gary said promptly.

"Pass," Jo said promptly. "Going, going, gone for the bargain-basement bid of fifteen."

"Oh, man," Tim said, "I can't believe you dumped it on me again. I'm going out the back door for sure." He reached for the glass Wy had set next to him and took a drink. "Okay, okay, what have we got?" When he overturned the jack of hearts that filled out the run in his hand, he whooped in triumph, to accompanying moans from Jo and Gary.

It proved to be the last hand of the game, as Jo won on points and tonight's rules said you didn't have to take the bid to win. Tim vanished into his bedroom and the latest Bon Jovi CD. At least he went in for real rock and roll instead of Ice-T and the Backstreet Boys. Parents, Wy was learning, had by virtue of their job description much cause to be grateful for small favors.

The toilet flushed and Gary came into the kitchen. "You got any tools?"

Wy looked at him and he held up a hand. "Sorry. Stupid question. You got any non-FAA-approved tools?"

"There's a toolbox in the closet next to the front door. Why?"

"You've got a leak in your bathroom."

"What?"

"Don't worry about it; I can fix it. You got any scraps of Sheetrock around?"

"Sheetrock?"

"Never mind, I'll take a look, see what you've got."

"Gary—"

"Don't bother," Jo said, taking a stool at the counter. "You know what he's like when he gets in fix-it mode. Where's Liam?"

"He didn't call?"

Jo pointed at the message machine. The red light wasn't blinking.

"Oh." Wy put water on to boil for the macaroni, and got cheddar and parmesan out of the refrigerator. "Jo—"

"You want me to go and you want me to take Gary with me."

"Well . . ."

"No." Jo gave her a sunny smile. "For one thing, I can't leave; I'm on a story."

"What story? You said you were here on a family visit yesterday."

"That was before somebody rolled a severed human arm with a gold coin clenched in its fist out into the middle of Bill's dance floor." She gave Wy an expectant look. "Come on, give."

Wy was reluctant. "I don't know. I think it's part of an ongoing investigation."

Jo made a face. "All right, all right, I promise not to use anything until Liam gives me the okay. What did you find up on that glacier?"

Jo, her green eyes alive with curiosity and her blond hair virtually curling tighter in anticipation, was hard to resist. Wy grated cheese and chopped onions and minced garlic as she told the tale. When she came to the end of it, Jo let out a long, appreciative whistle.

"Wy?" Gary called. "Have you got any spackle?"

"Who cares?" Jo said impatiently. Gary tramped down the hall and out into the garage, muttering beneath his breath. "It's really an old C-47?"

Wy shrugged. "That's what it looked like from where we were standing."

"World War Two?"

"Maybe. It's pretty busted up, and I'm not that familiar with DC-3s."

"I thought you said this was a C-47."

"They're the same plane. The DC-3 was used for domestic passenger service, the C-47 for the military, freight, troops. It's a hell of a plane. They're not making them anymore but they're sure still flying them. They're great for freight." Her eyes lit. "I'd love to get my hands on one for the business."

"And you got the tail numbers?"

"The last three numbers, all that were left before the break in the fuselage." She moved her shoulders uneasily.

"What?"

"I didn't like seeing that wreck." She thought. "If it comes to that, I don't think any pilot likes seeing any wreck."

"This is an old one."

"Doesn't matter. I can't help wondering, why'd they go in? Weather? They get lost? Instrumentation go out on them? Crew fall asleep?"

Jo, caught up in Wy's imaginings, said, "Think they knew? Or did they just hit and kerflooey, that's all she wrote?"

"They knew," Wy said flatly.

"How do you know?"

"The pilot knew, for sure, and probably the copilot

as well. They may not have known but for a split second, but they knew they'd fucked the pooch, all right."

"I found this light fixture on the workbench," Gary said, coming into the room. "Where's it supposed to go?"

"My bedroom, but Gary, you don't have to—" She stopped when he headed down the hall. She turned to his sister. "What's the other thing?"

"What?"

"You said, when I tried to kick you out of Newenham, that you couldn't go because 'for one thing, I'm on a story.' What's the other thing?"

"Oh. That."

"Wy?" Gary's was a voice crying in the wilderness. "Where do you keep your paint?"

"At the paint store! What's the other thing?" she repeated to Jo.

"Okay." Jo fortified herself with a long swallow of beer. "It's this. Liam doesn't have anything to be worried about. Does he? With you and . . ." She jerked her head toward the bathroom.

"No."

"He doesn't seem to know that."

"I don't follow you."

Jo's sigh was heavy and martyred. "If he were sure of himself with you, he wouldn't give a damn how many ex-boyfriends were hanging around."

"Oh, for God's sake, Jo, can't you let this alone? I told you yesterday I—"

"I know." Jo nodded. "I listened very carefully and I heard every word you said."

"So?"

"So, what I didn't hear you say was that you were

completely, totally, and irrevocably committed to Liam Campbell, forsaking all others, world without end, amen. If I don't hear you saying that, I'm pretty sure Liam doesn't, either."

Wy was confused. "I still don't get what this has to do with your bringing Gary down here to get Liam all riled up."

"You say you love him."

"I do."

"You say you want him."

"I do."

"But you won't say you'll marry him."

"I can't have kids."

"I know that. And you told him, and so does he, now."

"He wants kids."

"Does he want them more than you?"

"He says not."

"And you don't believe him."

Wy was silent.

"And all these years, I thought you were so smart." Jo gave her head a long, sad shake. "Somebody's got to hold your feet to the fire, girl."

"And you think you're just the person to do that."

"Who better?"

"Seen anything of Jim Wiley lately?"

Beneath Wy's amazed gaze, Jo's fair skin flushed a deep and unexpected red. "Up yours, Chouinard."

"Up yours times two, Dunaway," Wy said, delighted to turn the tables. "Come to think of it, I haven't heard any tales this past month of your latest conquests, and usually I get on average at least one call a week. Not to mention which, you're traveling with your brother, also a rare event, as you usually use your trips to see me as getaway weekends for you and your latest. You and Jim, hmmm. You wouldn't be seeing each other socially, by any chance?"

"In his dreams."

"Or in yours," Wy retorted, and then had to duck.

After dinner and coffee and still no appearance by Liam, Jo and Gary took their leave with suitable expressions of gratitude. During the time before and after dinner, Gary had found and fixed the leak in the bathroom, recaulked the bathtub, installed the new light fixture in Wy's bedroom, and put a ground fault interruptor in the outlet next to the kitchen sink.

"Handy, isn't he?" Jo said.

"Speedy, too," Wy said.

Gary gave Wy a long look. "With some things. With others, I take my time."

"Too much information," Jo said. "We're out of here."

Wy closed the door behind them and went back to Tim's room.

He was sprawled across his bed, head propped up on a pillow, reading.

"Hey," Wy said.

"Hey," Tim said without looking around.

Wy sat next to him. "What are you reading?"

He turned the cover of the book toward her, and went back to reading.

"*Little Fuzzy*," Wy said, pleased. "One of my favorites. For fun or for work?" Mrs. Cash, the English teacher for seventh, eighth and ninth grades at Newenham Public School, was teaching a science-fiction lit class this semester.

"Work."

"You like it?"

"Yeah."

She refused to let his laconic replies deter her. "What else is she assigning?"

"I don't know."

She stifled a sigh, and then was startled when he actually volunteered a remark.

"She made us watch television today, before she handed out this book."

"What?"

He angled a sly look up at her. *Star Trek.*

She grinned. "Which one, and which episode?"

" 'TNG.' The one where Data has to prove he's not a toaster."

"Ah." She thought. "So you're headed for a discussion on sentience."

"Looks like."

"How do you like the course?"

"It's okay, so far." He turned back to his book.

She looked at him, his hair cropped and spiked with gel in the approved current style, the blue jeans that now, mercifully, fit instead of hanging off his butt. His watch was the X-Men one she had given him for Christmas, to match the Wolverine T-shirt and his very own VHS copy of the movie, which by now was about worn out.

His desk was a disaster area, littered with textbooks and notebooks and CDs and a Walkman and a Game Boy, undoubtedly loaded with Tim's beloved Tetris and ready to go. On the wall was a poster of Euclid holding a pair of calipers, with a caption reading, *There is no royal road to geometry.* Next to Euclid was a poster of Jennifer Lopez holding nothing and wearing less.

On a short picture ledge, ordered specially for the purpose, sat a photograph of a girl with pale olive skin, a mass of straight brown hair, and tip-tilted, laughing brown eyes. The brass of the frame was newly shined, and the ledge, unlike any other level surface in the room, was dust-free.

Wy steeled herself. "Natalie's coming over tomorrow afternoon." She had learned the hard way not to refer to Natalie Gosuk as his mother.

His back stiffened into one hard, inimical line. "What time?"

"Four o'clock."

"You'll be here?"

"Yes. Every time. Always."

He put down the book and rolled to look at her. "I don't want to see her."

"I know."

"But you're making me."

"Yes."

"Why?"

It was the first time he hadn't shouted the question at her in a rage, and she wanted so badly not to blow the answer. "She's your birth mother, Tim."

"You're more my mother than she ever was or ever will be."

Wy thought of the shivering, wounded scrap of humanity she had found crouched beneath his mother's front porch on a flight into Ualik over two years ago, and said, "I can't argue with that."

"Then why?"

Hard as she tried, she couldn't go straight at it. "I

understand your anger at her, Tim. I share it. Anger is a good thing in many ways. Anger makes you fight back. A lot of times it's the difference between surviving and going under."

He looked at her

"It's just that, sooner or later, you have to accept what happened to make you angry, acknowledge it and move on."

"What if I don't want to? You bet I'm mad at her." His voice rose. "I hate her! And she deserves it!"

"Yes, she does, but are you going to spend the rest of your life angry with her?" Without waiting for an answer, she said, "You have that choice. It's up to you; you can live from now until you die blaming everything bad that happens to you on your lousy childhood and the awful things your mother did to you."

"It wasn't just her."

It was as close as he'd come to talking about the rest of it. "I know," she said gently, when what she really wanted to do was rip and tear. "But what I'm telling you still goes. You can't do anything to change the past. I'm not saying you shouldn't be angry, but you've got to learn to put it aside and move on. The jails are full of people who never learned to do that." Interesting, she thought, how sometimes she opened up her mouth and Liam Campbell came walking out of it.

In that maddening way teenagers have of making logic where none exists, he said, "You saying I'm going to jail if I don't let her visit?"

"No. I'm saying if you can learn to tolerate her company for a few hours a week, you'll be a better person for it." She hesitated. "She's an alcoholic, Tim." He shot up, knocking his book to the floor, and she held up a hand. "It's not an excuse, I know. But it is a reason. Sober, she might have been a completely different person. A completely different mother."

"She wasn't sober."

"No, she wasn't. And she lost her chance to be that person with you. But she's sober now, and she's reaching out. And you have to remember something."

"What?"

"Whatever else, she gave you life."

"It wasn't much of one."

"It is now."

His eyes held more bewilderment than rage. "I can't believe you're making me do this."

She said the only thing she could say. "I love you, Tim. I will always be on your side, no matter what."

She wasn't sure he believed her, but she was wise enough to leave it at that.

EIGHT

Liam rousted every one of Lydia Tompkins' neighbors within a ten-mile radius, starting with the one right next door, hizzoner Jim Earl, the mayor of Newenham.

"Lydia's dead? Well, shit," was Jim Earl's response. "Son of a bitch, that was one feisty old broad. There were some tourists camping out on the river below her house last summer, making a lot of noise and mess, and she took her twelve gauge down the bluff and ran them off. And made them take their garbage with 'em, too. Hell." Jim Earl, who was about Lydia's age, scratched a bristly chin. "What a flirt."

"She flirted with you?"

Jim Earl grinned. "Lydia flirted with everybody. She liked men and she made no bones about it. Didn't matter if they were young or old or fat or skinny, she liked 'em all. Drove her kids nuts after Stan Sr. died."

Liam remembered the overly elaborate crossing and recrossing of Lydia's legs at the post the night she'd decked Harvey with the sun-dried tomatoes. "Did she have a boyfriend?"

"Wasn't for lack of trying it wasn't me."

"Aren't you married?"

"Not so's you'd notice."

Liam waited but Jim did not feel the need to explain further. "Did you see her with anyone else?"

"Nah. There's a lot of coming and going down this road; it's the only road along the river. Kids drive down to the end and park at Peter's Point; there's a lot of traffic from that."

"Did you see anybody on the road on your way to work?"

"Well, shit, sure, everybody else on their way to work. Everybody who's got a job. Murdered, you say? Lydia? Man, that just plain makes no sense at all."

The story was the same all up and down the road. The good news was, fishing season was over, so everyone who lived year-round in Newenham was home. The bad news was, the smallest house sat on at least an acre, and most of that acre was thickly forested, deliberately so. People lived in the Alaskan Bush because they liked their privacy. Usually the only view was east and south, overlooking the river, the opposite bank, and the beginnings of Bristol Bay.

He woke Elizabeth Katelnikoff, a nightshift worker at AC, from a sound sleep. She was not pleased with him, but when he told her why he was there her irritation quickly changed to distress. She'd gone to school with Karen Tompkins, and had eaten her share of Lydia Tompkins' fry bread on afternoons after school. "No, I didn't see anyone. Or not anyone I don't know. Jim Earl passed me going to work. So did Dave Lorenz, and Sarah Aguilar, and Mike Engebretsen. I didn't see Eric Mollberg, but his truck was in the driveway, parked kind of crooked. Probably sleeping it off." She paused, and frowned.

"What?" Liam said. "Anything, Elizabeth. I don't care how silly you think it sounds."

"There was this white pickup ahead of me when I turned off on the River Road."

"Whose?"

"I don't know."

"Alaska plates?"

"Probably." She thought. "No, definitely Alaska plates. I would have paid more attention if they weren't, especially at this time of year."

"The gold and blue, or the Chilkoot? A vet's, maybe, the one with the purple heart? The University of Alaska plate?"

She closed her eyes, her face scrunched up in thought, and opened them again. "Nope. I just don't have a clue, Liam. I'm sorry."

"I want you to look up every white pickup registered in Newenham," he told Prince back at the post.

"What make?"

"I don't know."

"What year?"

"I don't know."

"That narrows things down." She caught his look and became very professional. "Magistrate Billington called. She wants to know how long she's going to have to keep that goddamn arm in her freezer." Prince cleared her throat. "Er, that's a direct quote. Says it's scaring Dottie."

It took a moment for him to place the arm Bill was

talking about. "Tell her we'll get to it once we find out who killed Lydia Tompkins." He picked up the phone, forestalling further comment, and called Mamie Hagemeister. "Mamie? Liam Campbell, down to the trooper post. Can you get hold of Cliff Berg or Roger Raymo and tell them I need some help canvassing a neighborhood?"

There was a brief silence on the other end of the phone.

"Mamie?"

There was a long sigh. "Liam, Roger moved back to California to join the state troopers there. He and his wife left Newenham last week."

"What?"

"And Cliff Berg went to work for Alyeska Pipeline last month. Good job in the safety department, at about three times what Jim Earl was paying him. And you know his wife never has liked Newenham; she's been chomping at the bit to get back to Anchorage ever since they moved here."

For a moment Liam was completely at a loss. Not only did he not know Mrs. Berg, he'd never actually managed to speak to Cliff face-to-face. Come to that, he'd only ever talked to Roger Raymo on the phone. He'd been in Newenham since the previous May, almost six months. In that time he had managed to miss connecting with the two remaining local law-enforcement officers who, besides Mamie and her night-shift counterpart down at the lockup, constituted what was left of the Newenham Police Department. And now, when he needed them most, they'd run out on him to better-paying jobs in Anchorage and Outside. It was difficult not to feel ill-used.

He rallied. "Who did Jim Earl hire to replace them?" Silence. "Mamie?"

"Nobody yet," she said.

"But he's got someone in mind."

"He doesn't consult with me about who he's going to hire and fire, Liam," Mamie said testily.

"He's not going to hire anybody, is he," Liam said with a sudden flash of inspiration. "What, the troopers are supposed to do it all, in town and out of it?"

She hung up without answering.

He wondered if her irritation was because she wanted one of the officer jobs. He hoped she got it, but Jim Earl was the cheapest bastard who ever lived, and if it were legally possible not to fill those officers' positions he wouldn't, not so long as the complaints on response time didn't pick up. They were going into winter, after two bad fishing seasons. Everyone was broke, and with the stocks of just about any creature in the Bering Sea with fins and claws so far down as to be in the toilet, people were scared. A lot of people, when they got scared, got drunk. When they got drunk, they got into trouble.

When they got into trouble, the cops got into it.

Only now there weren't any cops. Just him and Prince.

Everything inside the Newenham city limits was, ostensibly, the province of the now nonexistent NPD. Everything outside of it, from Anchorage to Togiak and including every unincorporated town and village between, was within the province of the Alaska state troopers. So it wasn't like they didn't already have enough to do.

He saw Diana Prince give him a curious look and

realized his knuckles were white on the handset of the phone. He sat down and replaced it with elaborate care.

He knew he was emotionally too close to the Lydia Tompkins murder. He'd fallen hard for her when she'd marched into the post, carrying her artillery in with her in brown paper grocery bags. She was so proud to have apprehended Harvey in the act of breaking into her car, so pleased with her own initiative. And the great legs hadn't hurt. He couldn't help but adore her, her character, her spirit, her courage.

And he couldn't help but hate her killer with every part and fiber of his being. He wanted to find him and break him in half. And after that he wanted to hurt him.

He almost wished he hadn't met her. He wished like hell he hadn't had to respond to the scene of her murder. If she'd lived closer to town, and had there been any cops in that town, the troopers wouldn't have responded to the call reporting her death. Everyone on River Road was outside the municipal boundaries of Newenham. The upside was they didn't have to pay municipal taxes. The downside was they couldn't vote in municipal elections. When Jim Earl scored a federal grant large enough to build a new city hall, he made sure that the second floor was made of apartments, of which he made equally sure the largest was rented to him before the last doorknob was installed. The apartment was his legal address, but the house on the bluff was where he lived. It was a polite fiction everyone was willing to maintain, since nobody else wanted to be mayor.

"Sir?"

"What?" He looked at Prince.

"I've entered all of the Tompkins family interviews."

"Did you talk to the kids?"

"Daisy and Rose? No. Betsy wouldn't let me. She said to come out to the house tomorrow, maybe then."

"Any of the others have kids?"

"No. Just Betsy."

"I would have bet my last dime Lydia Tompkins was grandmother to nineteen." He looked at the chair she had been sitting in the night before, and the rage was back like a hammer blow. "Son of a *bitch*."

"Sir?"

"Nothing." He mastered his anger and reached for the phone again. "Joe Gould, please. Joe, it's Liam Campbell."

"I don't do autopsies."

"I know that," Liam snapped. "I'm just asking. You'll get the body on the first plane out tomorrow morning? I want the medical examiner to get a look at her right away."

"He's not going to tell you anything I haven't. She fought with someone in her kitchen. She got hit, she hit back, she got hit harder."

"What with?"

"Fists only, it looks like to me. I think she fell back and hit her head on the counter. There is a sharp, straight wound on the back of the skull, and there was blood and hair on the edge of the kitchen counter."

Liam hung up.

"I brought her calendar and her most recent bank and credit card statements from the house," Prince said. She indicated a pile on the desk in front of her.

"Good." He was only half listening, having logged on to his own computer to review her witness reports.

"I called Elmendorf Air Force Base," Prince said. "Talked to the PRO and gave him those partial numbers you brought back."

Partial numbers. Oh. Right. The plane in the glacier. "What did he say?"

"He said he didn't know of any recent crash, but that he would check the records from World War Two."

"Good. Does he want the arm?"

"I didn't offer it. He did ask for prints. I told him we'd already sent them to the crime lab, but that the skin on the fingertips was pretty deteriorated." She hesitated. "I didn't tell him about the coin, either."

"Oh? Why not?"

"I want to keep it in evidence for a while. At least until we identify the body."

"What makes you think we will?"

"The crew roster. There are bound to be records that match up with the tail number. The crew have been missing in action for over forty years. Their families will be glad to know what happened to them. Might even find enough to bury."

"What's that have to do with the coin?"

"I don't know. But I don't want it part of the official record yet. Just in case . . ."

"Just in case what?"

"Just in case somebody on that plane was doing something they shouldn't have. Their families will be glad to know what happened, but—"

"Just maybe not all of what happened?" Liam said. Prince shrugged. "Maybe."

"Well," Liam said, saving the report and exiting the program, "I don't see that it can do any harm."

He dismissed Prince, who protested not too much, as she had an appointment to look at a house for sale on the Icky Road. Normally housing was tight in rural Alaska, given the high costs of transporting building materials and the fact that less than one percent of the land in Alaska was privately owned. The times weren't normal. Two lousy salmon seasons and a severely curtailed snow crab season the previous winter, and every other house had a For Sale sign in the window, the owner hoping against hope for a rich tourist to drive by in his SUV rental and fall in love with the place. Naturally, it was just his luck that the housing market opened up after Liam had spent his first summer in Newenham sleeping, sequentially, in his office chair, then on a gradually sinking boat, and now sharing Wy's twin bed, which was approximately fourteen inches too short for him.

ANCSA hadn't helped the housing situation either, or at least not in Newenham. The Alaska Native Claims Settlement Act of 1971, in exchange for a right of way through aboriginal lands down the center of the state upon which to build the Trans Alaska Pipeline, had paid Alaska Natives a billion dollars and 44 million acres of land. Once the land selection process had been wrestled through, with, of course, the requisite amount of billable hours by as many lawyers as was humanly possible, lands were deeded to the thirteen Native regions. The regions, in turn, had parceled out acres to their shareholder. Newenham, this land was located mostly on th to Ik'ikika on One Lake, all forty miles of it good long ways off to either side. The individual shareholder did what any sensible person would do: Once they acquired title, they built on it and moved out of town, as a result like the folks on the River Road escaping local taxation and representation both. The people left living in town were, perforce, mostly white.

Which meant that Newenham had a white mayor, an even whiter chamber of commerce, a mostly white city council, and until a week ago an all-white police department. Every time another family moved out of town, the city coffers suffered and so did city services. It made for a certain amount of resentment in the white population, which manifested itself in surprisingly little racial friction, a thing for which Liam was profoundly thankful.

He wondered how Lydia Tompkins had felt about the situation in which Newenham and so many other towns and villages across the state found themselves. He would have liked to talk to her about it, to have sat at her feet and soaked up as much of the local history as she was prepared to ladle out.

He looked at her chair and pictured her in it, bright-eyed, militant, determined, sturdy, stubborn, resolved. She'd had a good fifteen, twenty, maybe more years in her as she had sat in that chair. Someone had robbed her of those years, and robbed Liam of her acquaintance.

Cops took murder personally. Vengeance was too ~ong a word, and given the current state of the judi-system you couldn't really call it justice. Justice ⁱ have Liam beaning the killer with a baseball bat 's kitchen and then going away to leave him to his own blood.

He went to Prince's desk and opened Lydia's calendar, an Alaska Weather calendar. October's picture was of a night sky with stars showing through an auroral display of green and pink and orange and purple and white.

There was a dentist appointment here, a doctor appointment there, a city council meeting, on the date of which Lydia had written in small, bold print, *Take notes about when plow didn't come!* Liam wondered how far out the River Road the city grader was supposed to run.

The letters SC appeared with some frequency for about three months up until the end of July and then disappeared. Betsy and her family were over for dinner once or twice a month, the whole Tompkins clan every month. Lydia had written menus for each gathering on the dates: Salmon, asparagus, salad was one month; king crab, boiled and served with butter and mayonnaise, another; moose pot roast a third.

Three times a week, Mondays, Wednesdays and Thursdays, Lydia had a four-hour appointment with the initials MC. The only other regular entries were on the last Saturday of every month: the letters BC, a kind of food (Mexican, Thai, Italian), and what looked like titles of novels. He flipped backward through the calendar. July had been *Here on Earth*, August had been *The Red Tent*, September had been *The Poisonwood Bible*, and October was to have been *Tracks*.

He looked up at the clock on the wall. It was seven. He shut down his computer, locked up the post and climbed into the Blazer. There he sat, his hands slack on the steering wheel, and wondered without much interest what was for dinner. With slightly more interest, he wondered if Jo and Gary would be there.

Lights approached the post, flooded the cab, and passed on down the road. He heard a sound and rolled down the window.

The croak of a raven came from the top of one of the three spruce trees clustered together at the side of the post. He tensed, but it was somehow less derisive in tone than he was used to hearing, a series of soft clicks and something else pretty near a croon and maybe even a coo.

He decided to drive out to Lydia's house on the way home, see what he'd missed that afternoon. Never mind that Lydia's house lay upriver and Wy's house down. If it had been his and Wy's house, he might have gone straight home. If the bed in Wy's bedroom hadn't been a twin, he might have gone straight home and straight to bed.

He had proposed the purchase of a larger bed when he had finally moved out of the Jayco trailer parked on her front doorstep and into the actual house. Wy had avoided saying yay or nay and he had feared pressing the issue after John Barton's job offer. The Jayco trailer was still out there and still available for banishment, and any bed with Wy Chouinard in it was good enough for him, or at least that was the way he had felt at first.

He was suddenly very tired of being on his best behavior, of living his life on sufferance, of forever waiting for Wy to make up her mind. He loved her, didn't he? And he'd told her so, over and over again, hadn't he? What the hell else did she want?

This time the raven's croak was mocking and derisive. He rolled up the window so he didn't have to listen to it and headed for River Road.

The house was dark when he pulled into the driveway, the narrow windows in their old-fashioned wooden frames presenting a blank and bland appearance to the world. When no one answered his knock he stepped inside. The kitchen was sealed off with crime-scene tape. The living room was much as they'd left it that afternoon.

He walked down the hallway and into the bathroom. It was small and narrow, with shelves on every spare inch of wall and the floor space reduced by clothes hamper, wastebasket, and a freestanding electric chrome towel rack that heated the towels hanging on it. The tub had a rubber-coated wire shelf stretched across it, filled end to end with bath salts, soaps and oils, a loofah, a pumice stone and a manicure set.

One shelf held six different kinds of shampoo and conditioner, bottles and bottles of body lotion and a cut-glass heart full of cotton balls. Another shelf held thirteen kinds of nail polish, from bright red to dark green, and all the accompanying paraphernalia for putting it on and taking it off. Liam hadn't seen anything like it since he'd lived with Jenny. Wy didn't do nail polish or makeup. Not that he minded. Or that she needed it.

A washcloth hung from a dragonfly hook over the sink. A silver porpoise, a green frog with one leg extended behind him, and a bronze twig formed the door and cupboard pulls of the sink cabinet. O drawer was full of exotically scented cakes of s another full of spare toothbrushes and small tu' toothpaste. A third held several prescriptions inflammatory, something for pain, and an The anti-inflammatory and the pain pills years out of date, the antibiotic only seven months so. Hidden in the back of the drawer beneath an arm splint with Velcro fastenings was a vaginal moisturizer. The box was half-empty of tubes.

Liam shut the drawer again with more haste than finesse. He stood there for a moment, an unaccustomed flush on his cheeks at this unexpected and unwelcome glimpse into Lydia's personal life. She'd been seventy-four, for crissake. Probably had more to do with comfort than, well, than sexual activity.

Jim Earl's words came back to him: *Wasn't for lack of trying it wasn't me.*

He couldn't remember ever being disconcerted by a discovery at a crime scene before. The first casualty of murder was privacy, and in fifteen years of tossing crime scenes he had discovered pretty much everything there was to find out about people, good and bad. He remembered the five men on the short list for the murder of a twelve-year-old girl, and on the basis of what he had found tucked away in every suspect's house how he would have fingered any of the five except for the man who actually did the kidnapping, raping, torture and murder. He'd come out of that case, one of the first after his probation was up, with the conviction that nothing would ever surprise him again. "You don't want to know what your neighbors ~re really up to," John Dillinger Barton had told him ~rward, and truer words were never spoken. For a ~, when he walked down a street, he would study ~s passing him and wonder what they had se- ~ their basements, behind the headboards of ~ in the crawl space between ceiling and roof. ~tood stock-still, frozen into embarrassed immobility at the prospect of a seventy-four-year-old woman having a sexual relationship.

Although . . . nobody said it was a rule you ever had to stop having sex. He certainly couldn't think of a day when he would want to. Why should Lydia have been any different? He'd read somewhere that a lot of women became more comfortable with sex after menopause, after the possibility of bearing a child had passed. While men could father children into senility.

As it did often, but never often enough, the memory of Charlie came back to him. Charlie and his bright blue eyes and his red cheeks and his fat little fists and his dimpled legs kicking madly in the air and his gurgling laughter and his wounded cry when someone had the gall to put him down in his crib when it wasn't his idea to be left there at all, uh-uh, and he said so, loud and clear. His son. Jenny's son. Taken from him by a drunk driver before his second year.

If Liam had been climbing the golden staircase up till then, it was all downhill from there. He'd stopped feeling, had stopped caring, had just stopped, period, until one day it was just too much trouble to respond to a call and five people had frozen to death in Denali Park.

And then he had come to Newenham and found Wy again, and suddenly breathing out and breathing in were not quite the effort they had been the moment before. Was it only six months ago? The beginning of May, spring in the Alaska Bush. A time of renewal that had spread open its arms and included him in its embrace.

Or so it had seemed.

He wandered through the house, hat in hand. There

were photographs everywhere, including the bathroom, pictures of family, children mostly, baby pictures, school pictures, snapshots of the family
gathered around a Christmas tree, looking for Easter
eggs in the alders in the backyard, on the deck of a
seiner named the *Daisy Rose,* on the bank of the river
with the house visible at the top of the cliff. He recognized the children, tracing their faces back in time to
rosy-cheeked babies wrapped in the same soft white
afghan. There was a picture of a teenage Lydia on a
beach, posing with twenty or so others her age in a
shot that smelled of Senior Skip Day. Some of the faces
looked familiar to Liam, although he couldn't quite
place any of them. A tall, painfully thin boy had an
arm draped around her shoulder and was laughing
down at her. It wasn't the man in the family photographs. She looked straight into the camera with a
wide, joyous smile that in no way belied the determined set to her jaw. She had looked very like that
when she had marched into the post, all flags flying.

Her bedroom was ruffled and bowed within an inch
of its life, and he wondered if she'd had it redecorated
when her husband died. The curtains, comforter, pillow shams and padded headboard were trimmed in
eyelet lace, and there was a vanity with a tiny stool
padded in white velvet sitting before it. Dozens of bottles of scent in weird and varied shapes lined up in
front of a mirror with an elaborate gilt frame, and the
Kleenex box was hidden by a porcelain cover with
hummingbirds painted on it. "I am a female, female,"
Liam said, and then tried to remember where the line
came from. Oh, yeah. *Flower Drum Song.* Jenny and her
musicals.

The other two bedrooms had the lingering reso-
nance of adolescence, try as Lydia had to transform
them into a guest room and an office. The guest room
held a queen-size bed and a dresser, which were
nearly crowded out by a pile of stuffed bears, a large
cardboard box of basketballs and a shelf full of well-
thumbed picture books, including the entire Dr. Seuss
oeuvre. The office walls had been reserved for graduation pictures, four of them, eight-by-elevens in gilt
frames, mortarboards tilted to the correct angle, tassels
hanging on the correct side, Betsy slimmer and serious
and dignified, Stan bluff and hearty like his father,
Jerry thin to the point of emaciation and anxious about
what was going to happen to him now, Karen giving
the photographer an up-from-under look that said
plainly, *Know what it would be even more fun to do?*

For all her froufrou taste, Lydia had been a neat
creature. Her bills were filed by utility name in the top
drawer of a two-drawer filing cabinet. The bottom
drawer held tax returns going back thirty years. Liam
opened the most recent one and raised an eyebrow.
Stanley Tompkins Sr., unlike many of his Bristol Bay
contemporaries, must have saved his money from the
years when the Bristol Bay salmon runs were the
largest in the world. His widow had been very well-
off, although you'd never have known it. On the evidence feminine to the core, still, Lydia wasn't the
diamonds-and-champagne type.

Like the kitchen, the office was dated but functional. An old Smith-Corona electric hummed pleas-
antly into life when Liam pushed the switch. The office
telephone was a heavy black desktop model with a rotary dial. There was no computer, no fax machine, no

scanner, no printer. No answering machine. His heart warmed to her even more. Heaven, to Liam, was anywhere without an answering machine. He hated that little blinking red light that signaled messages waiting.

He went back to her bedroom, not because he wanted to search it further but because of all the rooms in the house it seemed the most hers. He was afraid he would collapse the vanity stool if he sat on it, so he perched, gingerly at first, on the edge of her bed. "Tell me what you know, Lydia," he murmured. "Who did this to you, and why?"

He thought of fetching paper and pencil from the office to lay out one of his grids, with Lydia in a box at the center and arrows pointing to possible suspects, but he couldn't summon up the necessary energy. He was suddenly so tired. He didn't think Lydia would mind if he closed his eyes for a few minutes.

He dreamed, dark dreams. John Dillinger Barton, disappointment and disapproval on his face. Charlie in the morgue, so tiny, so helpless, so white and cold and broken beyond repair. Jenny, day after day, month after month, quiet and abnormally still in her hospital bed, eyelids closed, face immobile except for what seemed like a tiny smile at the corners of her lips. Jim uncomfortable in a suit and a tie, standing next to an open grave.

Wy. She had the most marvelous mouth, lush, full-lipped. She didn't wear lipstick; a man didn't have to worry about getting all smeared up. He'd wanted to kiss her the first time he saw her, and only managed to keep his hands off her because, first, he was married and a father and, second, she was his pilot, en route to a crime scene.

It turned out she was just as attracted to him, and it hadn't been long before they'd both begun behaving very badly indeed, culminating in a long weekend in Anchorage, at the end of which she had broken it off and disappeared. He'd gone back to Charlie and Jenny knowing she was right, knowing that they were doing the right thing, knowing, too, that the sun didn't shine the same way it had before he had met her. He had tried for contentment. He hoped Jenny had never known, but the experienced philanderers he heard talking in the locker room at the club said wives always knew. God, he hoped she hadn't.

Wy would creep into his mind unbidden and unwelcome, once when he was making love to Jenny and doing his damnedest to do his best by her. Jenny came and then he did and all he could think of was Wy and her mouth and her hair and her arms and the way she made him feel.

He could almost imagine her there now, her teeth nipping at his jaw, her hands deft on his belt, that lush red mouth nibbling at his own. He was hard in an instant. He pushed up into her hand and she made a low, purring sound. Her breast was covered; with an impatient sound he nudged the fabric aside, fumbled for the snap on her bra and sighed his relief when her breast snugged into his hand. He turned his mouth in to her kiss. She sucked his tongue into her mouth, and his pants were no longer big enough to contain him, he could hardly breathe, he ripped at his zipper.

"Let me," she said.

The sound of her voice pulled him fully awake with a jerk that nearly dislocated his fifth, sixth, and seventh vertebrae. "What the hell?"

"No, let me," she said, sliding both hands inside his open fly and bending down. Her mouth was wet, warm, and eager.

He grabbed her arms and pushed her off him, ignoring her protest. He rolled off the bed and staggered to the light switch next to the door. When the overhead light went on it revealed Karen Tompkins, looking much more like a cat than a kitten now, one who was in lapping distance of the cream. Her hip-huggers were unsnapped and the zipper halfway down over a taut, smooth belly. Her sweater was pushed up over her breasts. Her eyes were heavy, and she smiled. She sprawled on her back, her legs spread, and she slid a hand between them and up, crooking a finger, beckoning him back to the bed.

He couldn't remember the last time he'd been this hard without Wy in the room. He caught sight of himself in the vanity mirror, his shirt unbuttoned, his pants unzipped, the head of his cock peeping out of the top of his shorts, still wet from her mouth. The fact that he was in uniform, or rather, almost out of it, was as shameful as the fact that he'd almost cheated on Wy. He stuffed everything back in and zipped up again with some difficulty.

Karen pouted. She had a lower lip a man could suck on until next Tuesday. Her mother had had the same lip, he remembered. He avoided looking straight at it. "Could you zip up, please?" When she stretched instead, giving a soft little moan while she was at it, he said, "Just put it all together again, Karen, okay?"

She sighed and slid off the bed, walking to within reach. Everything got pulled down and refastened, although it seemed to take her forever and she pouted the whole time. When she was done and giving him that patented come-hither, up-from-under look that she'd been working on since high school, he said, "What the hell do you think you were doing?"

She shrugged, and one side of the wide-necked sweater slid down a shoulder. "Who's been sleeping in my bed?" she said, and smiled a long, slow, seductive smile.

In that moment, she looked so much like her mother that it was difficult not to meld the two women in his mind. "It's not your bed; it's your mother's."

She shrugged again. The sweater slipped a little more. "It's not my fault if you choose to snooze in Mom's bed. Let's just say you were a temptation too strong to resist." She backed up a step and gave the mattress a testing shove. "Mmmm," she said, and smiled at him. "I've always liked this bed. And God knows Mom got enough use out of it. You sure?"

"I'm sure," he said grimly.

And he was.

Her breasts pushed at the sweater in a sigh.

Wasn't he?

"What are you doing here, anyway?" she said, wandering over to the vanity and picking up the perfume bottles one at a time.

He was a grown man, with adolescence far in the past. He no longer thought with his cock. If she was going to take things coolly, he was going to be even cooler. "I didn't have time to go over the place as thoroughly as I wanted this afternoon."

"Hmm." She uncapped a bottle and sprayed an infinitesimal amount on the inside of her wrist. She held it out to him. "What do you think?"

"Very nice," he said without leaning forward to smell.

" 'Very nice,' " she said, mocking. "Is that the best you can do? A woman wants her perfume to be irresistible."

"I looked at your mom's files," he said. "She was pretty well-off."

She shrugged an indifferent shoulder. "Dad was a good fisherman, and they saved their money."

"I didn't find a copy of a will. Was there one, do you know?"

She shrugged again. The sweater slipped all the way off her shoulder and halfway down her arm. She skimmed a finger down and pulled it back up very slowly, watching him all the while, one speculative brow raised, her mouth curved in a smug smile. "I guess. Mom said there was."

"Where is it?"

"I don't know."

"Did your mom have an attorney?"

"Probably Ed Kaufman. He's pretty much everyone's lawyer around these parts."

"Do you know who inherits your mother's estate?"

"It's divided three ways."

"Three?"

"Me, Betsy and Stan."

"Jerry doesn't get any?"

"Dad said he'd just piss away whatever he got left. The way he left things, when Jerry got too down and out Mom was supposed to help him. Now that Mom's dead, we're supposed to."

She wasn't exactly overcome with grief, Liam noted, and with tremendous relief felt that knowledge reach his shorts. "Who were your mother's friends around town?"

"Well, there was us."

His stare was patient, and he waited.

She pouted, what she obviously considered to be her very best thing, and when that didn't work pouted harder. "She had a book club that met once a month. They used to meet once a year in Anchorage or somewhere, too. I guess they'd know her best."

"Who were they?" He wrote down their names. "Okay, that's all, I think." He closed his notebook and pocketed it.

She followed him to the door. "Y'all come back now, you hear?" she called after him.

The Blazer was doing seventy-two on the unpaved surface of the River Road, ice, ruts, potholes, washouts, rock slides, snow drifts and all, in ninety seconds flat.

December 8, 1941

The news about Pearl Harbor came over the radio. The CO stood us down to listen. Sounds like the guys in Pearl really got it in the neck. Pearl was our main base in the Pacific. Whats to stop the Japs now? Im so thankful Helens back in Birmingham. They cant get to her there. The CO says we have to expect an attack and put everybody on alert. Were standing one in four watches on the aircraft in case of sabotage. March is bitching but then March is always bitching. I think he's got a girl in town, he's always off base when we arnt in the air. Im not sure Roepke really knows were at war hes always got his nose stuck in a book and when I asked him what he thought about Pearl he said, the barley, the onion, or the oyster?

Peters worried about family he's got at home. The way the brass talks they're expecting an invasion of Jap forces any minute and for sure the people in the islands and on the coast will get hit first. He wants to send money home and he asked me if I know anyone whos flying to Russia. He really harps on this Russia thing.

NINE

By ten o'clock Liam still wasn't home, and Wy was restless, the conversation with Jo replaying in her head. Was Jo right? Was Wy so untrusting that she was afraid to make a commitment? If so, was that something she could live with, or something she had to change? Did she want to change it? Which, when it came down to it, meant one thing: Was she ready to commit the rest of her life to Liam Campbell?

One thing seemed sure: Men left her. Men came into her life, made her love them, and left. Her father, Bob DeCreft, Liam.

She could get really angry about that if she wanted to. She could let herself get royally pissed off.

The conversation she'd had with Tim that evening came back. *Sooner or later you have to accept what happened to make you angry, acknowledge it and move on.*

Her father had given her life. Bob had given her wings. Liam had taught her to love. Would she change any of it, just to spare herself pain?

No. She would not.

There. It was amazing how much relief one un-equivocal answer provided.

There were other questions she needed answers to. Would Liam stay in Newenham or return to Anchorage? If he stayed, was she willing to make him a permanent part of her life? If he went, would she go with him? Would Tim?

She went out on the deck. It was crisp and cold, with frost already forming underfoot. The stars burned white-hot holes in the night sky and were reflected in the river below. They called it the Nushugak but really, it should have been called Bristol Bay Route 1. It carried boats up and down its one-hundred-fifty-mile length all summer long, and then it froze over and turned into a highway for snow machines, lasting until breakup. The river was the breath of life for Newenham and the hundred villages and homesteads and fish camps along its length. Wy liked living next to it. Sooner or later, everyone you knew floated or drove by.

Sooner or later, it brought everyone home.

She dropped into horse stance, to see if tai chi would give her some peace of mind, but they were working on the four Fair Ladies and she needed Moses to untangle her.

Or Liam.

Screw it.

She went back inside, started her computer and got on-line. She checked her Web site first, to see if anyone had posted a reservation. The Web site was a new innovation and had cost her a lot of money, but contrary to her fear that no one would search the Net for "air taxi—Bristol Bay," it was already paying off. Four cari-

bou hunters from Anchorage wanted a ride to
Mulchatna. Someone else wanted to take his girlfriend
and another couple out to a lodge at Outuchiwenat
Mountain. A pilot up in Niniltna she had met at the air
show in Anchorage the year before had written com-
plimenting her Web site and asking her who maintained it. She sent confirmations to the first two and a
name, phone number and e-mail address to the pilot.

She wasn't sleepy, and the house was very quiet.
The crack beneath Tim's door was dark. Maybe Liam
had driven back up to the crash site, although she
couldn't think why. On impulse she keyed into a
search engine and looked up DC-3s. The amount of information that came up made her blink.

The Douglas C-47 Skytrain was a redesign of the
civilian DC-3 twin-engine commercial airliner, which
she already knew. The RAF called them Dakotas, the
U.S. Navy the less romantic R4D. The military used it
to transport troops and cargo, including carrying para-
troopers over enemy territory, especially during the
Normandy invasion. She shuddered. Why the hell anyone would want to jump out of an airplane was beyond
her. The whole point was to stay in the air, where the
Wright brothers had intended you to be, until you were
ready to come down with, not without, your aircraft.

This of course led memory back to the previous
summer, when none other than Trooper Liam Campbell had jumped out of a Piper Super Cub into a lake
in hot pursuit of a felon getting away on a four-
wheeler. The Super Cub had been hers and she'd been
on the stick at the time, aiding and abetting the afore-
said trooper. Plus the felon hadn't been quite as felo-
nious as previously thought.

Which, of course, was completely different from parachuting into a war zone. She clicked on the first link in the list and thought she'd made a mistake when a site on Lend-Lease popped up. She knew what Lend-Lease was, sort of: It was the act under which the United States shipped war materials to friendlies in World War II before Pearl Harbor brought them directly into the war themselves. March 11, 1941, was when the site said the act had gone into effect. The Japanese attack had come barely nine months later. She thought of the glacial processes of the Federal Aviation Administration, and nine months didn't seem long enough to move the federal government into that much action.

They'd called it "An Act to Promote the Defense of the United States," and like all government documents, it went on forever. She waded through the *notwithstandings* and the *heretofores* until she got to what seemed to be the relevant clause. It began, of course, with

> Notwithstanding the provisions of any other law, the President may, from time to time, when he deems it in the interest of national defense, authorize the Secretary of War, the Secretary of the Navy, or the head of any other department or agency of the Government (1) To manufacture in arsenals, factories, and shipyards under their jurisdiction, or otherwise procure, to the extent to which funds are made available therefor[e], or contracts are authorized from time to time by the Congress, or both, any defense article for the government of any country whose defense the President deems vital to the defense of the United States.

Any defense article for the government of any country whose defense the President deems vital. That seemed

pretty broad, even for the president of the United
States. Someone should have been looking over Roosevelt's shoulder. Where was Congress? Where was
Jesse Helms? She was pretty sure her teacher had mentioned something about checks and balances between
the executive, legislative, and judicial branches of government in her high school civics class.

And then, after he caused them to be built, the act
said the president could sell them, transfer them, lend
them, or lease them. The act covered food, machinery,
and services. Harry Hopkins, FDR's good friend and
true, started the ball rolling before handing it off to one
Edward R. Stettinius Jr., of whom Wy had never heard
and probably never would again. Originally intended
to benefit China and the British empire back when
Churchill was still fighting like hell to keep it one, in
November 1941 the act was extended to include the
Soviet Union. Yeah, that had worked out well.

The budget for Lend-Lease was a billion three, back
when a billion three was serious money. Of course, in
the way of government programs everywhere, it
wound up costing much more than that, exceeding $50
billion in the end. Nobody ever paid it all back. Most
of the countries settled for lesser amounts within fifteen years, although the USSR didn't get to the table
until 1972.

She scrolled down. Well, well.

It turned out that C-47s came under the heading of
defense article.

She wondered, a little guiltily, if any of this stuff
should have been a surprise to her. She held a degree
in education, which had included a three-hundred
level class in Alaskan history. Had they studied Ler

Lease? Seemed like they ought to have, but she couldn't remember doing so. True, she hadn't been the most dedicated student ever to pass through the doors of the University of Alaska, Fairbanks.

Wy had gone to college at the behest of her adoptive parents, teachers both. The only classes she'd ever taught had been during her student-teaching internships, as the day after graduation she'd enrolled in flight school. She'd soloed after eight hours and from then on as much time as possible was spent in the air, filling up her flight log until three years ago when Bob DeCreft, in anticipation of his eminent retirement, offered her the Nushugak Air Taxi Service at a bargain-basement price. The sale brought her a Piper Super Cub, a Cessna 180, two tie-downs at the Mad Trapper Memorial Airport, a shed at same, and a two-bedroom, one-bathroom house on the Nushugak River. It also brought her a lot of goodwill in Bristol Bay. People were willing to take on faith anyone Bob DeCreft recommended.

Professionally, it was what she had been aiming at since she'd earned her pilot's license; a business small enough to run by herself that kept her in the air most of her working hours. Personally, there had been two benefits, one expected and one not: It got her out of Anchorage and away from Liam, at the time a much-married man and father, and, one day on a flight into Ualik, it had brought her Tim.

So she couldn't complain, and neither could her parents, retired now and living in Anchorage, with twelve weeks of each winter spent in a condo on a golf ourse on the Big Island. They couldn't say she had asted her education, independent businesswoman that she was now. But the fact of the matter was, she'd never been that good a student. It was probably more rebellion than anything else. She was maintaining an outward show of compliance by studying something her parents wanted her to, while determining inwardly to retain as little of it as possible.

She did another search, and discovered that World War II had been good to the territory of Alaska. During the war, the federal government had spent over a billion dollars on infrastructure, including docks, wharves and breakwaters in harbors up and down the coast. The Alaska Railroad was updated and improved, and roads were constructed, including the AlaskaCanada Highway, the only highway into Alaska. The Alcan had been built by the military during World War II—she knew that much—but she hadn't realized how much it had to do with Lend-Lease. Lend-Lease aircraft were supposed to be flown through Canada, following the route of the highway, on to Nome and then across the Bering Strait to Russia.

The phone rang, the business line next to the computer. "Nushugak Air Taxi," she said into the receiver.

"I'll be late tonight."

She looked up at the clock. It was ten minutes to twelve. "You already are."

"Surprised you noticed."

She winced away from the force of his hang-up. Ouch. Was he really that angry about Gary Dunaway being in town? Liam had never struck her as the jealous type.

But then, how well did she really know him? They hadn't had that much time together. A few months of flying him to crime scenes when she was on contract to the state's Department of Public Safety, four intense days in Anchorage, and the last six months, during which they hadn't exactly lived in each other's pockets.

She knew he preferred single-malt scotch, read poetry and history, could tutor Tim at math. He had allowed himself to be browbeaten into learning tai chi under the direction of that fiery little tyrant, Moses Alakuyak. He loved wearing the uniform of the state trooper; he seemed to expand inside it, some mysterious alchemy transforming him into more than a man. Call it a manifestation of the law of the land.

And he was good at it. Even after six months of laying it down, even as new to the area and to the people in it as he was, in a place where the previous trooper had made himself despised by his indifference and his indolence, Liam had earned the respect of town dweller and villager, hunter and guide, fisher and fish hawk, white and Native alike. The main difference, so far as she could tell, seemed to be that Liam loved the job. He seemed to love being a trooper the way she loved being a pilot, and in some way she had yet to explain to herself it was the reason Wy loved him most.

And, yes, she was in love with him—she knew that—madly, passionately in love with him, the love-story kind of love, the rip-your-heart-out-and-serve-it-up-on-a-platter-to-do-with-as-you-will, the Pyramus-and-Thisbe, Tristan-and-Isolde, Abelard-and-Heloise kind of love.

Although, come to think of it, most or all of those couples wound up dead. Or castrated. She placed the receiver in the cradle and pushed back from her desk. The screen of the computer went black, with points of light zooming into and then out of range. The traveling-through-space screen saver. She could wish for a little journey to the stars at the moment.

She got the Bushnells out of the desk and went out on the deck. The stars hadn't gone anywhere, Orion and the Pleiades and the Dippers and Cassiopeia, Taurus the Bull, the Great Square of Pegasus. It was cold out, below freezing, according to the thermometer fastened to the frame of the living room window, but she put the binoculars down and went into horse stance and forced herself through the form, blowing through the Fair Ladies like she knew what she was doing. The second time it was easier; the third time she was sweating freely and her thighs were trembling. She went through it a fourth time just to prove she could, and when she reached Step Up, Parry and Punch she really let loose.

"That Liam you knocking on his ass?" a voice said.

She slid into Apparent Close-Up and Conclusion, brought her right fist into her left palm, and bowed, once and low, in Moses' direction.

The old man was sitting on the top step of stairs leading from the deck to the edge of the cliff and the beach below. That beach was littered with shards of ice, which, in another snow and a few more high tides, would join together and reach out to the opposite shore, where the same process was taking place. In a month, perhaps less, the two would meet in the middle in a frozen handshake that would last the winter long.

"I didn't know you were there, *sifu*."

"Yeah, well, there's a lot of things you don't know."

His words were a little slurred, which meant he'd been drinking. Although she wasn't sure he was ever entirely sober, and he had to drink a lot before it affected him in speech or gait. He claimed to drink to drown out the sound of the voices that afflicted him with prophecy. He could tell the future, could Moses Alakuyak, and it never brought him any joy. Perhaps it was because people had always done what they wanted to in the first place, regardless of the best advice given them, and always would. It didn't help Moses' disposition any to watch lives going down in flames all around him, when the way out of the inferno was so clearly seen only to himself. He was a prophet without honor in his own country.

Still, that was no reason to allow him to attack unchallenged. "Is this my night to get beaten up by every man in my life?" she wondered out loud.

"It's sure as hell your night to get beaten up by me." He didn't sound like he was joking.

"Always a pleasure," she said. "You want something to drink?"

"Got any scotch?"

Liam did, single-malt, and Moses knew it. "I was thinking of something more along the lines of a mugup. You have any more to drink this evening and you're going to roll right off this deck."

"Who gives a shit?"

"Pretty much anyone who knows you, though I'm beginning to wonder why," she retorted. "Why don't you come inside?"

"I'm fine out here."

"You be fine out here, then." And she gave him the satisfaction of stamping back into the house and slamming the door behind her until the glass rattled in the frame.

He was still perched on the top step when she came back outside with two steaming mugs. This time she had her down jacket and her boots on, and she brought out a blanket, too, and wrapped it around his shoulders. It surprised her, and made her a little uneasy, when no scathing commentary followed on it being a fine thing when the wimmenfolks felt they had to swaddle up a grown man like he was some kind of baby too dumb to stay out of the cold.

They sat next to each other on the top step, if not in companionable silence then in silence. She'd made them tea and laced it well with honey. After an initial contemptuous snort, he drank without complaint.

Orion was well up in the sky, the Pleiades a bright cluster just out of his reach.

Wy loved flying on nights like this, when the stars went on forever and the lights on the control panel were a dim green glow, with no sun to create thermals to bounce over and the comforting drone of the engine the only sound. She hated to land on night flights, wanted to keep going as far as she could, as long as she could, wrapped in an immense cloak of warm, black velvet studded with bright, glittering rhinestones, just her, and the plane, and the night.

A meteor streaked across the sky, another, followed by a third. What day was it? That's right, October 21, the first day of the Orionid meteor shower. One day she wanted to be Outside in August during the Perseid meteor shower, maybe Colorado, high up in the Rockies, to see John Denver's "raining fire in the sky." Meteor showers were invisible in Alaska in the summertime; the days were too long.

Moses had been quiet for too long, too, when his expressed intent in coming here had been to give her grief. "What's wrong, uncle?" she said, using the honorific earned by every elder the length and breadth of the YK Delta just for outliving their contemporaries.

He raised his head and stared out across the river. "You asked me about your father."

Wy forgot to breathe.

His voice was dry and without expression. "His father ran out on him before he was out of diapers, and his mother did the best she could, but the booze got hold of her and she wasn't much use after that. Still, he was a cute little bugger, and smart, too. He managed to make it all the way through high school, supported them both working deckhand, and could have had a full-time job with just about anybody when he graduated. But he wanted to work the big boats, Alaska Steam, the ferries."

Moses paused for tea, and Wy discovered her hands had clenched around her mug. She unclamped them, one finger at a time, cautious not to make it obvious, terrified that even the smallest movement would distract him, change his mind.

"He worked for a couple of years, saving his money, and he was all set to go to school in Seattle when he fell in love."

Her mother.

"I have never seen any two people more in love in my life," Moses said, sounding almost judicial in tone. "They were crazy for each other, dancing the night away at the bars, necking in his truck out at the end of River Road, holding hands so they couldn't hardly get through a door when they needed to." He shook his head, and in the softest voice she'd ever heard him use, said, "No. That's not how I mean it to sound. That's not how it was. They were in love, girl. Head-over-heels, fly-me-to-the-moon, I-only-wanna-be-with-you love. You understand?"

Her throat tight, she managed to say, "Yes."

"Thought you might."

She waited as long as she could. "What happened?"

He shrugged. "What usually happens when two people fall in love? They got married."

"Was she pregnant?"

"What? No. They didn't have to get married; they wanted to. He told her all his plans, and she was all for it, so they were careful not to let anything happen to get in the way. They needed a place to live, though, so he used up his savings to buy them a little house, and he went back to work deckhanding, saving up enough to get the both of them Outside and him to school. She was miserable with him out on the water most of the time, but she handled it. Got herself a job down to the cannery on the slimer. Then she got herself an idea, and the next time he was in town and they had come up for air—"

His dry tone made her smile involuntarily.

"—she tells him. They could apply for a loan. They'd just opened up a local branch of an Anchorage bank, and he was a local boy with a good reputation. No reason somebody wouldn't lend him money. So they did."

You really are a master of the dramatic pause, you miserable old son of a bitch, she thought, not a respectful way even to think of one's elder and teacher. She was determined this time not to ask, but she didn't last thirty seconds. "What happened? Did the bank turn them down?"

"No." He shook his head and laughed, not a nice

laugh. "No, the bank didn't turn them down. It would have been better if they had."

"Uncle! What happened?"

"The bank manager told them she would have to sign the loan because she was the responsible member of the marriage."

She stared at him, again trying to make out his face in the dark. "Why?"

"She was white."

"What?"

"She was white, Caucasian, Polish-German-Scotch-Irish-English. A round-eye. A gussuk. Daughter to the BIA teacher couple in Icky. Think they were from Indiana, or some such."

Wy closed her eyes and bowed her head. "And he was native."

"Yupik as you and me. More. Myself, I think that was the beginning of the end. Oh, they went out to Seattle, and he came back with his certificate, and he got on the big boats. I imagine most of the big boats had mostly white crews and they weren't easy on him. He started drinking, and they started fighting. In the middle of all this, she gets pregnant."

"With me."

"With you. He ran off, Wy. Maybe he was just following the sterling example set by his own father. Maybe he just couldn't watch the world be mean to a child of his. I don't know. One day he was there; the next he was gone."

"What did my mother do?"

"She had you and farmed you out to your father's sister. Not the best thing she could have done, in the circumstances."

Wy remembered what little she could of her first years on earth, and bile rose up in her throat. No. Not the best thing.

"And then she left."

"Do you know where she is?"

He hunched a shoulder.

"What about my father? Do you know where he is?"

"Your father's dead, Wy."

She drew in a sharp breath.

"He quit drinking and eventually moved up to master on the Alaska ferry system. He divorced your mom and remarried. He had three kids by his second wife."

"I have half brothers and sisters?"

"Yeah."

"Where are they?"

"Outside somewhere. I don't know exactly where."

"Would someone in Icky know?"

"Probably. Whether they'll tell you . . ." He shrugged.

The red buoy at the mouth of the river winked on and off, on and off. Red right returning. On the very edge of the horizon she thought she could see the lights of a boat, too far away to see if it was coming up the river or passing it by. A meteor streaked across the sky. She took a long, shaky breath. "Thanks for telling me, uncle."

He grunted.

"Why now?" she said. "Why didn't you tell me all this when I first moved back to Newenham? You must have known from the beginning who I was, and who my father was. You knew I wanted to know. Why didn't you tell me?"

Another long silence, during which she got the impression, unusual in the extreme, that Moses was picking out the right words to use. "I hoped I wouldn't have to," he said finally.

She stared at him, trying to decipher his expression in the dark. " 'Wouldn't have to'? I don't understand."

"Remember last month, when you launched that two-bit kite into a gale-force wind to come after that boy of yours?"

Now she was angry. "Don't try to change the subject, old man." And then she added, "And six-eight Kilo isn't a kite."

"I'm not changing the subject," he said, his voice flat. "Do you remember?"

"Of course I remember. I nearly wrecked the plane, which would have taken out half my equipment inventory." And Liam had been with her.

"What made you do it, girl?" He sounded only curious, but she knew him well enough to know that, for Moses, curiosity alone was never a reason to do anything. "Gale-force winds, abrupt temperature changes, snow changing to sleet changing to hail changing to rain. It wasn't VFR; hell, it wasn't even good enough to be IFR. It was a National Weather Service wet dream. So what made you do it?"

"I . . ." She tried to think. "Jim and Jo had figured out that somebody was leaving bodies in a line leading to Old Man Creek. I knew Tim was there. I knew you and Bill and Amelia were there. I didn't think about it much, I just—"

He was inexorable. "Why did you come, Wy?"

"I guess . . . I couldn't not come, Moses."

There was a brief silence before he sighed and

shifted, the rough nap of the army blanket catching at
the shoulder of her parka. When he spoke again, his
voice, a deep, raspy husk to begin with, sounded like
gravel being ground together. "Something tell you to?"

Wy stiffened. "I beg your pardon?"

"Did something tell you to come to Old Man? Call
it instinct, intuition, a gut feeling."

"A voice?" she said.

He was surprised into a snort of laughter. "Yeah. A
voice."

She was almost amused. "I don't do voices, Moses.
That's your line of work."

He was silent for a while. "It's hereditary."

"What is?"

"Hearing the voices. It's passed down, generation
to generation."

She felt a pricking at the back of her neck. A flash
caught her eye, and she looked up to see another meteor, a second, a third. It seemed to be a long time before she could form her next question, and when it
came it was a weak "So?"

"So sometimes it skips a generation or two, according to the stories. Sometimes they just take a while to
make themselves heard."

"Moses—"

"I was the man who ran out on your father, Wy."

"What?"

"I'm your grandfather. Me, Moses Alakuyak. You,
born Wyanet Kukaktlik, to Eleanor Murphy and Doug
Kukaktlik, adopted by Mary Anne and Josep
Chouinard. You are my granddaughter. Mine by blo
and bone, if not by my presence in your life, u
three years ago."

The meteors were raining down on them now; every time one painted a streak across the horizon, a second burned into existence before the first's tail had faded. She said the only thing she could think of saying. "My father's name was Kukaktlik?"

"I didn't marry his mother."

She had wondered about the marital status of her parents. There had been hints here and there, a look from an Ickyite now and then. Icky was a notoriously upright village, and they wouldn't take kindly to illegitimate children. And she had wondered about the families they had come from. It wasn't as if she hadn't already suspected the truth, but last summer Moses himself had refused to answer the direct question.

And now he was volunteering information like there was no tomorrow. "You are my grandfather," she said, testing the sound of it on the night air. The stars did not alter in their courses. The meteor shower seemed to have tapered off. Everything seemed much as it was before she had said the words out loud.

And yet everything was changed.

"Yes," he said. "I wasn't going to tell you."

"Why?" she said in quick protest. "Why not? You knew I wanted to know who my family was, that one of the reasons I decided to come back to Newenham was to find out."

He sighed, a sound she had never before heard him make. "I got as drunk as I could before I came out here."

"Why?"

"Same reason as anybody looking for the courage to the right thing."

"Moses, I don't know what you mean."

heaved himself to his feet and stood looking

across the river at Bulge, the three-house village on the opposite shore, away to the south at the lights of an approaching boat, anywhere but at her. "I hear voices. It's a hereditary curse, according to legend. You're my granddaughter."

When she got it, she only wondered why it had taken so long. "Are you saying I'm going to start hearing voices?" Her voice scaled up.

"I'm saying I think you already do."

She searched frantically for something to say in reply to that, and came up empty.

"It's why I started teaching you tai chi in the first place."

She blinked, confused. "What? I thought . . . What are you talking about? You showed up on my doorstep one day and bullied me into horse stance and you wouldn't leave until I got it right, and then you left me standing in it until I actually fell over! I thought it was some kind of initiation, that you did it to everyone who moves to Newenham, and so I went along with it because I wanted to make friends."

"I was hoping," he said, ignoring her interruption, "that if and when they started in on you, the discipline would give you some peace. Be nice if you didn't have to start boozing it up. Boozing's hell on the liver, and you've got a kid to raise."

She was on her feet without knowing how she got there. She was so angry she stuttered. "You— I'm— This is bullshit, Moses. This is just total bullshit. Voices. Nobody hears voices; sometimes I think y don't even hear voices."

"Yeah, that's your mother talking throug" mouth, girl."

"Nobody talks through my mouth but me!" She pulled herself together and said tightly, "You know, Moses, you're going to have to make up your mind. Either the voices are talking or my mom is."

His voice was quiet and a little sad. "I knew you'd be pissed."

"Pissed?" She almost lost it, and only by an effort of iron will kept control. "I'm not pissed. You're just confused, Moses, is all. You said yourself you've had too much to drink tonight. I'm grateful to you for telling me about my parents, and . . ." She softened, touched his shoulder, wary of offering an embrace. "You," she said. "I have family now."

"Not a family you can take much pride in," he muttered.

"Stop that," she said. "I am proud of you. A lot of people are. Liam cares for you, Bill loves you with everything she's got, even Tim—"

"They'll come, Wy. They'll come when you least expect them, at the most inconvenient, inopportune times."

"Moses—"

"They'll come whether you want them to or not. I wish to god— Hell." He turned and walked away.

"Moses?" she said, coming down the steps after him. "Do you want me to drive you home?"

"I'm fine, girl. Track down that man of yours and take him to that itty-bitty thing you call a bed. He'll wipe the voices right out of your mind."

He disappeared around the corner of the house, and probably imagined what she heard next.

" least for a while."

boat was closer to the mouth of the river, and

she wondered in a detached sort of way where it was going, and why it had left the voyage upriver so late in the year. More meteors fell, but fewer and farther between, until at last they seemed to stop altogether.

Inside, the monitor was still flying through space. She shut the computer down and went to bed.

Liam never did come home.

TEN

Bill was curious about that coin.

She couldn't say why exactly. She didn't think it was because it was a gold coin. Maybe it was because she'd never seen any kind of a coin roll out of a dead man's hand before, but then that had to be a pretty rare experience for everyone privileged enough to witness it.

Diana Prince had left the coin with Bill, in the custody of the local officer of the court. Bill, after a hard day's work at magistrate's court, didn't want to deal with it, and so had left a blistering message on Liam's phone mail, with as yet no response.

The coin was in a plastic bag inside her desk drawer. She drew it out now and scrabbled around for a pair of reading glasses. Maybe it was the way her eyes, blue and intense and thickly lashed, looked out over the tops of them, measuring, challenging, their expression somewhere between a dare and an invitation. The man standing in the doorway, for one of the ~~few~~ times in his life feeling every one of his years, ~~saw~~ a sudden, excessive need for comfort, for satis~~factio~~n, for forgetfulness.

It was a weeknight, and the bar had closed at midnight. He closed the door behind him. When she heard the lock snick home, she looked up. "Well," she said, and sat back. She knew that look. Her heart skipped a beat. Twenty years, more, and her heart still skipped a beat, her nipples still hardened, the warm rush of feeling began between her thighs. Damned if she'd show it.

"Take your clothes off."

She stood up. "Make me."

He came around the desk at her and she kicked the chair out of the way before they fell on it. There wasn't time to get to her house, there wasn't time even to make it to the couch. He ripped her shirt open, buttons flying everywhere, and pulled her jeans down her legs, where they caught on the one shoe she hadn't been able to get off in time. He didn't kiss her or caress her, he pulled her legs apart and plunged in. She gasped and arched up, digging her nails into his bucking, heaving back. He bellowed out his pleasure and relief and collapsed on top of her, almost insensible.

They lay together, speechless, for a time. He stirred at last. "Christ." He raised his head. "May I come in?"

Her laugh was a bare thread of sound. "Depends. Who wants in, my man or the old crank who's been hanging out in my bar for the last month?"

"Both, I think." He propped himself on an elbow and smoothed the long strands of thick white hair back from her face. "I'm sorry."

She gave her hips an experimental flex. "You going to make it up to me?"

He laughed, burying his face in her hair. "You be

They dozed a little, impervious to the fact that they were half-dressed, on the floor, and that one of the wheels of the desk chair had rolled over a lock of Bill's hair.

"I told her," he said after a while.

"Finally got up the nerve?"

"Finally got enough beer in me."

She hesitated. "Moses?"

"What?"

"Are you sure?"

He nuzzled her breast. "I wish I wasn't."

So did she. "What do you think she'll do?"

"Get a lobotomy."

"Seriously."

He sighed and rolled to his back, swearing when he cracked his head on the couch. "I don't know. Up to her. I've prepared her as much as I can. I've delivered the bad news. She didn't believe it, but she's been told."

She rolled toward him, winced, and pulled her hair free from the caster. "Will it be as bad for her as it is for you?"

He shook his head. "No way to tell. Mine came to me young. They say my mother had them before me, but I don't remember her. And I haven't asked a lot of questions."

She knew why. Half the Bay thought he was god. The other half thought he was the devil. Bill had seen people turn away, step aside, retreat when they saw Moses coming, even though he never gave advice unsolicited. Everybody was afraid he might, though, and that this time it would be something they couldn't ignore.

"Man." He raised his head. "This is just pitiful. Lying under the desk, clothes half-off."

"I was ravished," she said primly.

He laughed, a wholehearted, rollicking sound that few had heard. "Yeah, right, that's why you didn't have any panties on underneath them jeans."

"What are you saying, sir?"

"I'm saying, ma'am, that I was honey-trapped. I didn't have a chance." He pulled her to her feet. "I'm hungry. Feed me."

They raided the kitchen, half-naked and giggling like a couple of kids, and brought their spoils back to the office and curled up on the couch. They fed each other olives green and black and pickles sweet and dill and pieces of cheddar cheese, washed down with enormous drafts of ice-cold beer. When they were done she licked his fingers clean, which led to other, more interesting places. This time it was long and slow and oh so sweet.

"This is all wrong, you know," she said drowsily, a little later.

"What is?" he said, facedown, body limp.

"We're too old to be enjoying sex."

"Who says?"

She ran one fingernail from his nape to the cleft of his buttocks, and was rewarded by a responsive groan. "Everyone under fifty."

"Everyone under fifty is wrong."

She smiled, closing her eyes and snuggling in for the duration. "They sure are."

The next morning as she was getting dressed and he was hindering her, he saw the gold coin on the desk. "What's that?"

"Remember that arm, and the coin that fell out of its hand?"

"Oh." He picked it up and looked at it, couldn't read the writing, and looked for the half glasses that had sidetracked him earlier. "Twenty dollars. And Lady Liberty in all her glory." He looked at her over the tops of the glasses. "This is gold."

"It looks like it, and it's heavy enough."

"Where did Liam say it came from, again?"

"John and Teddy found a wreck up near Bear Glacier, and tripped over the arm."

"They brought it back with them? Why?"

"Who knows why John and Teddy do anything?"

"Good question." He squinted at the coin. "I always was lousy at Roman numerals. What's MDCDXXI?"

"Beats the hell out of me. I'm strictly an Arabic-numbers kinda gal, myself."

"Up on Bear Glacier, huh?"

"Yeah." She took the coin and tossed it into the drawer. "You owe me breakfast."

"I owe you breakfast? You seduced me with those glasses of yours."

"You ravished me," she said. It was her story and she was sticking to it. They argued all the way to the Harbor Café, which they found packed full of fishermen, a morose group in stained Carhartt's and dirty white fishermen's caps pulled down low to hide their lack of hairlines. The air was thick with the smells of coffee, bacon and cigarette smoke. Bill and Moses sat and ordered enormous breakfasts, their digestive systems having long given up any attempt to dictate diet. It came and they ate heartily.

Replete, Bill stretched her arms, her breasts strain-

ing at the fabric of her shirt, to the rapt appreciation of
the fisherman sitting at the next table. Moses gave him
a hard-eyed look, and the fisherman reddened,
grinned and shrugged, as if to say, Who wouldn't? He
was maybe thirty-five.

"You're a vamp," Moses said out loud.

She did her best to look completely innocent. She
hadn't missed Marvin Engeland's admiration, or
Moses' reaction to it. She still had it, and she'd use it
however long it lasted. "I don't know what you're
talking about."

"Aw, what the hell, he's too old for you, anyway; he
wouldn't be able to keep up."

They staggered, laughing, out of the café together,
in time to bump into the four remaining Tompkinses
coming out of the building next door. It was a two-
story, prefabricated building, housing the offices of the
local State Farm representative, the Newenham Telephone Cooperative, Mario E. Kaufman, Attorney-at-
Law, Great Land Cable Television, the U.S. Parks
Service, and Vanessa Belanger, CPA. Betsy's eyes were
red but her head was high. Stan and Jerry were
solemn. Karen looked at Moses, then back at Bill, one
eyebrow going up, one corner of her mouth curving
into a knowing smile.

It took a moment for Bill to remember about Lydia.
"I was so sorry to hear about your mother," she said to
Betsy, the eldest.

Betsy inclined her head. "Thank you."

"I didn't know her outside of the book club, but
what I saw I liked a great deal."

Betsy smiled. "We're getting that a lot."

The Tompkinses had always been a clannish bu

not given to associating much with outsiders, but Bill had been a member of Lydia's book club, the Literary Ladies. It had been a going concern for almost thirteen years, and they'd stuck together through births, deaths, marriages and divorces. There was Bill and Lydia and Alta Peterson the innkeeper and Mamie Hagemeister the police clerk and Charlene Taylor the fish-and-game trooper and Sharon Ilutsik the hairdresser and Lola Gamechuk the cannery worker. They ranged in age from twenty-three to seventy-four. Some of them were married; some weren't. Some of them were mothers; some weren't. For one Saturday evening every month, they met to eat and talk about the book they had all read the month before, and the one thing they all had in common was the love of reading. "I know you're going to miss her," Bill said out loud.

Betsy nodded again, maintaining her dignity, and they climbed into her Toyota 4Runner and drove off.

"That is the weirdest damn bunch I've ever met, and that's saying some," Bill said.

"She was a beauty," Moses said. "It didn't translate into her kids, though. Even that Karen, little and cute as she is. She's just too damn hungry, and it shows."

"Who was a beauty?"

"Lydia. In high school, she was the girl everybody most wanted to."

"You, too?"

"Me, one," he said, and gave her a blatant pinch on the ass. "Let's go back to the bar."

"I have to; I have to get ready to open up."

"I'll go with you."

"No hanky-panky," she said sternly. "I have to work."

He grinned, the grin that from one angle fitted him with a halo and from another with horns and a tail. "Who, me?" But when they got back to the bar, he disappeared into the office and let her go to work, pulling the stools off the bar and the chairs off the tables, firing up the grill, emptying out the dishwasher. It was Dottie's half day, and Bill would be serving the lunch hour alone. She didn't begrudge Laura Nanalook's new start in Anchorage, but she'd been looking for a decent barmaid to replace her ever since. A few had come and almost immediately gone again. In the meantime, she picked up the slack. It was getting so she positively liked putting on that damn black robe and sitting in judgment of her fellow Newenhammers.

She gave the bar a last swipe and stood back, admiring its gleam. The tables in the booth and on the floor were spotless, the ketchup and mustard and A.1. bottles full, the salt and pepper shakers topped off. She had enough clean cutlery and dishes to feed an army.

It had been a rocky start, all those years ago. She had gotten on one plane after another until she had run out of cash. The bar had had a Help Wanted sign in the window, and she went to work that night. Two years later it was hers, along with a big, fat mortgage she'd paid off early. Newenham had been a boom-town in those days, boats so thick on the water you could walk across the bay and never get your feet wet. Hundreds of boats and billions of fish and no end of buyers from Japan, a country hungry for fresh fish. And in her bar hundreds of fishermen, ready to ster up with a fistful of twenties and ring the bell behind the bar. Those had been some wild and very profitable years.

Now there were fish farms from Scotland to British Columbia to Chile, and the North Pacific was being systematically fished out by processors with nets a mile, two miles long, ripping up the bottom of the ocean and every living thing with it, regardless of size or sex. The king crab had been the first casualty, then the herring, then the salmon. Now the fishermen were fighting over rights to fish the pollock, whose own population was already so low the Steller sea lion herds that fed on them were starving themselves out of existence. The fishermen's associations vowed and declared that the pollock population had nothing to do with the sea lions, but hell, it was perfectly clear to anybody whose livelihood wasn't on the line.

She wondered what was going to happen next. Alaska existed because of the exploitation of her natural resources: fish, oil, gas. What if she ran out? What happened then? And what happened to towns like Newenham, Togiak, Kodiak, Dutch Harbor, built on fish, whose continued existence depended wholly on the fishing industry?

Stan Tompkins was a fisherman—Lydia's son, or one of them. Jerry was pretty much a waste of time, sad when you thought how far he'd fallen from the start he had been given, but Stanley Jr. was a capable and prosperous man. She wondered what he thought of what was happening in the bay.

Lydia hadn't talked much about her children, although they had had some pretty raunchy discussions about sex, the seven of them. Sharon Ilutsik had

blushed a lot on those occasions, Bill remembered, and
Lydia would be inspired to more and better stories on
the strength of those blushes. "You're a dirty old
woman," Bill had told her once.

"And you aren't?" Lydia had retorted. "You and
Moses kind of set the bar pretty high." Which, of
course, had made Sharon blush more and the rest of
them laugh harder.

The clock ticked up to ten and she unlocked the
front door. The usual suspects were hanging around
outside, waiting, and she stood back out of the way.
Never get in between anyone and their first drink of
the day. She could have opened up at eight and the
same people would have been waiting. She got Chris
Coursey a Miller without being asked, and took orders for a Salty Dog, a screwdriver, and a Bloody
Mary, this last for Jim Earl, who looked like he needed
it badly.

Eric Mollberg shuffled in and sat down on his usual
stool. She brought him a bottle of Oly, and he shocked
her by refusing it and asking for a Diet Coke instead.
She poured it for him, making a heroic effort to keep
the inevitable commentary to herself. She remembered
the arm flying out of the bag, the hand opening, the
finger extending, the tip of it almost touching Eric's
nose, Eric's eyes bulging with horror, and felt a laugh
bubbling up inside her. To hide it, she went in the back
to check on Moses.

He was sitting in front of her computer, frowning at
the screen, and from the glow cast on his face he might
actually be operating it. She couldn't believe he even
knew where the on button was. When she went
around to see what he was doing, she suffered another

shock. He was on the Internet, and had by some miracle known only to the angels managed to get on Google. "What," she said faintly, "are you doing?"

"Doing a Net search, what's it look like?" he said, raising his head to look through the half glasses perched on his nose.

Her half glasses, she saw, which happened to be fluorescent pink with white tiger stripes and rhinestones winking from the corners. "I always want to rip your clothes off when you wear those things," she said.

He grinned. "I know the feeling." He tapped the gold coin, sitting on the desk next to the keyboard. "This thing might be valuable."

"How valuable?"

"Well, now, that depends. This coin is a double eagle, a twenty-dollar gold piece."

"So it's worth at least, I don't know, twenty dollars?"

Moses gave her a disapproving look and she subsided, for the moment. Those glasses did make him look awfully cute.

"They were the largest regular-issue gold coins ever made by the United States."

"What's a regular-issue coin?"

"I don't know, exactly. I think it means like nickels and dimes and quarters are today."

"Not commemorative."

"I think so. Anyway, there were two basic designs. The first one was the Liberty Head, with Lady Liberty facing left on one side with the date and an eagle with sun rays and stars on the other side. The reverse," he said, sitting up with an expectant look.

Knowing her duty, she looked suitably impressed.

"It was made from 1849 to 1907."

She looked at their coin. "Did we figure out what the date was on this coin?"

"Nineteen twenty-one."

"So not a Liberty Head."

"The other design is called the St. Gaudens type, named after the guy who designed it. Lady Liberty is back, only she's in full figure and standing, again on the dated side, and a flying eagle on the reverse."

"And it was made—"

"From 1907 to 1933. And there's something called a mint mark that is supposed to be right below the date."

Bill squinted, but Moses had her glasses and she couldn't see anything more than some indecipherable squiggles. "I'll take your word for it."

"Twenty-dollar gold pieces," Moses went on in a professorial tone, "are the most commonly found gold coins today because people hoarded them when they were made. Each coin contains about an ounce of gold, and the price of the coin depends on the price of gold bullion. Gold is soft, so the coins that actually saw the inside of somebody's pocket are pretty beat up. They can be worth anywhere between three hundred and four hundred dollars." He sat back and said proudly, "This one's in pretty good shape, so far as I can tell, so I figure it's high-end."

"Wow." Bill looked at the coin with more respect. "I wonder whose it was?"

"Who belonged on the other end of that arm, you mean?"

"Yeah."

He shrugged and pulled off her glasses. "You'd be

amazed the kinds of things people haul around in their pants. I know a guy carries a big blue glass marble around—I mean it's two inches in diameter. Says it's his good-luck piece. Every time I see it I'm glad for him that it hasn't broken. Ouch." He winced at the thought of what kind of damage a broken marble in the pocket might do. "I know a woman carries an ivory carving of a sea otter everywhere she goes, changes pockets only when she changes her pants. It's her, I don't know, totem, I guess."

"Like a good-luck charm?"

"Could be."

"And you're thinking this gold coin was a good-luck charm, too?"

He looked at the coin. "If it was meant to bring good luck to its owner, and the owner was attached to that arm, it sure failed of its purpose."

"No kidding." Because he seemed more contemplative than driven, she said, "You got a feeling about this?"

He thought about it before he replied. "No," he said, seeming a little surprised by his own answer. "I think I'm just interested." He slanted a glance up at her. "I'm allowed to be interested without its requiring me to prophesy, ain't I?"

"You is." Somebody shouted for beer on the other side of the door. "Don't hurt the computer," she said over her shoulder, and shut the door on his oath.

The customers had doubled in number and she took her first three burger orders. As she served the third she became aware of a conversation going on in a booth in the back, featuring Evan Gray. One of her minor frustrations was that Moccasin Man was as adept at getting out of jail as he was at getting into it in the first place.

"It's true," he was saying to the rapt audience gathered around him. "They were smuggling gold into the Asian theater, gold for the resistance forces fighting with the Allies. Thousands, hundreds of thousands of dollars' worth. Maybe even millions."

"And you think it's up there?"

"You saw that coin. You know where it's from. I was over talking to John Kvichak and he's thinking about going back up to the crash himself. Hell, it's only Bear Glacier; we can drive to Icky and four-wheel it the rest of the way in."

"Bags of gold so heavy you'll strain yourselves carrying them down the hill, is that it, boys?" Bill said.

They jumped and looked around. "Oh. Bill. Hey."

"Hey, yourself. You thinking of mounting an expedition up to that plane crash John and Teddy found?"

Moccasin Man gave her his best grin, a vast expanse of white enamel, a heated promise of full-blown sexual fulfillment, and a total lack of sincerity. "Well, hell, Bill. We were just talking."

"The site's being treated as a crime scene, Evan. I don't think the troopers are going to be best pleased if you bunch of yahoos go up there and start messing around in search of this mythical gold."

Evan looked amazed. "Why, Bill, we'd never do that." He winked at the other men. "Would we, boys?"

There was a chorus of agreement. Over her shoulder Bill saw the men at the bar cocking a collective ear, even Eric Mollberg, who looked anxious, as if he hadn't quite remembered how to interpret data sober.

Better and better. She could only hope that Liam

had covered the ground thoroughly and that there was no evidence left to be messed up.

Or that the glacier would calve on top of the Gray gang upon their arrival. Cheered by this vision, she returned to the grill and watched through the pass-through as the Gray gang sidled out the door.

ELEVEN

Liam hadn't been able to go home the night before, not even as far as the Jayco popup in the front yard. He was embarrassed and ashamed of his reaction to Karen's advances. It bothered him that even in his sleep he hadn't been able to tell Karen from Wy. He knew it was irrational but it was how he felt. He didn't want to see Wy until he had calmed down. He wanted a shower before he saw her. He wanted to dip his penis in a jar of disinfectant before he saw her.

He didn't want Wy to see him, was what it amounted to. He was afraid she would be able to read what he'd been doing all over his guilty face. Besides, Jo and Gary might still be there, and if she couldn't read him Jo sure as hell could. The reporter had the most unnerving stare Liam had ever encountered, one that cut right through any bullshit he might be able to throw up about where he'd spent the last hour.

Besides, he told himself, with Gary there maybe didn't want him in the house.

He knew it wasn't true, but it was an ex grabbed at. He went back to the post. He wc sacked out in the front seat of the Blazer, but he didn't want anyone driving by the following morning to see him. The chair behind the desk was on casters but it was well padded and leaned back pretty far, and it wasn't like he'd never slept in it before. He loosened his tie, propped his feet on the desk, and prepared to wait out the night.

His mind wouldn't let him alone. Images of Lydia giving him the once-over, the pure female appreciation in her eyes even more unsettling when she depreciated thirty years in age and became her daughter Karen. The gold coin rolling out of the dead, desiccated hand, winding round and round and round on the dance floor of Bill's Bar and Grill. Wy's expression, comprised of horror at the sight of the arm and guilt at the presence of Gary in the booth with her. The slab of ice separating from the face of the glacier, falling he could believe almost intentionally right on top of the two of them.

The snarl of John Dillinger Barton over the phone: "What the hell's keeping you; get on the goddamn plane!"

He grieved again for Charlie, but the grief was no longer the crushing, debilitating force it had been. Instead it brought his son back in all his round-cheeked, dimpled glory, and he was grateful, would always be grateful. He wanted to remember Charlie, always and forever. His son. Likely the only child of his body he would ever have.

He must have dozed off at some point, because the thing he heard was a loud *bang!* For one disorimoment he thought he was back at the foot of ier. "Look out, Wy!" he shouted, and dove for

Only he fell out of his chair instead, into a sticky pool of coffee spilled the day before that he could swear he had cleaned up. He lay where he was, swearing feebly.

"That's my boy," he heard someone say.

Oh, no.

He raised his head cautiously to peer over the edge of the desk.

It was.

Col. Charles Bradley Campbell of the United States Air Force, eagles and all.

But wait, there was more. Colonel Campbell had not come alone. Behind and slightly to the right of the erect figure in immaculate blue was a slender young man in neat chinos and a light blue button-down shirt with a dark blue tie under a dark blue windbreaker. He had neatly cut straight black hair and round, no-rim glasses perched on the end of a thin, high-bridged nose through which he peered at Liam with some puzzlement.

Liam got to his feet. "Hi, Dad."

Charles smiled. "Hello, son. Great to see you again."

Uh-huh. Liam shook the hand extended to him and offered no explanation of his swan dive out of the office chair. Charles was tactful enough not to ask for one. "You must have had a late night."

"Yeah." Liam glanced surreptitiously at his watch. It was past ten. Where was Prince?

Firm footsteps sounded on the stairs, and the door opened to admit Prince. "Charles!"

"Diana," Charles said, a wealth of information in that single word.

Prince recovered fast; Liam had to give her that. "How nice to see you again," she said, eyes cast demurely down.

"How very nice indeed," Charles said.

More footsteps. Already the morning was not turning out well, and when he saw who it was, he groaned inside.

"Liam," Jo said, "I need to talk to you about this crash site. How do I get to it, and—"

At that moment Col. Charles Bradley Campbell sprang into her dazzled view. Liam, while not a vain man, knew that he was good-looking, and knew that he looked like his father, but although he'd had his share of women there was something about the elder Campbell that made them go down like ninepins in his presence. Jo, the hardest of hard-nosed reporters, all but went over flat on suddenly very round heels.

Charles was a tall man, as tall as Liam, and the similarities didn't stop there. His eyes were as blue, if less warm, his dark red hair, if shorter in style, as thick and as yet not gray even at the temples. His jaw was as firm, his shoulders as broad, his waist and hips as trim, his legs as long, and he looked just as good in the snug jacket and slacks of his dark blue air force uniform as Liam did in his trooper blue and gold.

Liam, looking at Charles through Jo's eyes, remembered his state of deshabille and snugged up and straightened his tie. It was pretty much all he could do without a dry cleaner.

For her part, Jo, not a woman easily impressed, for the first time received an inkling of what was itching at her friend Wy. What she didn't see in Liam was manifestly obvious in Liam's father. "Jesus," she said, looking from one man to the other and pleased that her voice was light and steady. "The apple sure didn't fall far from this tree."

Charles Bradley Campbell grinned, a quick, lethal grin with razor-sharp edges. "Why, thank you, ma'am."

Liam, Jo was interested to note, looked less than thrilled. "What are you doing in town, Dad?"

Charles looked wounded. "What, I can't drop in once in a while to visit my son?"

"Drop in all the way from Washington, D.C.?"

Charles smiled with all the warmth and charm at his command, both of which were considerable. "Newenham's just like everywhere else, son. A plane ride away."

The man standing in back of him made a discreet noise.

"Why, I'm forgetting my manners," Charles said. "Special Agent James G. Mason, trooper Sgt. Liam Campbell."

"Special agent?" Liam said.

James G. Mason's smile was slow and a little shy. "Of the FBI."

"FBI?" Jo said. "What's the Feebs doing in Newenham?"

"Good-bye, Jo," Liam said.

"Come on, Liam—"

"Allow me to introduce you around. Jo Dunaway, reporter for the *Anchorage News*," he said to his father, who was too smooth to show alarm. The FBI man looked confused, but that may have been cosmetic. "Good-bye, Jo," he repeated. At his look, Prince went to the door and held it for her, not without some small feeling of triumph at being the woman left behind with Col. Charles Bradley Campbell.

Liam waited for the disgruntled footsteps to fade well out of hearing. "Special Agent Mason."

"Sergeant Campbell."

"How can I help you?"

The agent looked at Charles, who shrugged. His glasses slipped farther down his nose and he pushed them back up again, a nervous habit. "Well, we heard you had found the wreckage from a plane crash."

"And this merits attention from the FBI?" And the air force, he thought, looking at his father, who looked blandly back.

"Well"—Mason flushed slightly—"er, yes, we think it does. Um, we think it might be the wreckage of a plane that crashed into Carryall Mountain the night of December twentieth, 1941. It was a C-47, a Lend-Lease aircraft meant for Chiang Kai-Shek's forces in China."

"And the FBI is interested in this crash—why? Is there some indication that this was other than an accident?"

If possible, Mason looked even more apologetic. "The special agent in charge in Anchorage sent me down as an observer, just in case."

Liam looked at Charles. "There were three people on board, a pilot, a copilot, and a navigator. We bring our boys back."

It was simply said, and Liam had no doubt that Charles, a career man to whom the United States Air Force was life and breath, meant every word. Nevertheless, he couldn't escape the feeling that something had been left unsaid. "I imagine you want to go up there."

Charles nodded. "Can you take us?"

Prince looked chagrined. "Our plane is still on floats."

Charles looked at Liam and smiled a slow, knowing smile. "Know an air taxi we can charter?"

Liam, expecting a Fury when he called, found Wy vague and distracted. Well, if she couldn't be bothered to ask where he'd spent the night, he sure as hell couldn't be bothered to offer the information. He explained the situation in crisp and businesslike tones. "Can you get the Cessna in there with everyone on board?" There was a long silence. "Wy?"

"You want to fly back to the C-47 wreck?"

"Yes," he said. "I just said that. Didn't I just say that?"

"I don't know. I . . . yes, I guess so." She seemed to pull herself together. "All right. How much do they weigh?"

"A hundred eighty," Charles said.

"One forty-five," Mason said.

Liam heard pencil scratching on paper. "We'll make it."

Liam remembered the tiny dirt strip carved out of the snow, no bigger in his fevered memory than a Band-Aid, and carefully kept anything he might be feeling from showing on his face. "She says it's a go," he said, hanging up. "Need a ride?"

"Thanks, the commander out at Chinook was kind enough to loan us a vehicle."

"You flew into Chinook?" Chinook Air Force Base was forty miles south of Newenham. It was a small base, fully manned only during the height of the Cold War, and would have been closed years earlier if

senior senator from the state of Alaska hadn't had
enough seniority to head up the military appropria-
tions committee.

It certainly offered Liam's father far too easy access
to Newenham, and to Liam.

"Of course."

"You fly in with him?" This to Mason.

"Yes," Mason said.

"What did you fly in on?"

Charles grinned. "Nothing like an F-15 to shrink the
spaces between places, Liam. You ought to let me show
you what mach speed looks like from the inside."

"Thanks anyway," Liam said. One of the sorest
spots between father and son was the son's complete
inability to appreciate the magic of flight.

"You coming with us?"

Liam couldn't have put his finger on how he knew
Charles didn't want him at the crash site, but he did.
He looked down at the list of names belonging to
Lydia's book club. He looked up at his father, into the
blue eyes so like his own, so determinedly clear of
guile.

He handed the list to Prince. "Talk to them all, see if
she was worried about something, fighting with someone; you know the drill."

"Yes, sir," Prince said, very glum.

"See you later," Charles told her.

She brightened visibly.

Liam followed Charles and Mason in the Blazer, out
the gravel road to the airport, ten miles from Newenham, complete with hangar and tie-downs and Gift
Shoppe. Wy was waiting for them, 68 Kilo fueled and
ready. They climbed in and took off.

It was a much shorter ride this time, and a much louder landing. Liam was certain they were going to end up in the trees, a place they had already been in a plane once this year, thank you very much, when a hard kick to the rudder swung the tail around and they rolled mercifully to a stop.

"Nicely done," Charles drawled over the headphones.

"Thank you, Colonel," Wy said.

"Charles, please." He smiled at her. Liam, watching from the backseat, noticed that while she inclined her head in acknowledgment she didn't smile back. Maybe that was why he loved her, the one woman left in the world Charles Bradley Campbell had yet to charm.

Give him time.

They hiked up the trail to the glacier, encountering fresh bear scat and a gray-muzzled cow moose, who gave them an incurious stare before moving placidly into a stand of diamond willow. It was overcast today, and colder. Their breath made little clouds that hung in the air, only to swirl, disperse and vanish as the line of people walked through them.

"It's going to snow," Wy said, looking at the horizon.

"How much and how long?"

She measured the clouds with narrow eyes. "A couple of feet by morning." She saw Liam's face. "I'm kidding."

All the same, he kept an uneasy eye on the horizon after that. The last thing he wanted to do was take off into a snowstorm. They'd had to land in one the month before. He wasn't enthusiastic at the possibility of repeating the experience.

They emerged from the trees into the clearing at the foot of the glacier.

"Where is it?" Charles said. Behind him, Mason was staring upward, openmouthed.

"There," Liam said, and pointed.

Charles looked. "Jesus H. Christ," he said, but it was more prayer than curse.

The face of the glacier looked to the southwest, and even in late October one day of sun had done enough melting to throw the outline of the plane into even starker relief, most of the fuselage, what was left of the right wing. The glacial backdrop was stunning, too. The cloudy day brought out the colors hiding in the ice, green, purple, a little red, a hundred different shades of blue, from powder to navy. Some trick of the light made it seem as if the tail of the craft were protruding, and at the same time made the whole thing look semitransparent, almost phantasmic. And why not? Liam thought. It was indeed an apparition, the specter of a time gone by and a war long since won. Only the spirits of the men who had been her last crew had the right to walk here.

Charles took an involuntary step forward.

"Hold it," Wy said, barring his way with one hand. "That glacier calves. The whole thing could come down on top of you at any moment."

"We've got to get up there."

"You can't."

"How'd you find the wreckage, then?"

"It's falling off the face of the glacier a little bit at a time," Liam said. "A couple of hunters were passing by, and stumbled over some . . . pieces."

"We've got to recover the bodies." Charles seemed aken out of his usual sangfroid.

"They're dead, Dad."

There was a spark of anger in Charles' eyes when he turned to look at his son. "There are three of our own up there, Liam."

Parts of them might be, Liam thought. "Who were they?"

Charles seemed to pull himself together. "Capt. Terrance Roepke of Minot, South Dakota. First Officer Aloysius"—all three of the men winced—"March of Pasadena, California. Flight Engineer Obadiah Etheridge of Birmingham, Alabama. All U.S. Army Air Corps."

"What were they doing over the Yukon-Kuskokwim River Delta in a C-47 on December twentieth, 1941?"

"You ever hear of Lend-Lease?"

"Yes. Sure. Of course. Okay, refresh my memory."

"It was Roosevelt's way of funneling equipment and supplies to the Allies before we actually got into the war. The C-47 was a standard piece of Lend-Lease equipment."

Liam nodded at the wreck. "Where was this one going?"

"Russia."

Wy's brow creased. "Weren't most of those planes ferried through Nome by way of Fairbanks by way of the Alcan?"

"Yes."

"What was this one doing so far south?"

"I don't know. Bad weather, instrument failure, extreme cold, any of those things. We're talking 1941, real seat-of-your-pants flying, especially up here." Charles looked and sounded a little wistful. "These guys had to be good, or good guessers."

Liam looked up at the glacier. This crew hadn't been that good.

Mason, finally having gotten his mouth closed, grabbed Liam's arm and pointed involuntarily. "Look!"

As they watched, a section of the glacier shuddered and split from the main body of ice. It was so large it seemed to take a long, long time to fall. At about the time the first piece of ice hit the ground, the first *boom!* hit their eardrums, followed by a loud, continuous thundering crunch of ice striking bottom and breaking up.

The ghost of the C-47 seemed to ripple. They held their breath, watching, but the plane stayed where it was. "We've got to get up there," Charles said. "We've got to get those men out."

"Sooner or later they'll come to us, Colonel," Wy said. At his look she added, "You can't climb up the face of the glacier for the same reason. You can't rappel down from the top for the same reason. The whole thing is just too unstable. Really the only thing you can do is wait." She paused, and then, because she too was a pilot, repeated gently, "They'll come to us."

There was a brief silence. "How long?"

Wy shrugged. "It's a glacier. It's also October. It's going to get colder very soon, and it's going to snow a lot. I'd leave any recovery attempt until next year. Check it out in the spring, see what kind of a snowfall there has been, see how long it will take to melt off. Try to get in sometime between then and when the glacier goes into full calving mode. No guarantees it won't have, and no guarantees the whole thing won't slide off the face of the glacier the moment we fly out of here, but at least nobody else gets killed."

They stood staring at the glacier. After a moment, Wy touched Liam's arm. "Liam? Do you hear it?"

"Hear what?" Liam became aware of a faint buzzing noise, increasing in volume. It got louder and louder, until he looked over his shoulder at where the trail ended at the edge of the trees to see five four-wheelers burst into the clearing. Their drivers saw the little group and the man in the lead shouted out a warning but it was too late.

"Look out!" Liam said, and picked up Wy around the waist and leaped left. Charles and Mason both jumped right. The vehicles skidded to a halt.

Paul Urbano looked at Liam picking himself out of the blueberry bushes, his uniform smeared with blue stains, and said, "Oh, shit."

Teddy Engebretsen, John Kvichak, and Kelley Mac-Cormick looked as if they were trying to will themselves into invisibility.

The fifth man, Evan Gray, laughed out loud.

Peering around him, her short cap of blond curls ruffled and adorned with the odd desiccated birch leaf, so did Jo Dunaway.

December 10, 1941

That plane that went in four days ago? They found two of the guys! Both pilots were kilt in the crash but there were two other guys on board and although they were hurt they fixed up some kind of wooden slats they call skis (they use these skis to travel over the snow in Norway, I hear) and strapped them to their knees and feet and crawled out. They only made it three miles but that was enough for them to be seen from the highway and be picked up. The story is it was fifty-eight below. I cant believe they're alive. Nobody can.

I wonder if Ill ever be abel to tell my son what I did in the war. I cant even tell them at home where I am. Its this big secret that were giving planes to Russia and China. Like March said the other day, theres hundreds of planes going through Nome every day, do the brass think the Germans and the Japs havent notised? He was taking a talley on a tablet and saw I was watching is why he said it. He said if I can keep cownt anybody can.

TWELVE

First on the list of Lydia's book club members was Bill Billington. As Newenham's one and only magistrate, she was a walking, talking database on the community and its citizens. She knew who was sleeping with whom, where all the bodies were buried, and if the check really was in the mail or likely to be anytime in the near future.

Besides, Diana Prince had skipped breakfast, and the best lunch going was at Bill's. She bellied up to the bar a little past one o'clock and grabbed a stool at the end. The lunch crowd was already thinning out, although she didn't know where everyone was going. Over to the Breeze Inn to play pool, probably. Winter in southwestern Alaska, particularly for the unemployed, could be just one long, cold, dark stretch of boredom and inertia, and after the last two pitiful fishing seasons, there wasn't a lot of incentive to work on boats or hang gear for the next one.

She wondered where Col. Charles Bradley Campbell was sleeping that night. She wondered if he would find a way to let her know.

"What can I do you for?" Bill said, running the bar rag in Diana's direction.

"How about a steak sandwich, fries, green salad with bleu cheese on the side? And a Diet Coke with a wedge of lime, if you've got it. Lemon if you don't."

"Coming right up."

"And talk, when you have a few minutes."

Bill raised an eyebrow, and went into the kitchen to slap a slab of meat down on the grill. The air was filled with the satisfying sound of charring beef. She made Smokey Pete another vodka martini on the rocks, blended four margaritas for a group of giggling young women who were celebrating the twenty-first birthday of the last of them to become legal, and stuck her head into the office. Moses was dozing on the couch. She pulled a throw over him and closed the door silently behind her. She assembled the steak sandwich, loaded the plate with fries, and delivered it just as Prince was forking up the last of her salad. "What's up?" she said, pulling her stool opposite Prince's.

"Liam wants me to ask you about Lydia Tompkins' book club. Says you were a member." Prince wiped her hands on a napkin and got out a notebook. "Says you, Lydia, Alta Peterson, Mamie Hagemeister, Charlene Taylor, Sharon Ilutsik and Lola Gamechuck were all members."

"That's right."

"How often did you meet?"

"Once a month."

"All of you pretty close?"

"Pretty close."

"Did she mention that she was having trouble with

anyone lately, her children, business acquaintances, friends?"

Bill blew out a sigh. "I still can't believe she's dead. I would have bet my last dime she would have outlived the youngest of us."

"Bill?"

"Sorry. Children. Stanley Tompkins left Lydia very well-off. One or the other of them had money before they married; some said it was Lydia, but I don't buy that. Her father was a local fisherman who never made it very big, who drank a little too much, and who fathered a few too many children ever to be seriously in the chips. Stanley, now, I think she married Stanley because he was her father's exact opposite. A very hard worker, and from the stories I hear tell from the old farts had an absolute genius for finding fish. Clarence knew Stanley pretty well."

"Clarence Saguyuk?"

"Yeah. Anyway, when Stanley died, he left Lydia well dowered and all the children well provided for. None of them have to work unless they want to." She indulged in a snort. "And most of them don't."

"What do you mean by that?"

"Stan Jr. is the only one of them with a real job, but even he plays at it. You ought to take a look at that boat of his sometime, the *Arctic Belle.* It's got all the bells and whistles on it, thousands of dollars of electronic equipment; I think he bought the first GPS in the Newenham boat harbor. He gets a new reel practically every year, he's always upgrading his skiff, he gets one hole in his gear and that's it, got to hang some new and right now, too. He's the nicest one of the kids, certainly the easiest one to talk to, but he's fifty-five going o twelve. Or fifty-six," she added. "I don't keep track of my own age, let alone anyone else's."

"Does he live beyond his means?"

"I don't think so. I'd bet Karen does, though. She's a shopper, that girl; she never walks in here in the same outfit twice running and she's always got some new piece of gold-nugget jewelry hanging off her."

"Is he married? Stan Jr.?"

Bill shook her head. "No. He's had a thing going off and on with Carol Anawrok for years, ever since high school. It stopped while she was married to Melvin Delgado, and then started up again after Melvin died. It stopped again while she was married to Keith West, and then started up again after Keith died." Bill shook her head. "Both cancer of the lungs. Carol keeps marrying smokers."

"And the rest of the kids?"

"Betsy's the oldest, about fifty-six or -seven, I think. Her husband is David Amakuk, whose family moved down from New Stoyahuk. He's a foot shorter and two feet wider than she is. They met in high school, married the week after they graduated. He runs the *Daisy Rose*, a drifter I think Betsy financed. He does pretty well out of it, generally comes in just under high boat. They have two daughters, Daisy and Rose, both living in Anchorage now. Jerry's the other son." She paused.

"What's wrong with Jerry?"

"Everything."

"That sounds pretty comprehensive."

"He's one of those lost souls, no ambition, no direc-
~~on. He's been up before me on possession I don't
~~ow how many times, and DWIs, too. I took away his

driver's licence and I threatened to suspend the rest of the family's, too, if they didn't keep him away from a steering wheel. Stan Sr. tied up Jerry's inheritance so that he'd get an allowance from Lydia, so he wouldn't blow it all on one toot at the Great Alaskan Bush Company in Anchorage. Which Jerry is capable of doing, if nothing else. His apartment is in Lydia's name; she pays all the bills. Paid."

"Did Jerry resent having his money tied up that way? Would he threaten Lydia to get more?"

Bill reflected. "He was more along the lines of pathetically grateful, would be my guess. The most wretched thing about Jerry is that he knows just how worthless he is. He knows he'd be homeless in a heartbeat if he had control of his own money." She shook her head. "I remember one time, during one of the possession busts or whatever it was, he told me he had a home and a fixed income, and that he wasn't a vagrant. He was proud of it."

"Great."

Bill regarded Prince not without sympathy. "Yeah, I know, you'd like a motive. Sorry about that."

"There was no forced entry. It's likely she let whoever it was in."

"Who in Newenham locks their doors?"

"Yeah, well, okay, never mind. There's a fourth child, isn't there?"

"There would have been, if Karen had ever been a child."

"I beg your pardon?"

"That kid was sprung full-grown from the head Zeus, and when she landed she was hot to tro ready to go. She's very pretty, which doesn'

During her high school years alone, there were three accusations of statutory rape brought against three different boys, all dropped for lack of evidence. She moved into one of the Harborview Town Houses the week after she graduated from high school, I think the better to see which boats are in and which crews are available for plucking. She doesn't have any other vices of which I'm aware, doesn't smoke, doesn't drink much, doesn't do drugs—does the local provider, though; she and Evan Gray were an item a while back, but I think she wore even him out. She surely likes her men."

"Anything kinky going on there? Something that might result, say, in blackmail? That she needed money to pay off? That she might go to her mother for? And her mother might refuse her?"

Bill laughed. "Karen would consider it advertising."

Prince sighed. "Okay. What about her friends? What about the ladies who lunch?"

"The Literary Ladies," Bill said.

"Sorry. The Literary Ladies. Stand by one." Bill made a round of the house. The girls in the booth were getting very giggly, and so was their designated driver. Bill served up a round of sodas and forced a jumbo order of nachos on them. She came back and settled in across from Prince.

"The Literary Ladies were formed in 1988, November, I think." She smiled at a memory. "First book we ~~read~~ was Toni Morrison's *Beloved*, because it won the ~~Pulit~~zer that year. Scared the shit out of everyone, and ~~almost~~ busted up the group right there. One woman ~~would~~ come back—what was her name, Margaret,

Melody something? Anyway, we never saw her again. I haven't seen her since, as a matter of fact, so she must have moved away."

Prince was more interested in the current members, and said so, with emphasis.

"All right, all right. There's me. There was Lydia, of course. There's Alta Peterson, who owns and minds the hotel. There's Mamie Hagemeister, you know her, and there's Charlene Taylor and you know her, too. They're all originals, except for Charlene, who joined when she was posted to Newenham, back in, oh, 1992, I guess. Sharon and Lola are newcomers, the youngsters in the group. Sharon joined when she was still in high school, and about two years later brought Lola in. Sharon does hair down at the Prime Cut and Lola works in the cannery in the summer and answers the phone for the Angayuk Native Association in the winter."

"You're all pretty close?"

"Pretty close," Bill said cautiously.

"You don't seem sure."

"Close for getting together only once a month," Bill said.

"Any disagreements?"

Bill raised one eyebrow, but Prince refused to back down. "Of course we fight. Lola married the wrong man, we told her so, and she stopped coming for the duration of her marriage, about thirteen months, I think it was. Charlene arrested Sharon's cousin Richard for fishing inside the markers up Kulukak River, and Sharon stopped speaking to Charlene un*' I found him guilty, and then she stopped speakin* me instead. Alta was pissed at Sharon because Sh gave Alta a punk-rock haircut without permission, and she stopped speaking to her until it grew out."

"Anybody ever get mad at Lydia?"

"Nope. Not that I remember. Well."

"What?"

"She used to tell raunchy stories that embarrassed the hell out of Sharon and Lola."

"Raunchy stories?"

"Yeah, I think she liked giving them the needle. Especially the younger ones. Hell, if half the stuff she said about her and Stan Sr. was true, she wasn't even bragging."

"What kind of stuff?"

Bill grinned. "One time, when the kids were off on a basketball trip to Anchorage, Stan Sr. borrowed a pair of handcuffs off Martin Gleason—a city cop here, before your time—stripped Lydia butt-naked and kept her chained to their bed for twenty-four hours, during which he invited five guys over to play poker in the kitchen. He visited her between hands, with the other guys thinking he was using the john. She said after the second time all he had to do was walk into the room for her to come. Lola just about died."

"Jesus." Prince remembered Mrs. Lydia Tompkins, a short, plump, bright-eyed woman who had most definitely achieved elder status, and tried to reconcile that picture with the sexual dynamo Bill was describing.

"Yeah. I want to be Lydia when I grow up." Bill paused. "It must have about killed her when Stan Sr. died."

"So you never had any disagreements with her self?"

"Oh, hell, yes. You can't be even once-a-month friends for over twenty years and not fight. Not if the friendship is real. I told her she was spoiling Karen and she was mad at me for, oh, about five minutes, I think it was. But Lydia could never stay mad at anyone for long."

Bill sighed. "I should be angry at who killed her. I should be breathing fire and smoke up one road and down another, as far as roads go in this town, until I sniff out the bastard and annihilate him. But all I can think of is that I've lost a friend, and all I can feel is tired."

It was the closest Prince had ever heard Bill come to admitting to human weakness, and she didn't know quite what to say in response. She fell back on formula. "You can't think of anyone who would have wanted to hurt her?"

Bill shook her head.

"Can you give me directions to Lola's house? I can track down everyone else."

"Okay." Bill drew Prince's notebook to her and began to write.

Alta Peterson, owner and proprietor of the Bay View Inn, Newenham's only hotel, was long-limbed and lean in the best Scandinavian style of construction, and wore tiny little round glasses through which she was peering at a copy of *Girl with a Pearl Earring*. The book was propped in her lap. Her feet were propped on the check-in counter. She wore a lime-green sweater over a pair of polyester slacks the color of Welch' grape juice, and an orange chiffon scarf in an artistic knot at her throat.

Prince narrowed her eyes against the glare and cleared her throat.

"Diana. What can I do for you?" Alta did not leap to her feet. This was Newenham. It was October. Jo and Gary Dunaway and Special Agent James G. Mason were the only three customers she had at present, and she wasn't expecting Diana to bring her any more.

"You hear about Lydia Tompkins?"

"Yes."

"I'm talking to everyone who knew her."

"Uh-huh."

"Bill Billington tells me you were a member of Lydia's book club."

"Yes."

"You were good friends?"

"Yes."

"Before she died, did she say she was having trouble with anyone? Anybody threatening her, anything like that?"

"For what reason?"

"I don't know; I was kind of hoping you could tell me."

Alta closed the book, marking her spot with one forefinger, but she didn't pull her feet off the counter. "Lydia Tompkins was a good and true friend of mine from the time my husband first brought me to Newenham. If anyone had threatened her and I had heard about it, I would have sought them out and kicked their behind. What's more, I would have had to stand 'n line to do it."

"She had a lot of friends?"

"She didn't have anything but friends."

"You remember her talking about any problems she might have had with her children?"

"No."

Alta had elevated the monosyllabic response to an art form. "Well, if you remember anything—"

"If I do," Alta opened her book again.

Prince took the hint and left.

Mamie Hagemeister was Alta Peterson's polar opposite in temperament. She burst into tears at her desk at the local jail and had to be ministered to with Kleenex and a can of Coke from the machine down the hall. "She was the greatest gal," Mamie said, blowing her nose. "One time I was sick with the flu, really sick, and she came and got my kids and kept them for three days so I could sleep. She did things like that for everybody. And she did things in the community, too. She taught Yupik at the grade school, and ran the fund-raising drive for the new fire truck, and donated time down at Maklak Center. She had an uncle who was a drunk." With a rare flash of pragmatism, she added, "Everybody in Newenham has an uncle who's a drunk. But Lydia did something about it." Dissolving once again into tears, she said, "I just don't know who would do such an awful thing. Everybody loved Lydia."

Prince's ears pricked up at the news that Lydia had volunteered at the small clinic attached to the tiny hospital that treated drug and alcohol abusers. Users were notoriously unstable people, quick to take offense and slow to take responsibility, with a tendency to hit when they were high and apologize later when were sober and about to be jailed for the th

There was a possibility that Lydia had offended someone and that it had resulted in a confrontation in her
home. Counselors in the big city had unlisted phone
numbers and had mail sent to a box at the post office.
In small towns like Newenham, it just wasn't that hard
to find someone.

Charlene Taylor was in the air, tracking down a
rumor of a group of hunters going for bear in an area
the Fish and Game had closed to hunting the month
before. Prince moved on to Prime Cut, Newenham's
lone beauty salon, located in the minimall that housed
the Eagle grocery store. Sharon Ilutsik was blow-
drying Jimmy Barnes' hair. Jimmy Barnes, a rotund,
bouncy little man and Newenham's harbormaster,
greeted Prince with some embarrassment and was out
of the chair a second later. Sharon sighed a little over
his tip, and then he came bustling back in, even redder
of face, to mumble an apology and shove a couple of
bills her way. She brightened and accompanied Prince
to the espresso stand next door to order a double
skinny latte with vanilla flavoring. Prince managed
not to gag and got a cup of coffee, added cream and
sugar with a lavish hand, and they sat down at one of
two faux-wrought-iron tables.

"Lydia Tompkins," Sharon said. "Yeah, we were
friends. I usually only saw her once a month, at book
club, except when she came in for a haircut. You could
use one, by the way," she said, giving Prince a critical
once-over. "You're getting a little shaggy around the
rs and the back of your head."

Prince ran a hand through her short, dark curls. "I'll
an appointment after we're done here. When did
see Lydia?"

"At the last book club. Saturday before last."

"Did she seem upset about anything? Anything at all, it doesn't matter how unimportant it seems to you."

"No. Although—"

"What?"

"Her daughter showed up about halfway through the evening. I remember because we were right in the middle of sitting down to dinner and Lydia ran her off. Karen was not best pleased." Sharon sipped her latte. "But then Karen is never best pleased by much, unless it's a man and he's about to take his pants off."

"That's a little harsh."

"Harsh but true," Sharon said cheerfully. "Karen defines herself by the men she sleeps with. I swear the girl has notches on her bedpost. It's probably posts, plural, by now."

"Like her mother."

"Lydia didn't sleep around," Sharon said sharply. "She and her husband had plenty of fun, and she liked to tease us with stories about it, but she wasn't at all like Karen. She was a one-man woman." She paused. "At least, she was while Stan Sr. was alive."

Prince stared. Mrs. Lydia Tompkins, plump, seventy-four, mother of four, grandmother of two, brainer of muggers with jars of sun-dried tomatoes, was doing the nasty with somebody? *I want to be Lydia when I grow up,* Bill had said. So, suddenly, did Prince. "You mean she took a lover?"

"Why not?" Sharon said, bristling. "She was old. She wasn't dead. Nobody says you have to stop having sex when you hit fifty. Look at Bill Billington and Grandpa Moses."

Prince had fallen into the way of regarding Bill as more of a contemporary and an ally in the good fight against evildoers, but when Sharon said it out loud, of course it was true. Bill and Moses were both older than God, and couldn't keep their hands off each other. She readjusted her thinking. "So you think Lydia had a lover."

Sharon hunched a shoulder. "I don't know. I probably shouldn't have said anything."

"Yes, you should," Prince said firmly. "Who was he?"

"I don't know. I went to her house about four months ago, and somebody had sent her this big bouquet of flowers, tulips, lilies, roses; it was gorgeous. You know we don't have a florist here, so somebody had to have Goldstreaked it down on Alaska Airlines. I thought at first it was one of her kids, but she blushed when I asked her, and said no, a friend had sent them for her birthday. She never did say who, but I got the impression the friend was a guy." Sharon studied the milky stuff swirling around in her cup, and looked up with a smile. "It was kind of cute, you know? Here she was, seventy-four years old, little old Grandma Lydia, and she's getting flowers from a guy. Kinda makes you not be afraid of getting old yourself, you know?"

Lola Gamechuk, thin, dark, and careworn, answered the phone six times while she talked to Prince. Five of the calls were from her daughter, Tiffany, who didn't like her baby-sitter and wanted Mom to come home right now. The sixth call Lola put through to Andrew Gamechuk, the current president of the Angayuk Native Association and Lola's cousin. Andrew interrupted his game of one-on-one with a sponge basketball and the hoop mounted on the wall of his office, which Prince had been watching through the open door of his office, to take the call. After a moment he got up and closed the door. Prince looked back at Lola.

"How well did you know Lydia?"

"Not very."

"You were a member of her book club."

"I saw her once a month."

"Never any other time?"

Shrug. "Sometimes in the store."

"Did you know of anyone who was bothering her, someone who might have held a grudge against her, who might have wanted to hurt her?"

Silent stare.

"Lola," Prince said, surrounded on every side by Yupik storyknives and finger fans and dance masks and feeling whiter than white, "all I want is to catch the person who did this to Lydia. Did you know that she worked down at Maklak?"

Lola, who had been staring fixedly at her desk, met Prince's eyes for the first time. Hers were a deep, dark blue, framed in wings of straight black hair that curved gently beneath her jawline. With some sleep and a little animation, Lola Gamechuk could knock the world on its collective ear with that face alone. "Everybody knew that."

"Did anyone there get mad at her for any reason?"

A long silence. "Maybe."

Prince tried not to pounce. "Would you know of anyone who maybe had done that?"

A longer silence. "Ray."

"Ray who?"

Lola looked at her fingers. "Ray Wassillie. Sometimes he drinks too much. Sometimes when he drinks too much he gets mean."

"Was he mean to Lydia?"

Lola's face closed up. "I don't know."

That was all she was going to say. Prince packed up and left, trying not to look as if she was running away. The Yupik mask mounted on the wall next to the door laughed at her from within a circle of ivory and fur and feathers. She glared at it as she went out, but the grin didn't change.

"Lola was married to Ray Wassillie for about a century one year," Charlene told her, unfastening her gun belt and placing it in the second drawer down in her desk. She turned the key in the lock and put the key in her pocket.

"Oh, hell."

"Don't be mad at her. He treated her pretty badly. She told us once she never would have left him if he hadn't hit the baby."

Prince remembered the phone calls. "Tiffany?"

Charlene nodded. "Tiffany wasn't even two months old, colicky, cried a lot. Ray came home drunk and lost his temper. I saw the marks. Lola gets back every way she can. Can't say I blame her much."

"Christ."

"Yeah." Charlene stretched. "Man, it's windy up top. It was a bitch keeping her on course. My shoulders feel like they've been frozen."

"You catch them? Mamie said you were tailing ome hunters going after bear in a closed area."

Charlene made a disgusted face. "No. I checked all

the likely strips but I couldn't find the plane. I'll go up again tomorrow, but you know what it's like. I might as well be on foot, for all the good I can do." She touched her toes and sat down. "So you want to know about Lydia."

Charlene and Bill would be her best sources; Prince had known that from the beginning. Bill, as magistrate, would take an impartial, innocent-until-proven-guilty view. Charlene, on the other hand, was a cop. She worked where the human rubber met the road. Cops never took anything on faith, and disbelieved every story that was told them on principle until and unless they could confirm that the story told was fact in all its essentials, and even then remained wary and unconvinced. Cop shops bred skeptics. Skeptics cherished few illusions about human nature, and therefore were seldom disappointed. "Tell me about Lydia," Diana said.

Charlene linked her hands behind her head and stared at the ceiling for inspiration. "Lydia Tompkins. Seventy-four years old. Widow of Stanley Tompkins Sr. Mother of Betsy, Stan Jr., Jerry and Karen. Born in Newenham, went to school in Newenham, married another Newenhammer. Never went farther than Anchorage when she traveled. So far as I know, never wanted to. Had an excellent relationship with her husband."

"So I've heard."

Charlene laughed. "I'll bet. Gets along with her children. Stanley Sr. made a lot of money fishing and, unlike most of his fellow Bay fishermen, invested well and left a tidy sum, evenly divided between all concerned. Lydia could have spent a lot more money than she did. You've seen her kitchen."

"Yes."

"Right out of 1957, isn't it? We used to tease her that Mamie Eisenhower was going to come walking out of it one day with a plateful of pork chops. She could have afforded to remodel it once every five years, but she said everything still worked."

"Was she a miser?"

"No, just frugal. She was very generous with her grandchildren. She was very generous with her friends, come to that. She gave the Literary Ladies Christmas and birthday presents every year." Charlene nodded to a large painting by Byron Birdsall on the wall. A narrow creek crooked its way between snow-covered banks, leading the eye to Denali, gilt in the setting sun. The creek seemed to shimmer with life and the whole painting radiated an inner glow. "I saw that in Artique one year and came home raving about it."

"Wow."

"Yeah. She was generous to a fault. Especially to her children."

"How so?"

"Karen and Jerry regularly run out of money. All they had to do was ask."

"Did fishermen really used to make that kind of money? The kind of money that would set a whole family up for two generations?"

Charlene gave her a tolerant look. "Given the year you came to Newenham, I suppose it's hard for you to imagine, but yes, salmon fishermen, especially the seiners, used to make that much money. Some of it was luck but mostly it was experience—experience and good equipment. Stanley Sr. had both. He worked deckhand on his father's gillnetter from the time he was six, according to Lydia. And that was back when the law said you could only fish under sail."

"No kidding?" Prince had a brief vision of the bay covered with white sails skimming over a deep blue surface.

"No kidding. So, anything else?"

Prince gathered up her notes. "Not for the moment. I'll call if I think of anything else."

"Me, too. Diana?"

Prince paused, one hand on the doorknob.

Charlene's voice remained pleasant and even. "I'd take it as a personal favor if you found this son of a bitch and strung him up by his balls."

Diana touched the brim of her flat-brimmed hat. "I'll do my best."

THIRTEEN

The phone rang as he was getting out of his blueberry-stained uniform and into the last clean one hanging in Wy's closet. Since Wy didn't own a lot of dress-up clothes, most of hers were folded into the dresser drawers and he had most of the closet for his own. It hadn't been like that with Jenny, a true disciple of the women's department at Nordstrom. He remembered having to hang his uniforms in Charlie's closet, and thinking that that would be a problem in fifteen or sixteen years.

He wondered what kind of a teenager Charlie would have been. Probably not as high-maintenance as Tim Gosuk, but you never knew. He'd dealt with enough parents in severe shock at their offspring's behavior to know that all biological, sociological and anthropological studies to the contrary, much of the time procreating was a crapshoot. He'd read another study recently that claimed that a bad kid in a good neighborhood had a better chance of succeeding in life than a good kid in a bad neighborhood. The author of that study had obviously never been to the village of Ualik, where Tim had gotten his start.

The phone rang. He heard Wy answer it in the living room.

She was upset about something, and it wasn't his not coming home last night. He'd finally told her that he'd spent the night at the office, and she'd nodded without much interest, her mind obviously elsewhere. He'd expected irritation, even anger. What he hadn't expected was indifference. It unsettled him.

It made him wonder where Gary had spent the night.

"Liam?"

He buckled his belt and padded out to the living room, snagging his shoes on the way. He tucked the receiver in between his shoulder and his chin and sat down on the couch. "Campbell."

"Sir, this is Prince. I have interviewed all of Lydia's book club members."

"Yeah?"

"No hope there; they were all pretty tight. But she did do some volunteer work down at the Maklak Center."

The *MC* on Lydia's calendar. "Any run-ins with clients?"

"They're closed for the day. They open again tomorrow at eight."

"Baloney. Nose around, find out who works there, call them at home."

"Yes, sir. Also, one of Lydia's friends thinks she might have had a gentleman caller."

"A what?"

"A boyfriend, sir."

Liam remembered the frankly female appraisal in Lydia's eyes the night they had met. "I wouldn't bet the farm against it. Got a name?"

"No. One of the Literary Ladies—"

"The who?"

"The book club, that's what they called themselves. Anyway, one of them saw a bouquet of flowers Lydia got. She said it was a birthday present from a friend, and that she got the distinct impression that the friend was male and that the relationship was romantic."

"Any indication it was a local guy?"

"No. But Charlene Taylor says Lydia never went farther from Newenham than a Costco run to Anchorage."

"So a local guy. How did the flowers get here?"

"Sharon—Sharon Ilutsik, the one who saw the flowers—didn't know, but she figured they were Goldstreaked down from Anchorage. There isn't a florist in Newenham, and this was a professional arrangement."

"She remember the date?"

"No, but Lydia said they were a birthday present."

Liam got his shoes tied and stood up, changing ears. Wy was standing out on the deck, staring across the river. The wind had picked up and was teasing curls out of a fat braid, forming a bronze corona around her head. Clouds, low and thick and dark, were scudding by, and Liam thought he saw a snowflake in the dimming light. "Okay, Diana," he said, "find out Lydia's birthday and call Alaska Airlines to check their records to see when the flowers came in. Should have been paid by credit card, if he called it in to Anchorage."

"Will do. You coming back in?"

"No. I've got a dinner date with my dad."

"Lucky you." She meant it.

"Yeah." He didn't.

He hung up and joined Wy on the deck. "Hey."

She looked up at him with a faint smile showing through the escaped wisps of hair. "Hey, yourself."

"How was your day, dear?"

She laughed, as he'd meant her to. "Not bad. Got a flight from the U.S. Air Force, a thing that hardly ever happens, since they prefer to fly their own. Not to mention the FBI. We small-time air-taxi outfits just love federal expense accounts."

He grinned. "I should start taking a commission."

"Right after you take your first flying lesson."

"That'll happen."

"I can hardly wait."

A gust of wind whistled overhead and tugged at their clothes. She was in a blue plaid shirt tucked into blue jeans cinched down by a wide leather belt. Her hiking boots were stained with salt, mud and wax, held together by a new pair of shoelaces, red-and-white-striped like a barber pole. It didn't vary much from what she had been wearing the day before, or three years before. It had to be one of the most unseductive outfits he'd ever seen on a woman of his acquaintance, and he didn't understand why his first, last and only inclination was to rip it off.

As if he had spoken his need out loud she looked up and met his eyes.

"Where's Tim?"

Her eyes widened. "Basketball practice."

"When will he be back?"

"They're going out for pizza after." Her knees were shaking. She wasn't sure how much longer they'd hold her up.

His eyes narrow and intent, he reached out a hand and unbuttoned the top button of her shirt.

"Not out here," she said, her voice weak, her head falling back.

"Why not?" He unbuttoned the second button.

"In the wind, and the snow, and the cold?"

"I'll keep you warm." He lowered his mouth to her throat.

"Someone will see."

"Let them," he said, and bit her.

Liam Campbell was a civilized man and an intuitive and generous lover, but that evening something feral had gotten off the chain. He took her down to the deck with hands that were rough and impatient, and he knew it and didn't seem to be able to control it. He ripped open her shirt and pushed up the T-shirt and bra beneath it and put his mouth on her breast, sucking hard. She made a sound deep in her throat, her own hands fumbling with his clothes, but he would have none of it. He didn't want her participation; he wanted her submission, and he pulled at her jeans until they tangled around her feet, unzipped his, and pushed inside.

"Liam!" The word was almost a scream.

He managed to hold it together for one frantic, heart-thumping moment. "Don't let me hurt you."

"You aren't. You won't. You couldn't." She pulled one foot free of her jeans and hooked it around the small of his back, tilting up and pulling him deeper. "Do it."

She screamed for real this time, a sound swallowed up by the wind and the snow and the dark. For a split second he could feel everything as if with a separate sense. The sudden quick flush of heat rising up from her torso. The kiss of snowflakes on his ass. The long, lovely line of her throat as she arched up into him, like she couldn't bear an inch of space between them.

"Do it again," he muttered.

Her eyelids fluttered. "What?" Her voice was slurred.

He thrust again. "Come on," he said, "come again for me, baby."

"No, Liam, I can't—"

"Sure, you can."

And she could.

And then he followed her into the dark.

Neither of them moved for long moments afterward, lying in a stupor of sexual satisfaction on the deck, the wind gusting to twenty-five knots, the temperature dropping another degree every minute, the snow moving from a snow flurry to a snowfall. Liam thought he could stay there, in that position, on top of that woman, forever, and he might have, if she didn't eventually exhibit some signs of being unable to breathe.

"I'm sorry," he said, and shifted his weight to his elbows.

She smiled without opening her eyes. "Don't be."

"Okay." He nuzzled her neck.

He felt a laugh catch in her breast.

"The only time a man is sane," he said, belatedly going for a little foreplay with her ear, which he knew she loved, "is the first ten minutes after orgasm."

She laughed out loud this time.

He raised his head and smiled down at her. "It's true."

"Says who?"

"Says Dapper Dan."

"And who, may I ask, is Dapper Dan? Not that I'm contesting his thesis." She raised her hips and exercised a muscle or two.

"Oh, man, I'll give you a week to quit that." He gave her a hickey, just to reestablish his supremacy. "Dapper Dan was a friend of Damon Runyon's."

"Why'd they call him Dapper Dan?"

"Because he was very dapper, and a very successful ladies' man."

"Not unlike someone else we might name."

"The only woman I want to be successful with now is right here. Lying under me, as a matter of fact."

She raised a hand to trace his eyebrow, nose and lips. He sucked her finger into his mouth. She shivered, and he smiled.

But when they managed to pull themselves off the deck, get dressed and go back inside, the constraint came back. "I'm supposed to meet Dad for dinner at Bill's."

"Tell him to come here instead."

"He wants to talk about that wreck on the glacier, and he doesn't want civilians around when he does."

She grimaced. "Okay."

"Wy?"

"What?"

"You seemed a little out of it when I got home. What's going on?"

She made a wry mouth. "So much for my powers of concealment."

"I love you." He said it simply, without flourishes. "I'll always see more than you want me to."

Her eyes softened. "Oh, Liam."

"There is something, isn't there?"

"Yes."

He took a deep breath. Damn the torpedoes. Remember the *Maine. Tora, tora, tora.* "Is it about the job John offered me in Anchorage?"

She looked as relieved as he did to finally open up the subject to discussion. "No."

"All right, then." He had not spent so many years walking through the fire to get to her to give up without a serious fight. He'd go to war for Wyanet Chouinard. He just didn't know if he'd live in Newenham for her.

She seemed to make up her mind about something. "I'll banish Tim to his room the minute he gets back. We'll talk then, really talk." A half smile. "Don't be late."

When he was gone the house seemed very empty. She checked for messages on the answering machine. A teacher in Togiak wanted a competitive bid for bringing four students and herself into Newenham over the Thanksgiving weekend for the Bristol Bay Academic Olympics. Dagfinn Grant had given her a quote and she thought it was too high. Wy, knowing Finn, thought it probably had been, and called her back. They arranged fares and pickup times to their mutual satisfaction, and Wy filled in the dates on her calendar. She'd been looking for a toehold into business with the various school districts. This was a start.

Ronald Nukwak had called from Manokotak, needing a ride for his family to Newenham for a wedding. That one she let go, reluctantly, because Ronald already owed her for seven round-trips, Manokotak to Newenham and back again. If one of the kids had been sick, she would have rolled out the Cub, but this wasn't an emergency. She hated losing Ronald's business, not to mention pissing off the half of Manokotak to whom Ronald was related, but she had bills to pay, too.

She heard enough of the next message to understand the speaker was calling from Ualik, but they were on a cell phone that faded in and out. Somebody wanted a ride, but she didn't know who and couldn't figure out when, so she let that one go, too.

She closed her calendar and leaned back with a sigh. The first time she'd flown into Ualik and landed on the runway that also formed the main street of the town, she'd found Tim Gosuk crouched, shivering, beneath his own porch, hiding from his next beating. The village hadn't improved in the interim. The last time she'd been there her fare had been late getting to the plane, and during her wait two men had staggered by, and a third had stopped and threatened her, followed by two small children, who also smelled of drink and who threw snowballs at her. She wouldn't have minded the snowballs so much except that they hit the plane. She had run them off, and they'd come back with their father just as she was loading the passenger, a woman who was also drunk and who she was very much afraid was going to throw up en route. The father cursed her most foully and, what really scared her, got in front of the plane after she'd started the engine. She knew from firsthand experience what a prop could do to a human head, and she was just about to cut the engine when he staggered off again. The kids threw snowballs until she was in the air.

She had been incredibly lucky that no one had managed to lay hands on a gun. It wouldn't have been the first time a stranger to a village had been attacked. Alcohol, the blight of the Alaskan Bush, was almost always involved. Usually the incident wound up involving the community health representative, the troopers, and sometimes the medical examiner. She was glad she couldn't understand the last message, and then she was ashamed that she was glad. They were her people, after all, Yupik, Alaskan, Bush rats. That she hadn't wound up an alcoholic herself was due only to the fact that, at least once, the cards had fallen for her instead of against her. God knows she carried the gene.

The time she'd spent with Moses on the deck the night before came back to her, along with his words.

"No," she said out loud. "Not now. Later, when Liam comes home."

She picked up a copy of *The Fiery Cross*, her current book, but she was too restless to read. Liam was reading *Nathaniel's Nutmeg*, but that didn't hold her interest either. She clicked on the television. Ninety-nine channels and nothing on. She paced. Finally she went to the computer and got on-line, checking the Nushugak Air Web site for messages, finding none.

Then she remembered the Web site she had visited when she was looking up stuff on Lend-Lease, before Moses came over. She clicked on the bookmark and found the page of links. One went to the full texts of the various Lend-Lease acts. Another went directly to the United States Navy's Web site, and the cargo ships that plied the Atlantic run funneling Lend-Lease materials to Britain, in the teeth of the U-boat wolf packs. There were links to the air force and the army as well. She followed another link and fetched up at a site sponsored by McDonnell Douglas, these days aka Boeing, which contained a brief history of the C-47.

In 1941 the Army Air Force (recently transmogrified from the Air Corps) selected it as its standard transport aircraft. The floor was reinforced and a large cargo door added, and hey, presto, the Skytrain was born. It could carry up to six thousand pounds of cargo, a fully assembled jeep, a thirty-seven-millimeter cannon, twenty-eight soldiers in full combat gear, or fourteen stretcher patients and three nurses.

All the Allies flew it, on every continent and in every major battle of World War II. By 1945 there were more than ten thousand of them in the air, answering to the nickname of "the Gooney Bird." General Dwight D. Eisenhower himself called it one of World War II's most important pieces of military equipment.

Her eyes dropped down to the specs with professional curiosity. It had a wingspan of ninety-five feet, six inches and was seventeen feet high. Its maximum ceiling was twenty-four thousand feet, with a normal range of sixteen hundred miles and a maximum range of thirty-eight hundred miles. It weighed thirty-one thousand pounds and cruised at one hundred sixty miles per hour, powered by two twelve-hundred-horsepower Pratt & Whitney engines. It was a three-holer, pilot, copilot and engineer, although she thought they'd been called navigators back then.

There was a picture, too, black-and-white, the aircraft gray with the barred white star on the fuselage just before the tail, and the tail numbers small and white on the vertical tail above and behind it. It was a shock to see what the wreck on Bear Glacier had looked like whole and proud.

Twenty-four thousand feet. And according to Colonel Campbell, they were on their way to Russia, to Krasnoyarsk, so already they were way the hell and gone off course. She wondered what the weather had been like that night. She did another search and raised the National Weather Service's site, which was excellent but was more focused on forecasts than on history.

Well, hell. You could see Carryall Mountain from Newenham, couldn't you? She tried to picture the horizon in that direction. She thought so. If you could, and if it had been clear that night, someone might actually have seen the plane auger in. There were a lot of Alaskan old farts in Newenham, a lot of people who'd been around from well before war had broken out. The plane must have made one hell of a bang when it went in, and that wasn't something you forgot.

She'd make a few calls tomorrow, she promised herself. She shut down the computer and resumed pacing away the minutes until Liam got home.

FOURTEEN

Charles was already at Bill's, vamping every female in sight. Tasha Anayuk, Natalie Gosuk's roommate, was leaning up against the booth, gazing into his face as if he was the answer to all her prayers. Bill made sure his glass never ran dry. And Jo Dunaway was sitting across from him.

"Liam," Charles said, catching sight of his son and breaking into a warm and well-practiced smile.

"Dad." He nodded at Jo.

Special Agent James Mason was sitting next to Charles, and nodded to Liam, his round-rimmed glasses slipping down his nose again.

Liam wondered about those glasses. They looked like plain glass, and the brown eyes behind the glass seemed to be very shrewd. During an interrogation, a perp might find those glasses less alarming than the eyes.

Jo had a notebook out, he noticed, and several pages were already filled with her cramped scribble. A curl fell over her eye and she flipped it back with an impatient gesture. "You giving an interview?"

Liam said to Charles, careless of the incredulity in his voice.

"The air force brings back its own," Charles said, smile gone. "No matter how long they've been gone. I think that's a damn good story, and one the public has a right to know."

"Their families are all likely dead by now. Why not leave them where they are, declare the area a grave-yard?"

Jo and Liam both waited for Charles' answer. He made a show of thinking it over, and when the silence had drawn out long enough to be anticipatory, said simply, "They're ours. They were members of the force when they took off from Nome that evening. They were members of the force when they went off course. They were members of the force when they slammed into that glacier. Just because they're dead doesn't make them any less ours. We don't leave anyone behind. We defend the nation and we protect our own."

Liam could see that Jo, hard-nosed seeker of truth that she was, was nonetheless impressed by this speech, and Tasha was either in love or getting ready to enlist, or maybe both. Liam ordered a beer.

Jo flipped through her notes. "I think that's all for now, Charles. If I have any further questions, may I call you?"

The smile was back and full-bore. "Of course. But why don't you stay and have dinner with us?"

Her gaze rested for a speculative moment on Liam's face. "Sure. Why not?"

"I can't stay long," Liam said.

Mason took a gulp of beer.

*   *   *

They ordered, ribeye for Charles, filet mignon for Jo, New York for Liam, steak sandwich for Mason. All the fishermen whose boats were still in the water had taken one look at the horizon and had stayed inside the breakwater that morning, so there was no fish or shellfish on the menu that night. Charles ordered a bottle of wine, and Liam, recognizing the signs, wondered if he ought to give Jo some kind of alert. He decided not to. He didn't like her job, but he liked her just fine, and in spite of the crap she'd dumped all over him on Wy's behalf he was glad Wy had such a staunch friend. But she was a grown woman who made her own choices.

He winced away from the prospect of Wy's best friend and his father in the sack together, but then he'd winced at the reality of Diana Prince and his father in the sack together and it hadn't killed him. His father was a rounder. If a woman was even halfway presentable and even a tenth of her was willing, it was as inevitable as the sun rising in the east that Charles would hit on her. Liam still thought the impulse to nail everything in sight came from Liam's mother's abandoning the both of them for a German nightclub owner when Liam was barely six months old, but that was his father's problem to work out, not his. He didn't do therapy. He kept his nose buried in his beer and spoke only when spoken to.

The bar was about half full, mostly of drinkers. Moses was at his usual table, playing chess with Clarence Saguyuk, another old geezer who looked twice Moses' age and had maybe half as many teeth. Neither factor seemed to affect his playing ability, if the forest of pawns, knights, rooks and one queen at his elbow was any indication. Eric Mollberg sat a little behind Clarence, a glass in one hand. He looked almost sober. Maybe he was finally coming out the other end of the tunnel. Liam had been down that same tunnel and he knew just how long it was.

Moccasin Man was holding forth in his usual booth, too, and Liam saw him make at least two sales. Gray was getting bolder with every day that passed without an arrest. Fine by Liam. Pretty soon Evan Gray would have enough rope to hang himself, and Liam would be there, ready to haul on the other end of it.

He wished with all his heart that the politicians in Juneau and Washington, D.C., would get a clue and legalize and tax all drugs, from dope to crack to ecstasy. If people wanted to go to hell in a pile of white dust or at the end of a needle, let them, instead of overworking law enforcement and overcrowding the jails to the point that every third bust was a drug bust and that the U.S. had more people in jail today than the Soviet Union ever did in all their gulags combined.

The result was the Evan Grays of this world, with marijuana stashed somewhere in or near Newenham and a profitable and growing retail business. Admit him to the ranks of businessmen and be done with it, and while we're at it, tax the hell out of him, Liam thought, watching Tasha Anayuk slide out of the booth opposite Gray, tucking something into her pocket. She saw Liam watching, and instead of flushing and scurrying away like the lawbreaker she was, she flashed him a brilliant smile and a little wave.

"Don't you think, Liam?"

"Sorry?" he said, turning back to his father. "I didn't hear you."

"There ought to be a museum dedicated to Alaska's World War Two effort."

Liam cut a piece of steak. "Why not?"

"Really," Charles insisted. "The Alcan was built to support Lend-Lease planes to Russia and China. The war in the Aleutians drew enough Japanese strength north to make the victory at Midway possible." He was at his most winning and it was all directed straight at Jo Dunaway, who was looking, in spite of herself, a little dazzled. Although that could have been the face Jo always put on when she got ready to seduce more information out of a source than they had previously known they had. According to Wy, such sources were legion, and Jo left them all lamenting their failure to recognize this fact.

"Maybe you could get in touch with the air museum in Anchorage," Jo said. "They're underfunded and going out of business every other week. If you could find a sponsor, they'd probably greet you with open arms."

"It's a thought," Charles said, with a warm smile that applauded such a wonderful idea and the wonderful person who had had it.

Be careful what you wish for, little girl, Liam thought. Half a steak to go, some chitchat, and he was out of here.

"Liam."

"Dad?"

"How have you been?"

"Fine."

"Catching a lot of cases?"

"No more than usual."

"Now there's a modest statement if I ever heard one,

Colonel," Jo said. "Just last month Liam busted a serial killer who's been kidnapping and murdering women around these parts for the last twenty-five years."

Charles nodded at the stripes on Liam's arm. "I noticed the promotion. Good job."

"Thanks."

"Still flying out to the Bush?"

"Yes."

"Still hating it?"

"Yes."

Charles fortified himself with a drink. "I know I've said it before, but it bears repeating."

"No, it doesn't."

Charles plowed on. "If you learned how to fly, if you learned the reasons why planes stay up in the air and how to keep them there, you wouldn't be nearly as afraid to travel in one."

Liam made no reply.

Jo met Special Agent James Mason's eyes. Special Agent James Mason had been careful to keep his mouth full of food during this exchange, which made Jo think highly of both his intelligence and his sense of self-preservation.

Clearly there was a problem of communication going on here strong enough to overwhelm any residual parent-child affection. She wondered how hard Charles had pushed Liam to learn to fly as a child. She wondered how hard Liam had resisted. But that wasn't all there was to it. On the surface, Charles was trying to reach out to his son, and Liam was refusing to see the outstretched hand. On the surface, Charles appeared fatherly and, well, maybe not loving, but at least proud and friendly.

Liam, on the other hand, looked sullen and churlish and about twelve years old. Charles had done something to make Liam angry, and Liam had not forgiven him for it. Charles was pretending it had never happened. Liam was reminding him.

She wondered what it was, and if there was a story in it. She was immediately, if only mildly, ashamed of herself. Looking for the story in everyone she met was an occupational hazard. There was always a story, though, and it was never the story the person wanted told. Some were worthy of her editor's attention and some weren't. A very few she kept to herself. She nearly always got the story, though, and she idled away a few moments, letting Charles' questions and Liam's monosyllabic replies join the slipstream, while she pondered what this one might be. Had Charles broken a law? Had he broken it in his son's posting?

"Where's the arm?" Charles said, and she woke from her reverie.

"At the crime lab in Anchorage."

Jo looked down at her plate. Her filet mignon stared back up at her. With a shrug, she took another bite.

"I should take custody of it."

Liam was uncertain of the protocol involved, but on general principles he decided that the arm should stay in the custody of the state of Alaska. "They'll take fingerprints. Did they take fingerprints in World War Two?"

For the first time Charles looked uncertain. "I don't know. I think they relied more on dog tags back then. Seriously, Liam, I can take charge of the arm and fly it back to D.C. I'll turn it over to the FBI lab." He hooked a thumb at Special Agent James Mason. "They'll track

him down. It's what they do, and really, it's only a
matter of deciding between which of the three. It was
a military plane, the property of the federal government. The FBI probably has jurisdiction." He looked
expectantly at Mason.

Mason, caught with his mouth full, chewed and
swallowed without any noticeable embarrassment.
"The only interest the FBI might have is if the wreck
was anything other than accidental. We don't really
think it is." He smiled, and Jo noticed because she was
incapable of not noticing that it was a very nice smile,
if not of the full wattage of Colonel Campbell's, then
with its own amount of shy charm. "I'm here mostly
on a field trip. My boss wants to get as many of the
Anchorage-based agents into the Bush as possible.
This was an opportunity for him."

An expression passed over Charles' face that was as
unpleasant as it was fleeting.

"I think I'll stick with the plan, Dad," Liam said.
"The ME will turn it over in due course."

"There are families waiting for word, for some kind
of closure. These men have been missing a long time.
They deserve an honorable burial as soon as possible."

"It's not like the families don't know how or when
they died," Liam said. There was no answer to this.
"Oh, and I guess you'll probably want the gold coin,
too."

"The what!"

Charles' exclamation was somewhere between a
bark and a shout. It had a parade-ground kind of feel
to it, and if activity in the bar did not come to a halt, it
slowed down and heads turned their way.

Liam, not expecting this reaction, said, "The gold

coin in the arm's hand. It, uh, fell out." He didn't say where or when.

Charles had himself under strict control. The smile was gone, though, and Jo gave him a long, thoughtful look. This was the face behind the gun sight on his jet. She wouldn't care to have that face on her tail. He lowered his voice. "There was a gold coin in the hand?"

"Yeah." Liam, for his part, didn't know what this was leading to. "It's an American twenty-dollar gold piece. Bill's got it."

"Get it."

Liam raised an eyebrow at the snapped order, but he got to his feet and walked to the bar, aware that most of the bar was eyeing him, openly or covertly. Moses was one of the former, that connoisseur of upheaval and disaster, and he grinned at Liam as he walked by. Eric Mollberg was one of the latter, nearly tucking his head beneath his arm to avoid eye contact. Clarence took advantage of Moses' distraction by nipping off with Moses' other knight. Liam and rest of the bar learned some new Yupik when Moses turned back and discovered the loss.

"Well?" Bill said.

"He wants the gold coin."

Bill jerked her head. "Top drawer, in the office."

"Thanks." He found it and brought it back.

Charles almost snatched it out of his hand and then seemed to notice the odd looks he was getting. He laughed. It didn't convince them. He saw it. "I'm sorry," he said. "It took me aback a little. I have a list of personal effects from the families, things the flight crew might have had with them on board. One of the copilot's grandchildren said he remembered his grandmother talking about a lucky gold piece that her grandfather had carried. It had quite a legend attached to it, was supposed to have been won from Wild Bill Hickok in the poker game before the one he got shot in, and been in the family ever since. In the normal course of events, it would have gone to the son and then to the grandson. It'd be nice to get it back to him."

It was a charming story, told with style and just the right touch of sentimentality. It was a pity that the only person at the table who believed it was the storyteller himself. He seemed to want to move on, and quickly, too. He looked at Liam and said, "Does anyone else know about this piece?"

Liam thought back to the scene in the bar two nights before. "Pretty much everyone in Newenham by now, I'd guess."

"Damn it. Liam, we can't wait until spring to recover the bodies. We have to do it now."

"Dad, I told you, and so did Wy. That's pretty much next to impossible. It's October—hell, it's almost November. Winter's coming on. It's snowing right now. That airstrip isn't maintained, and there's no way to get the wreck down off the glacier even if it were."

"We'll use helicopters. I'll call Elmendorf, see what's available. And there's an Air National Guard base, too—Kulik, isn't it? I'll ask them what they've got."

"I know those guys, Dad," Liam said evenly. "They're on call for rescues all over the state. I don't think they're going to volunteer their crews and their equipment to recover bodies that have been lying there for sixty years. We're coming up on storm season. They'll have plenty of work on their hands rescuing the living."

Charles' eyes narrowed. "Those guys who came busting up on the four-wheelers when we were out at the wreck . . ."

"What about them?" Liam said, wondering where this was going.

"They were treasure hunting."

"They said they were caribou hunting."

"Crap. They knew about this gold coin and they went looking for more where it came from."

Liam couldn't deny it. "So?"

"So if we don't get that wreck out of there you're going to start losing Newenhammers who think there might be gold in them thar hills."

Liam remembered the slab of ice that had nearly killed him and Wy the previous morning. "You'll lose just as many going after it."

"Not if I round up good equipment and good equipment operators. Leave it to me." Charles stood up and threw down a couple of bills. "Excuse me. I've got some calls to make."

The three of them watched him stride out the door. When it closed behind him, Liam looked at Mason and said, "What's going on?"

"I don't know," Mason said. "I don't," he added when he saw Liam's skepticism. "My boss heard about the wreck and called the commander out on Elmendorf. The BOC told him that Colonel Campbell was flying in. My boss asked him to ask Colonel Campbell to let me hitch a ride to Newenham. He said okay. I have to say we were all a little surprised. I mean, the United States Air Force doesn't exactly hand out rides on an F-15."

"So the inference is he wanted you here. Why?"

Mason was using a french fry to mop up the last drop of steak juice and was very intent on the job. "He said that cooperation between federal organizations was essential to the smooth working of government, and that he was happy to be able to contribute to it, in however small a way." He met Liam's eyes with a bland expression in his own.

"What can you do here?"

"Not much," Mason said. "I don't have a lot of authority over the sixty-year old wreck of a military plane. If it was sabotaged, or the flight was in any way related to espionage of some kind, then I could step in, maybe. And only maybe." He smiled. "In Alaska the FBI is more concerned with Russians importing underage girls who come thinking they're going to be part of an ethnic dance group and who wind up shaking it down in the strip clubs."

"Were you on that case?" Jo said.

"From the start." Mason didn't sound happy about it.

"Were the girls in on it?"

"The older one, the twenty-year-old, maybe. The two younger ones, no way."

"Are they still in jail?"

Mason winced. "We prefer to call it protective custody."

"Waiting on the INS?"

"That, and the fact that we need them to testify against the guys who brought them into the country."

Liam reached for his wallet. "I'm due home."

"Give Wy my love."

"Where's Gary?" Liam said, suddenly noticing her brother's absence.

"Relax," Jo said. "He's doing some patchup work for a guy he knows in Ik'ikika."

Liam tried not to show his relief.

She waited until he was inches from a clean getaway. "What's going on with your father, Liam?"

"I know as much as you do, Jo. And sometimes I think," he added, a trifle grimly, "a lot less."

"Man," she said.

"What?"

"Sons and their fathers."

"What about them?"

"Tell the truth. You guys just sit around thinking up ways to fail each other, don't you?"

"Go to hell," Liam said, and marched to the bar, wallet in hand.

Jo watched him go, admiring the straight spine that managed to broadcast every ounce of the offended dignity that he was feeling.

Fathers and sons, she thought.

There oughta be a law.

She was unaware that she'd said the words out loud until Special Agent James Mason said, "Against what?"

"Many things," she said, recovering. "Many, many things."

"There already are," he said. "And speaking as a member and on behalf of the law-enforcement community, I have enough laws to make people mind already. My old man used to say that every time Congress enacted another law, they took another little piece of our freedom away."

"Sounds like a right-wing reactionary to me."

He laughed. "It's early," he said, reaching for his jacket. "You're at the Bay View Inn."

"Yes."

"So am I. I've got a bottle in my room. Want a drink?"

She looked him over with care. He met her eyes without guile, something to mistrust in any member of any law-enforcement agency. "Sure," she said.

After paying his tab Liam paused at the chess table. "Get the hell outta my light," Clarence said. Eric Mollberg had gone to the bar for a refill. Moses looked up and growled, "What?"

"Do you know who did it?"

Moses moved his last pawn to the last row and exchanged it for his queen.

"Do you?"

"Check," Moses said. Clarence swore loudly.

"Goddamn it, old man," Liam said.

"Goddamn it, yourself," Moses said. He reached for a bottle of Oly and flatfooted it. "Beer!" he bellowed, and behind him Liam heard the bar cooler open. "I don't know," he said finally, glaring up at Liam, who seemed to have planted himself like a rock.

"You'd tell me if you did."

"It doesn't work like that. You'll find him." He tried for one of his fallen-angel smiles, not quite succeeding. "Besides, you're not a believer, boy. What you doing bothering the old shaman when you know you're going to do whatever the hell you were going to do in the first place? Go on home. She's waiting for you."

"I am." Liam didn't move.

"Go on, then! Quit interfering with my chess game."

Clarence gave a sudden cry that sounded just like the cackle of a raven, and moved his rook. "Checkmate."

"Fuck," Moses said.

Clarence sat back in his chair and looked up at Liam beneath shaggy brows. "You talking about Lydia?"

Liam shifted his gaze from one side of the table to the other, and nodded.

"You should have seen her when we was all young," Clarence said. "That girl had boys buzzing around like mosquitoes, wanting to suck that juicy little thing dry."

Moses uttered a sharp bark of laughter. "Including you."

"Including you," Clarence retorted. His beady little black eyes sparkled and he all but smacked his lips. "Those were the days. Get hold of a truck and drive your girl and your friends and their girls to Icky and have an all-day party on the beach at One Lake. You remember that party out the beach that one summer?"

Moses grinned.

"Yeah," Clarence said. "I see you do. Bet Leslie and Walter and Silent Cal and Stan do, too."

"Stan's dead."

Clarence frowned. "Stan's dead?"

"Going on five years."

Clarence was outraged. "Goddamn! How's a man supposed to get drunk with his friends if they keep dying on him!"

"What about Lydia at the beach?" Liam said.

Moses and Clarence got matching faraway looks on

their faces. "We went up to the fish camp used to be at Icky."

"Wasn't Icky," Moses said. "The fish camp was out the end of River Road."

"It was up Icky way, this fish camp," Clarence said, glaring. "A bunch of the guys and the girls in the school. We took some beer, and somebody had some records and had figured out a way to run a record player off his pickup battery. We stayed up there two days and two nights, dancing and singing and laughing and pulling fish out of the river." Clarence looked at Moses. "Remember the eagles?"

Moses nodded. "Couple eagles sitting in this cottonwood snag, old Silent Cal got too close and one of those eagles hoisted up its tail feathers and shot a stream of yellow shit straight into old Silent Cal's face."

Both old men shook with remembered glee, until Liam was afraid Clarence at least might go off into an apoplexy.

"I think he thought he was going to get lucky that night," Clarence said, mopping his eyes. "But his girl wouldn't have anything to do with him after that." He winked at Liam. "Not to say she didn't get lucky herself."

Moses leaned forward and leveled a forefinger. "Clarence, you are a dirty old man."

"I wasn't then."

Again both men fell into choking fits.

"When was that?" Liam said.

"Oh, hell," Clarence said, knuckling his eyes. "Long time. Long time ago. Before the war."

"Not long before," Moses said instantly.

"Long time before," Clarence said, glaring.

"We weren't that old long time before the war, old man."

"Set up the pieces; we'll see how old I am!"

Liam left them to it.

December 15, 1941

Its cleer but god its cold they say its thirty-seven below the coldest in twenty-five years. Our mechanic Billy hes from Duluth in Minnesota hes a good guy he lost a filling the other day just by breathing in. He can only do a twenty-minute shift and even then he has to work in mittens. It took him two hours to replace a plug yesterday.

Haven't written for a while because we spent a week tdy flying out of Anchorage One day we went to Adak to pick up eighteen patients. 1250 miles and usually eight to ten hours flying time. There was a front hanging off Umnak and it was rough as hell. The nurse was a pistol she piled blankets all over the patients to keep them from bouncing around and give her parka to another. Roepke brought us down to 50 feet. Everybody puked. He brought us back up to thirteen thousand and the cabin temperature dropped to twenty below but at least it smoothed out. He put her down at Naknek in a forty mile an hour crosswind he had to really crab her in. Man that was no fun. While we were on the ground another Gooney crashed and burned on landing. The crew got out okay. We overnighted. The whole flight took two days two hours and ten minutes.

Came back to find a letter from Helen. She lost the baby. Says shes sick and needs money to pay the hospital.

Went to Petes for dinner when we got back. Hes a good guy knows not to talk to much. Wanted to know about Krasnoyarsk and what it looked like and how many people lived there. Told him it looked like Nome.

FIFTEEN

Diana Prince caught a call just as she was headed out the door at the end of the day. Someone had made a charge of child abuse against Bernadette Kusegta, who ran a small day-care center out of her home. The complainant, one Gloria Crow, accused Bernadette of interfering with her three-year-old daughter, Tammie. Kusegta, plump and attractive, with her black hair permed into a mass of large curls, looked white beneath her brown skin. She sat, unmoving, her eyes fixed on a point somewhere beyond the large room decorated in primary colors. It was heaped with toys and books, and a small inflatable swimming pool filled with about four inches of water sat on the floor, one lone rubber duck floating in the middle of it.

"Well, go on, arrest her!" Crow said. "What are you waiting for?" She was slender and sharp-featured and vibrating with rage.

"When did you see the marks, ma'am?" Prince said.

"Tonight! When my baby came home! She was crying and holding her bottom!"

"Did she say that Ms. Kusegta had hurt her?"

"No, but who else could have done it? Go on, arrest her! She hurt my baby!"

"You said, 'When your baby came home,' ma'am. From that, I'm guessing you didn't go get her."

"No! So what?"

"Who did bring your daughter home, Ms. Crow?"

"Leslie did; he picked her up on his way home."

"Is Leslie your husband?"

"He's my roommate."

"What's his full name?"

"Leslie Clark."

"And when he brought your daughter home, she was crying and holding her bottom."

"Yes!"

"And then you looked and found the marks."

"Yes! I know she did it; she was the only one who could have! Arrest her right now!"

"Where is your daughter now, ma'am?"

"She's home, of course! I came here as soon as I saw what that bitch did to her!"

"Is Leslie there with her?"

"Of course! Did you think I'd leave my baby all alone?"

Diana flipped her notebook closed. "I'll need to talk to your daughter, ma'am. Right now."

They made it in the door before the boyfriend started beating on the little girl again, but only just. He was now in the lockup, protesting his innocence in spite of the similarity in size and shape between his hands and the marks on Tammie's defenseless little bottom. Bernadette Kusegta's face had regained some of its natural color, and Gloria Crow was still insisting that Leslie could never have done such a thing, that she would have known if he could, that she would never have let him in her house or left her daughter with him if she'd known. Diana took statements and called Bill Billington for an arraignment at ten a.m. the next morning. It was almost ten before she was through, and she was tired and heartsick and wanted nothing so much as a long, hot bath. Preferably with bubbles, but if no bubbles were to be had she might pour in a bottle of Lysol.

She had her hand on the knob of the door when the phone rang. It would have forwarded to Liam's cell after the second ring, but she seemed to be constitutionally incapable of walking out on a ringing phone. Cursing herself, she snatched it up. "Alaska State Troopers, Newenham post."

The voice was loud enough to make her wince away from the receiver. "Ma'am! Ma'am! Please, calm down, I can't understand a word!"

There was a gulping kind of sob. "Please help me; I think my sister's dead."

"What happened to her?"

"Oh, God, Karen, please, Karen, don't do this, please don't do this!"

"Ma'am? Where are you?"

"We're at my mother's. Please help us, please!"

"Where is your mother's house, ma'am? Ma'am?"

"Oh, God, I think she's dead." The voice dulled and flattened. "Oh, Karen. Oh, Karen."

"Ma'am?" Diana clenched the phone so hard her arm ached. "I need you to tell me where you are. Ma'am?"

After a long, silent moment, when she thought the caller might have hung up, the woman told her. Diana told her she was coming, called Liam, and called Joe Gould.

She got to Lydia's house five minutes after Joe and a split second before Liam. The three of them stood once again in Lydia's kitchen, looking at another body on the same floor.

"Strangled, this time," Joe said.

"What was your first clue?" Diana said, her voice hollow. Karen's eyes were open and bulging, her tongue protruded from her mouth, and her throat was one livid bruise.

To Liam's everlasting shame, his first reaction at the sight was relief. Now Wy would never know what had happened in Lydia's bedroom.

Joe did not change expression.

This time there had been a fight. The kitchen table and chairs were knocked over, drawers had been pulled out and dumped, cupboards opened and emptied on the floor. Broken dishes and spilled rice crunched underfoot, and the body was coated with powdered chocolate. "Let's check the rest of the house," Liam said.

It was trashed. The bed had been ripped apart and the mattress dumped to the floor. The drawers to the filing cabinet had been opened and dumped. The shelves in the medicine cabinet in the bathroom had been swept clean, bottles of Bayer and boxes of Band-Aids and bars of scented soap winding up in the sink or toilet and all over the floor. Betsy Amakuk sat on the couch in the living room, where all the books had been pulled from the shelves. She was weeping into Stan Jr.'s shoulder. Stan Jr. patted her awkwardly. He looked angry. Jerry wasn't there.

"Somebody was looking for something," Diana said.

"No shit," Liam said, and returned to the kitchen. Joe Gould was zipping Karen into a black plastic body bag. "To the airport, Joe, straight to the airport and no stopping." He dialed Wy's number on his cell phone. When she answered, he said, "I need you to take the Cessna to Anchorage tonight. Right now, in fact. Can do?"

"Are you coming?"

"Yes. You'll be transporting a body." Silence. "Wy?"

"Whose body?" she said, but he got the feeling she was only killing time.

"Karen Tompkins."

"What?"

"Karen Tompkins, Lydia's daughter. We just found her. I need to get her body to the ME in Anchorage tonight. Can you take it?"

Another silence. "I— All right. I'll call Bill to stay with Tim and head for the airport to start pulling seats."

"Meet you there." He hung up and looked at Prince. "You know the drill."

"I do."

"We'll do a turnaround and come straight back."

"Okay." She was straining toward the door, eager to start questioning the neighbors.

"Go," he said, and she bolted for the door like the starter pistol had been fired.

"Give me a hand," Joe said, and Liam went to Karen Tompkins' black plastic–clad feet. They lifted her easily and bore her from the room. Liam glanced back at the isolated island of faded linoleum in a sea of broken crockery, spilled flatware and a layer of white flour, an eerie reverse print of the dead woman's body.

They were in the air half an hour later, the second and third rows of seats pulled and stacked in the shed next to the tie-down. "Karen Tompkins?"

"Yeah."

"Lydia Tompkins' daughter?"

"Yeah."

"What happened?"

"It looks like somebody strangled her."

She made a noise of distress. "Why?"

"I don't know yet."

The storm had cleared, and the moon rose in time to light their way through Lake Clark Pass, a narrow gorge hedged about on all sides by very tall, very steep mountains already covered with snow. They landed at Merrill ninety minutes later, to be met by the meat wagon. Brillo Pad was driving.

Brillo Pad, aka Dr. Hans Brilleaux, had a very thick, very wiry, very curly head of very black hair, hence the nickname. Brillo Pad was fifty-six years old and very proud of his hair's continued thickness and lack of gray. "Liam," he said, big white buckteeth flashing in a grin. His face was swarthy and his nose was large and red-veined.

"Hans Brilleaux, Wy Chouinard."

Brillo Pad gave Wy the once-over. "Delighted. You folks staying the night in Anchorage?"

"You done with Lydia Tompkins?" Liam said.

"Who?"

"Lydia Tompkins," Liam said, enunciating the

name in careful, independent syllables. "The woman I sent you two days ago."

Brillo Pad tore his eyes from Wy and said, "Sure. I knew that. Ah, yeah. Head injury, whacked her skull pretty good, causing internal bleeding and a clot. Bam. On the physical evidence of the body, good chance it was accidental, not intentional. She clawed him, but no skin or blood, only fibers. If I had to guess, I'd say they came from a Carhartt's jacket."

"Great."

"I know, not many of those around Alaska, are there?" He helped Liam maneuver the body bag out of the 180. "Who's this?"

"The first woman's daughter. How quick can you look at her?"

Brillo Pad whistled long and low. "Daughter, huh? Man, you're the reason I've been in business the last six months."

"I'm figuring the same guy did both women. Any hard evidence you can find, say fibers from the same coat, would be most helpful."

"I'll take her straight to the lab, see what I can see. So, are you staying in town tonight?"

"We're going home," Liam told Brillo.

"Okay. I'll give you a call when I've got something."

He drove off, and Wy got clearance from the tower. They were back in the air five minutes later.

Liam felt a sense of relief as the lights of the big city receded behind them, and wondered at it. "It's easier flying at night," he said over the headset.

She looked at him in the darkness of the cabin. "You're not as afraid to fly in the dark?"

"I don't think I am. Or at least not as much as I am during the day."

"It's a miracle," she said lightly.

"Maybe it's just that I can't see how far up we are." He peered out of the window, saw a flare burning on one of the Inlet oil rigs far below, and straightened hastily.

"Or maybe you're just tired of being scared and your little monkey brain has decided enough is enough."

"Maybe," he said, unconvinced. He was glad, though, to be spared some of the usual terror. He wasn't relaxed enough to doze, but at least he wasn't holding the aircraft up by the edge of his seat.

It was dark and warm in the cabin. Outside the stars were very bright, competing with the new moon, and both lit every rugged peak and every hanging glacier of the pass in bold relief. The moonlight reflected off the snow and lit the cabin of the aircraft with enough light to read by. He was very conscious of Wy's shoulder brushing his, of her strong hands, relaxed and competent, resting on the yoke, of her long, jeans-clad legs stretched out in front of her, the soles of her feet just touching the rudder pedals. He turned a little in his seat so he could watch her.

She glanced over. "What?"

"Nothing. I just like watching you work, is all."

Her teeth flashed in the dim light. "Since when?"

"Since tonight, I guess."

She held up a hand and turned a knob on the tuner. A woman's voice gave a recorded weather report. When it began to repeat, she turned it off.

"I love you, Wy."

She reached for his hand and brought it to her lips. "Same goes."

He brought her hand to his mouth and kissed her palm. They flew on steadily for a few moments, content.

"Liam?"

"What?"

It was odd, but the question she had been dreading to ask came out more easily than she had imagined. Maybe everything was easier at five thousand feet. "Are you going to take that job that John Barton offered you?"

"I don't know." His answer, too, was much less tense than it might have been.

"Do you want it?"

Did he? Did he want to go back to the fast track, to being John Dillinger Barton's fair-haired, handpicked successor, well up on the ladder to the top?

He remembered the answer he'd given Brillo Pad when the ME had wanted to know if they were staying the night in Anchorage. *We're going home.* It was natural now, or so it seemed, for him to call Newenham home. He thought of the people he would never have met if not for his fall from grace and his transfer to Newenham. Bill Billington, a magistrate unlike any other he had ever encountered. Moses Alakuyak, that not-quite-dried-up little demon. Charlene Taylor. Newenham had given him Wy back. Newenham had given him Tim.

He thought then of the mighty river flowing past their deck, of the great bay it emptied into, of the rolling muskeg and the hundreds of lakes and the ragged peaks and glaciers and hidden valleys beyond.

Of the little herd of caribou that he had been told wandered into town in the early spring when they overran their calving grounds. Of the walrus hauling out in herds on the beaches of an island just miles down the coast. Of the hundred tiny towns and villages, cabins and fish cabins and lodges sprinkled across this vast area with a lavish hand, each one housing some gem of a person like Leonard Nunapitchuk, who refused to be a victim, who remained stubbornly in his own house even after his wife had been murdered in it by the same man who had kidnapped and murdered his daughter.

"You know, Wy, I don't know the answer to that one, either. Three years ago I wouldn't have hesitated; I would have grabbed it and ran. I had a wife, and a son, and a career where there was nowhere to go but up. And then I met you. Wy?"

"What?"

"If I take the job, will you come with me? You and Tim?"

There was a brief silence. "I don't know, Liam. This is honest. I don't know."

He laughed then. "Yeah, well, we're not the most decisive couple on the block, now, are we?"

"I guess not." She laughed, too, a little. "Liam."

"What?"

She took his hand again, and his curled around hers in a comforting grip. "There is Tim."

"There certainly is. I wasn't thinking we'd leave him behind."

"I know."

"I like him, Wy. I like him a lot. And without sounding too egotistical, I think he likes me. I'd like to be his father. And," he added pointedly, "I'd like to make it official."

"Yeah, yeah, yeah," she said. "Man, I never knew anyone more hot to get married than you."

He leaned over to kiss her. " 'Hot' doesn't even come close," he said with his best sexy growl, and then his mike got tangled up with hers and they both started to laugh.

"Tim can't get into any more trouble in Anchorage than he has in Newenham," he said, sitting back. "Same cliques, same drugs, same joysticks. He can go to the malls and the movies, and it'll be harder to keep tabs on him if he finds a friend with a car, but otherwise it's not that different."

"It's a lot bigger than Newenham. The school's bound to induce big-time culture shock. And then there is Natalie."

Liam shook his head. "I never would have thought to hear you using Natalie Gosuk as a reason to keep Tim in Newenham." He was gentle but inexorable. "Are you sure she isn't just an excuse to keep you there, too?"

She was silent. They were out of the pass and were losing altitude, on approach across the Nushugak into the Newenham airport.

"Do you know the words in the wedding service, Wy? 'Forsaking all others, so long as you both shall live.' That's what I want. 'Forsaking all others.' And all other places. We don't have to move to Anchorage; that's not what I'm saying."

She didn't sound angry. "It kind of sounds like that, Liam."

He was exasperated. "Do you get anything about

me at all, woman? I love you! I've always loved you! I would have walked out on my wife and my child if you'd asked me! But you didn't ask!"

She stared at him. "Don't you get anything about me?" she said at last. "I wouldn't have wanted you if you'd been able to do something like that. One of the reasons I love you, that I've always loved you, is that you're an honorable man. I knew all I had to do was drive to Glenallen and knock on your door. I always knew that."

"But you didn't."

"So I didn't love you enough to? Is that what this is about? I let you back into my life, Liam, into Tim's life. You're important to both of us now."

"I want to be essential."

"You are. You were then." She was silent. "Or . . ."

"What."

She took a deep breath. "I don't know, Liam. Love is supposed to be unselfish. If you love, you're supposed to want what's best for the person you love."

"And?"

"And if I'd loved you enough then, I shouldn't have asked you to choose between me and Jenny and Charlie. If I'd loved you enough, I should have bought the house next door to yours, so you'd never have to be far away from your son."

His feeling of comfort vanished. The plane seemed very high in the air and nowhere near as steady beneath his butt as it had been a moment before. "You're telling me you didn't love me enough."

The silence that followed seemed to him to be very long. "I guess I didn't."

The next question was as difficult but came much more quickly. "Do you now?"

If he hadn't been listening so intently for her answer he might have missed it. "Wy?"

"Did you hear that?"

"Hear what?"

"The engine seemed to miss a beat."

"What?" Liam sat up, peering at the prop, instantly focused on where they were.

"There! It happened again!"

She was adamant so he listened. A high-pitched drone whined past the outside of the aircraft. The Cessna seemed to shudder, although it might have been Wy's hands clenching on the yoke. "What the hell?"

"What is it?"

Her hands were already a blur of movement. "I think someone's shooting at us."

"What!"

"I said I think—"

There was another whine, followed this time by the unmistakable impact of metal on metal. The prop began to shudder, and the cowling and indeed the entire front of the aircraft with it. "Hang on!" she shouted, and kicked the rudder and put the Cessna into a shallow dive and a spiraling turn.

It was an unnecessary command; Liam had his hands clenched around the edge of his seat and with every muscle strained upward, keeping that plane in the sky. Oh, God yes, anything but down, please, please, I'll never get drunk again, I'll do all of Miranda every single time no matter how the Supreme Court rules, I'll marry and settle down and live a nice, quiet life, just please don't let this plane go down with me on board.

But when he risked a glance out the window, down seemed to be coming up very fast indeed, and now he cursed the light of the moon that so clearly illuminated the river beneath them. No, not into the river—it was too cold; they'd never survive long enough to make it to the shore—and then the shore was beneath them—oh, no, not the shore, they were going to crash, the plane was going to hit the ground and break into pieces and they were going to break into pieces with it, not the shore, please not the shore. Wy's face was tight-lipped and grim, the yoke shook back and forth in her hands in time with the shaking of the propeller and the cowling and the whole front of the plane, Oh, god, he thought he was going to be sick.

The ground rushed up at them and suddenly he saw a stretch of open ground, oh, God, was it an airstrip? It was white with snow or frost but it was long and straight and there were no trees in the middle of it, no trees for the plane to run into, no trees to decapitate him or impale him or skewer him, a Campbell shish kebab. "Is it an airstrip?" he shouted.

"Shut up!" she shouted back, and the ground rushed up, filling his range of terrified vision, up, up, up, until they hit down, hard, bounced once, hit again, and then, miraculously, all three gears were on the ground and she had cut the engine and they were running out the length of the airstrip, this blessed airstrip that had appeared out of nowhere to aid and to succor them in their time of need.

The Cessna rumbled and rolled and thumped and chunked over hummocks of ice and snow and what might have been a fallen tree and finally stopped.

It was very quiet in the cabin of the little plane.

Liam could hear himself inhale, exhale, inhale. His heartbeat was clearly audible, too, a rapid thudding sound, like a drumbeat, slowing now.

"Liam."

"What?"

"I'm sorry I told you to shut up."

"It's okay. Everything's okay. I'm fine. You're fine, and I'm fine, and we're on the ground, oh, God, how I love the ground, and everything's fine." He was light-headed, a little dizzy.

"Liam?"

"Really. I'm fine. I'm just—I'm fine."

Another silence. "Wy?"

"What?"

"Why does the plane always break when I'm on board?"

She ruffled up. "It doesn't always break. It's only broken once before when you were on board. And it didn't break this time; somebody broke it."

She opened the door and climbed out. He followed.

One end of the propeller had been hit, it looked by, yes, by a bullet. The squared-off end of the prop was not quite holed but sort of splooshed, dented, cratered, if you could call something that small a crater.

Liam could. "I have to sit down," he said, and staggered over to a tree trunk.

"Me, too," Wy said, and followed him.

They both sat down at the same time, not bothering to clear off the trunk, and as a result the snow on the trunk wet their pants through immediately. They didn't move, except that Liam put his head between his knees.

"You okay?"

"I'm fine," Liam said, his head still between his knees. "Where are we?"

"Bulge. The village across the river. Their front street."

"Oh." He peered around, and now that the terror had cleared from his eyes he saw the three little houses, shacks, really, clustered at one end of the airstrip. "Where is everybody?"

Wy let her head fall back and closed her eyes against the glare of the moon. "Nobody lives here during the winter."

"Yeah? Summer cottages."

"One room, river view."

He turned his head, still keeping it low. "You sound almost cheerful." She looked it, too, as near as he could make out her expression in the moonlight.

"I am," she said, and laughed out loud and opened her eyes.

He sat up with caution. "What's so damn funny?"

She laughed again, a joyous sound. "I didn't know it was coming!"

"What?"

"I didn't know anybody was going to shoot at us!"

He stared at her. "Okay," he said. "I didn't, either, which goes without saying, as I'd much rather shoot it out on the ground, although I'd rather never shoot it out at all. What the hell are you talking about?"

"I didn't know anybody was going to shoot at us, and I didn't know we'd have to make an emergency landing! I didn't know anything about it! I didn't hear any voices, or feel any feelings! I didn't have any visions!"

"Wy, honey," Liam said, "you've got a first-aid kit

in the plane, don't you? Is there any, well, you know, Valium in it?"

"I'm fine, Liam," she said, and got up to do a neat dance step, of necessity shuffling a bit because of the snow, but still . . . "Listen," she said, coming to sit back next to him. She seized his hands in both of hers and kissed him soundly, a loud smack that echoed off the sides of the plane and back at them, and made her laugh again.

"Wy—"

"Moses came to see me last night," she said.

"Wy, let me get the first-aid kit. You've got some whiskey in it, don't you? I think you could use a drink, and I know I could."

He tried to stand up and she wouldn't let him. "Wait a minute, Liam. I know I sound crazy, but listen. Moses came to see me last night, and he told me he was my grandfather."

"Oh." All that meant to Liam was that the little martinet was going to be his grandfather-in-law. He could only imagine how much Moses was going to beat up on him now. There were probably one hundred additional movements in tai chi that Moses had been saving up to torture him with, and he'd have to learn them all. "Maybe I don't want to marry you after all."

She laughed again, a clear, full-throated sound that rang down the airstrip like a bell. "He's a shaman."

"I've noticed," Liam said dryly.

"No, no, listen." She shook his hands. "Listen, Liam. I'm his granddaughter, and he hears voices."

"Wy, I don't—"

"He told me I was going to hear them, too."

"—think— What? What do you mean?"

"I mean just what you think I mean. He told me that hearing the voices is hereditary in our family, that sometimes it takes a while for them to kick in. He told me the reason I made us come to the fish camp last month is because I knew Gheen was coming and that Tim was in danger."

He looked at her and remembered how determined, how in fact implacable she had been to fly into the teeth of thirty-five-knot winds, blowing snow and fog and the year's first winter storm. She was going to go; nothing anyone could say or do short of busting up the plane with a crowbar was going to stop her. He had been angry with her, and terrified, because he knew he'd have to go with her. "Did you?"

She rounded on him. "Of course not! I told Moses last night that all I did was follow the trail of dead bodies that crazy bastard left. It was pointing right toward Old Man Creek. It didn't take any voices to see that; it was right there on the map!"

She looked as fierce as she sounded; there was plenty of moonlight to show him that. "That's why you were nervous about the flights," he said.

"What flights?"

"The one to the glacier this morning and the one to Anchorage tonight. You were looking for advice from the voices if you should fly or not."

"Voices," she said with scorn. "Imagine. I'm a pilot, Liam. I'm not a shaman. Besides, a shaman is a man. All the shamans I've known are men."

"How many have you known?"

"That's not the point. Okay, one, all right, Moses! But I've never read about a woman shaman, or heard about one, and besides, I don't believe in any of that stuff anyway. He's my friend, and my tai chi teacher, and it turns out he happens to be my grandfather, too." She made a visible effort to calm down. "He's also a drunk, and he was drunk on his ass last night. He probably didn't have a clue what he was saying."

He always had before. Liam kept that thought to himself.

"And besides," Wy added, "if any voices were going to kick in they would have kicked in before this flight. They would at the very least have kicked in before we left Anchorage. I haven't got any; I don't care whose granddaughter I am."

Suddenly, right over their heads, a raven cawed loudly. They both jumped. Wy leaped to her feet and shouted, "Yeah, your mother, you little black bastard!"

She marched off.

Liam stood up and brushed at the seat of his pants, searching out the cawer in the tree above. He'd been there the month before, or someone very like him, and had followed them down the river in the skiff. They would have missed the mouth of Old Man Creek if it hadn't been for the raven.

Although it wasn't necessarily a he. It was impossible to tell a male raven from a female raven from a distance. Liam had been making it his business to read up on ravens. As a practicing law-enforcement professional, he preferred his science straight, unencumbered by myth or legend, but it was hard to get away from either in this country. He read Bernd Heinrich and Richard K. Nelson, and he learned that Alaska Natives regarded the raven as a trickster, not a helper. You had to watch Raven or he'd steal you blind, food, home, woman, children, the sun, the moon and the stars, for that matter.

All Liam knew was that something big and black and winged had come between him and disaster three times in the last six months, and he was grateful. There was a series of soft croaks from a branch above him. He thought he caught a blue-black gleam of raven wing, a glimpse of a beady eye.

He also thought he might be going a little insane. Disneyham was finally getting to him. He followed Wy to the plane.

She had the toolbox out of the plane and was rooting through it. She stood up as he approached, hacksaw in hand. "What are you doing with that?"

She got a plastic crate out of the back of the plane and went to the front, upended it, and climbed on top.

"Wy?"

She put one hand on the prop and rested the hacksaw on the end, to just before the bullet nonhole.

"Wy!"

She started to saw. She might even have been whistling.

"Wy!"

SIXTEEN

Karen Tompkins' town house was on the south end of the complex, looking directly over the small boat harbor. There was a kitchen, a living room, and a dining room downstairs, and two bedrooms and two bathrooms upstairs. There was no yard in front, only two parking spaces. It was exactly like the other seven units in the building, with a narrow deck running across the front and five sets of evenly spaced stairs providing access. There was a small wrought-iron table with two matching chairs on the deck in front of Karen's.

Inside, there was a lot of pink. The sheets on the bed were pink and satin. The towels in the bathroom were pink and fluffy. The china dishes in the kitchen cupboard had pink roses on them. The purple leather couch had pink plush accent pillows. The carpet was maroon, and the walls were hung with watercolor paintings of flowers and hummingbirds and butterflies.

The bed was king-size. So was the tub in the master bath. Two drawers of the dresser were devoted to toys intended to be played with in both, some of which raised eyebrows all around.

There was a calendar hung over the kitchen counter, with a dentist's appointment coming up on November second, and that was about it. Envelopes were tucked into the calendar's pocket. Diana shuffled through them. Bills, electric, gas, garbage, telephone, all due at the first of the month. An Alaska Airlines Visa bill, carrying a thirteen-thousand-dollar balance and a two-hundred-dollar periodic finance charge.

In the spare bedroom, which didn't look as if it had seen much use, there was a plastic box with a handle on top, the size to fit letter-size files. Inside were Karen's birth certificate, her high school diploma, her bank statements, the deed to the town house. Nothing looked out of the ordinary.

There was no clue as to who her most recent bed partner had been, but from what Diana had heard so far, you could pretty much throw a dart anywhere within the Newenham city limits and hit someone who'd spent time between Karen Tompkins' sheets.

She had interviewed Betsy Amakuk and her husband at Lydia's house, although Betsy was nearly incoherent with grief. She'd lost a mother and a sister within the space of two days, so Diana didn't blame her. Her husband said they'd been home that evening, sorting through Lydia's bills, which they'd fetched from Lydia's house that morning, and writing Lydia's obituary for the newspapers. Betsy had made a quick run back to her mother's house to look for Lydia's birth certificate to run with the obituary, and had found Karen dead on the kitchen floor. No, they couldn't think of anyone who wished Karen harm.

"She had a lot of boyfriends," Betsy had said in an exhausted voice. "She liked men, sure. But she wouldn't have stayed with anyone who threatened her, or hurt her."

Diana thought of the toys found in Karen's house and reserved judgment.

She had interviewed Stan Jr. at his house, a ranch-style home with two bedrooms and one bath in the Anipa subdivision, painted forest green with white trim and a corrugated metal roof. Inside there was a lot of overstuffed furniture, a fireplace, a kitchen of near-sanitary cleanliness, a large bathroom with a soaker tub and terra-cotta tiles. It looked very comfortable, and very expensive. Stan Jr. was pale and tightly controlled. He shook his head when she asked him if he knew of anyone who might have wanted to hurt Karen. He'd seen her with a number of different men, most recently with Roger Hayden, who worked for the Newenham Telephone Cooperative.

"When was the last time you saw them together?" Diana asked.

He thought. "About a month ago, I guess. They were having dinner at Bill's."

Lastly, Diana had interviewed Jerry at his place, a cramped, barely one-bedroom apartment in a six-plex next door to the Last Frontier Bank. It was painfully neat, partly because it looked like Jerry didn't own much. He scurried into the bathroom after letting her in, probably flushing his stash down the toilet, and she wandered around, poking her nose into this and that. The kitchenette cupboards held four place settings of flowered melamine and a set of Ecko pots and pans. The glasses and flatware were from Costco, and it all looked brand-new. The refrigerator was almost empty but for half a loaf of cheddar cheese, a carton of eggs with one left, and a quart of two-percent milk with a week-old expiration date. The lesser part of a case of Rainier beer filled up the bottom shelf.

The bedroom held a full-size bed, neatly made with white sheets and a flowered comforter that no man had picked out. The dresser drawers were only half full of underwear and T-shirts and socks, and a spare change of bed linens. The closet was echoingly empty, a blue suit, two lighter blue shirts, a pair of black oxford shoes, a pair of sneakers. The suit was inexpensive and so new it still sported a tag. Betsy had probably bought it for him for Lydia's memorial service, scheduled for the following Saturday afternoon.

The baseboard heating clinked as it came on, and the smell of burning dust filled the air. She went back into the living room and sat down gingerly on the nubbed fabric of the hard, narrow couch. On the wall opposite was a velvet painting of the Beatles back when they shaved. Copies of *Alaska Magazine* were stacked in two neat piles on the pressboard coffee table. There was a stereo, in her opinion the only evidence of human habitation, and a collection of CDs, the Beatles, the Beach Boys, the Rolling Stones. Jerry was a rock-and-roll boy.

There wasn't a book on a shelf, or a family photo in a frame, or a birthday card or a graduation announcement on the refrigerator. She'd never seen a lonelier or unlovelier five hundred square feet in her life. It depressed her just to look at it.

The sound of the toilet flushing for the third time faded away and Jerry emerged from the bathroom, ostentatiously drying his hands on his jeans, and sat down on the matching nubby chair next to the couch.

"I'm sorry to bother you so late at night," Diana said, "and I'm sorry to have to ask these questions at a time like this, but can you tell me the last time you saw your sister Karen?"

His thin, anxious face seemed to sink in on itself, but she couldn't tell if it was from grief for his sister's death or apprehension at having to deal with a cop. "Last night, I think. Or was it this morning?" He stopped. "I can't remember, exactly. I can't believe she's dead." He leaned forward. "Are you sure she's dead, ma'am? I mean, couldn't you have made a mistake? Could it maybe have been someone else who got killed?"

"I'm sorry, Jerry. It's Karen. Your sister Betsy found her. There's no mistake."

His eyes were shiny with tears. "She was so cute when we were little. I liked her best of all. We used to hide together from Bossy Betsy."

"Jerry, I really need you to concentrate. When was the last time you saw her?"

"I don't know," he said helplessly. "I think— Oh, wait. It was when we went to the lawyer's."

"What lawyer?"

"Ed. He wrote Dad's will. And Mom's." A tear rolled down his face. He smeared it with the back of one hand, leaving a shiny track down one stubbled cheek.

Diana made a note. "Did Ed read the will to you this morning?"

"No, but he told us what was in it." As an afterthought, he added, "Karen was mad."

Diana sat up straighter on the very uncomfortable couch. "Mad about what?"

"Oh, I don't know. Mom gave away something Karen wanted."

"Do you remember what it was?"

He screwed up his face. "A picture, maybe? It was old. I didn't care."

He was lying; it stuck out all over him. Karen might have been mad about something, but it hadn't been a picture. "Betsy and Stan Jr. were there, too?"

"Yeah."

Diana made a note. "Jerry, was anybody mad at Karen, that you know of?"

"Nobody ever got mad at Karen," he said earnestly. "Everybody loved her. Why, every time I went over to her house, there was somebody there hugging her and kissing her."

Diana gave him a long, thoughtful look. He meant it, every word. "Do you remember who you saw there the last time you were at her apartment?"

He shrugged, and she gave it up for the night. "Okay, Jerry, thanks. I might have to talk to you again." She got to her feet. "Are you going over to Betsy's?"

He looked at his feet. "I don't know."

Translated, that meant that he knew he usually wasn't welcome. "She'll want you there, and you shouldn't be alone. I'll give you a ride over." It was impulsive, and with this family she didn't know if Betsy really would want him, but she couldn't leave him alone in that cold, bare excuse for a home, mourning the loss of the only person left in his family who seemed to give a damn. Or at least Jerry thought she had.

She left him in Betsy's driveway and returned to the

post to type up her interviews. She hadn't discovered a hell of a lot about who might have killed Karen, but some areas of interest did present themselves.

Karen had been upset at the meeting with the attorney. Why? Neither Betsy nor Stan Jr. had mentioned it, only Jerry. She made a note to call them both in the morning, and Kaufman, too.

Karen slept around, most recently with Roger Hayden, the telephone guy. It was almost three o'clock, and Diana was bone-tired. She'd call him in the morning, too.

Karen owned the town house free and clear, no mortgage. Unusual for someone so young, and so unemployed. She also had a very healthy bank balance. If it had all come from her father, and if the other three kids were in the same financial health, Stan Tompkins Sr. must have been a very good fisherman indeed. Diana made a note to ask Kaufman if Karen had a will. If Karen hadn't, as too many people of her age did not, it would be interesting to see where her money went. She'd call Brewster Gibbons, too, to get an update on Karen's bank account. If Karen had so much money, why hadn't she paid off her Visa bill?

Either Special Agent James G. Mason was older than he looked, or he'd had some excellent and intensive tutoring in the horizontal arts. Jo, deeply appreciative, lay flat on her back and stared at the ceiling while she waited for her vision to clear and her heartbeat to return to normal.

"I believe I have just discovered the secret of the universe," Special Agent Mason said. His head was at her feet.

She discovered she had enough energy left to laugh.

"But my thesis may require further investigation," he added, and crawled up the bed to flop down next to her.

Later they conducted a raid on the pop and candy machines down the hall, and curled up on the bed to tear into Doritos and Reese's peanut butter cups, and spiked Diet Cokes with what was left of Special Agent Mason's whiskey.

He touched an experimental finger to her skin. "You know you actually glow when you come?"

"You roar like a lion. My eardrums will never be the same."

"Can't help it. Always do."

"Louder with me, though."

He grinned. "Oh, yeah. Way louder."

She leaned forward and caught his lower lip between her teeth. He angled his head. When she pulled back, she licked her lips and said, "Mmmm. Who taught you to kiss like that?"

"Did the top of your head lift completely away?" he said, as complacent as a twenty-seven-year-old special agent for the Federal Bureau of Investigation can be, stark naked and in bed with a newspaper reporter six years his senior. She pinched him and he caught her hand. "Behave yourself. Or at least wait until I've finished my drink."

"You're no fun." She stuffed pillows behind her and leaned up against the headboard. "You going back to Anchorage tomorrow?"

"I don't know. Colonel Campbell hasn't said." He looked at her, amused. "Is this where I get pumped for information?"

Jo put on her best Scarlett O'Hara voice. "Only if you want to be, sugar."

He reversed to sit next to her, and picked up her hand to trace the lifeline in the palm. "I'm in a pretty good mood at the moment. Pump away."

"Why is Campbell so interested in that wreck?"

"I don't know. I don't, Jo. I really am just along for the ride. It's not every day somebody so low on the food chain gets a ride on an F-15. My number came up and I lucked out."

"That's you. What about him?"

He linked their hands together. "He's determined to haul out this wreck. I repeated everything that pilot friend of yours said to him, but he is determined." He paused.

"What?"

"I think he was always going after it, even before the trooper said anything about the gold this evening. Colonel Campbell was on the phone all afternoon. Every time I tried to call him to find out when we were leaving the line was busy. After a while I figured it must be out of order and I went to his room. I heard him talking through the door." He kissed her hand.

"Don't stop there." He turned with a grin and kneed her legs apart. "I didn't mean that and you know it."

He kissed her, eliciting a long, low purr. "I do like the sounds you make when you're getting some, Dunaway."

Her toenail made a line up the back of his leg. "Tell."

He explored her ear with the tip of his tongue. "It sounded like Colonel Campbell was ordering up some kind of helicopter, one equipped for high altitudes, low temperatures and rough terrain, capable of hovering for long periods. And he wanted it stripped. One pilot, one loadmaster, and nothing else."

She shivered and bit his shoulder. "Room for cargo."

"Be my guess." His lips traveled to her earlobe.

"And this was when?" She hooked one leg around his waist.

"This afternoon. About three o'clock." He moved over her, settling fully into that good old standby, the missionary position, and smiled into her eyes.

She shifted her legs and slid her hands down to his ass. Her voice was a little breathless. "Four hours before dinner, when Liam told him about the coin, which seemed to trigger Colonel Campbell's decision to recover the wreck, which he seemed until then to be willing to leave until next spring, or forever."

"Yeah." He sounded distracted, his attention elsewhere.

"Ahhhh," she said.

"Any more questions?" he whispered.

"No."

"You sure? I can talk and fuck at the same time."

"Not tonight you can't."

"Jesus!"

"Told you."

December 17, 1941

March says were making a special trip to Krasnoyarsk
not a ferry job this time were bringing the same plane back
instead of catching a ride. I asked Roepke and he said how
did I know so I guess we are. I saw the CO talking to
Roepke and they shut up when they saw me and the old
man was pretty snappish when he told me to get back to
work.

No letter from Helen. I wish I could call. I hate not
knowing whats going on I hate it I hate it. I hope shes all-
right. I hope Moms with her.

I talked to Peter. I'm going down to his house again
tonight.

SEVENTEEN

He couldn't believe she'd talked him back into the plane.

He couldn't believe the plane had actually made it back into the air. He couldn't believe it had actually managed to stay in the air over the river to Newenham. Most of all, he couldn't believe it had brought them safely back to earth, rolling out down the length of the one runway the Mad Trapper Memorial Airport boasted with the engine vibrating like a three-legged washing machine.

He especially couldn't believe it when she kicked an abrupt right rudder and they swung off the runway before they'd reached what he would have considered a safe taxi speed. "What the hell are you doing?"

"I don't want anyone to see us. I got enough problems without filling out forms in quintuplicate for the goddamn FAA."

He bit his tongue as they narrowly missed a Beaver tied down at the end of a row of small planes, swung in behind it and taxied briskly down to Wy's shed.

When she killed the engine he sat there for a moment, staring at the sign nailed to the top of the shed. NUSHUGAK AIR TAXI SERVICE, and Wy's phone number, beneath which new paint added in smaller letters, WWW.NUAIRTAXI.COM. He felt he'd never really looked at it before, noticed the brightness of the colors, even in the dark, the inventiveness in the arrangement of the words, the sheer artistry in the lettering.

In fact the whole night felt pretty damn good to him. He stretched out his legs and touched the rudder pedals. "What do these do again?"

"They push the rudder back and forth. Liam, don't—"

"And what does the rudder do, exactly?"

"The force of the wind against the rudder pushes the plane in the direction you want it to go," she said, dumbing it down for her audience.

"You're so cute when you're playing teacher." He grabbed Wy and kissed her, hard. Since she was halfway out of her harness, this proved awkward, but doable.

"Whew!" she said, emerging. "What was that for?"

"General principles," he said, and grabbed her again.

She squirmed. "We've got a perfectly good bed at home."

"It's a twin."

"It's a bed."

"I've always wanted to lay you in a plane."

"Don't con me, Campbell; the only thing you've ever wanted to do in a plane is get out of it."

He was fumbling at the buttons on her shirt. "We're on the ground. Against all odds, against any realistic expectation, we were shot out of the sky and we made it home alive and in one piece. Gimme."

She giggled. He couldn't remember the last time he'd heard her giggle, if ever. They were always so everlastingly serious about everything. "I wanna have some fun," he said. "I want you to have some fun. Come on, Wy." There wasn't a lot of room and the damn yoke kept getting in the way. He finally found the lever that pushed the seat back. It gave suddenly and his seat slid back with a bang. She was half-on and half-off his lap, half-dressed and half-not, and she was laughing so hard that she was no help at all.

"Shit." He rested his forehead on hers. "What am I going to do with this?"

"No point in wasting it," she said. In some fashion best known to pilots she managed to eel backward down into the rudder well, and he forgot the world.

"Oh, yeah," he said lazily, a little later. "That wasn't exactly what I had in mind, but it'll do. I owe you."

She snickered, buttoning her shirt up cockeyed. "You'll pay, Campbell. Oh, yeah, you'll pay. Come on, let's get out of this bucket and go home."

"I've got to check in," he said.

"Why?" She almost wailed it.

He stepped from the Cessna and snatched her up into a comprehensive embrace. "Because it's what I do. Come on."

They drove to the post in the Blazer, and if the state of Alaska had been peering in the windows it would have been shocked at the behavior going on in the front seat of this vehicle, purchased and maintained for the purpose of enforcing the law and apprehending the violators thereof. Once Liam pulled off and for a few breathless moments Wy feared that they were going to do something Liam could arrest them for. A little farther down the road he drove into the ditch, churned through the snow, uprooted a birch and a couple of alders, and skidded back up on the road. "Keep your hands to yourself next time," he said severely.

The post, not surprisingly, was empty, since it was nearly four o'clock. "Five minutes," Liam said, giving Wy a brief, fierce kiss.

Inside, he found Prince's notes in the computer and scrolled through them. The stuff on Karen was interesting. Mad about something in the will, was she? Something Betsy and Jerry and Stan Jr. got that she wanted? Something even loser Jerry noticed she wanted? Badly enough to confront one of them for it? Bad enough to start a fight over it, and lose?

And no visible means of support and a paid-up mortgage, or what looked like one. Although the Visa bill was odd.

The most likely scenario was that the person who had killed Lydia had killed Karen. Lydia had died of a blow to the head suffered in a struggle that could likely have begun without murderous intent, according to Brillo Pad. Lydia's death could have been involuntary manslaughter, not murder.

Karen's death was murder, though. He thought again of her body's outline on the kitchen floor. A murder that had been made to look as if it had been done by someone caught in the act of robbing the house. Thereby suggesting a stranger. Which, ergo, suggested no such thing.

He sat down at his desk and pulled a sheet of paper from the printer. He penciled a square in the center and labeled it *Lydia*. He penciled another square just

below it, labeled it *Karen* and connected the two with a
line. He made three other squares and labeled them
Betsy, Stan Jr. and *Jerry,* and connected them to Lydia
and to Karen.

In the upper right-hand corner he made another
square and labeled it *the boyfriend* and connected it to
Lydia.

The boyfriend hadn't come forward. Could be
scared. Could be guilty. Could be nonexistent; witnesses had been wrong before, and Sharon hadn't seen
the boyfriend, only his flowers. Or flowers Lydia said
had come from him. Had Prince tracked down those
flowers yet? He found a note in the file. She'd called
Alaska Airlines Goldstreak; they hadn't gotten back to
her.

He made another box and labeled it *blackmailer?*
and connected it to Karen. Karen lived a pretty high
and free lifestyle, according to just about everyone.
So far as he could tell, he was the only functional
male in the bay who hadn't slept with her. Ripe for
blackmail. Look at that Visa bill, at total odds with
the paid-up mortgage and bills. If she had money,
and it wasn't going to pay her Visa bill, where was it
going? Except then there was the bank account, a
very healthy ten grand. And why would her blackmailer kill her, thereby killing his cash cow? And it
wasn't like she tried to hide what she did, and she
didn't have anyone to hide it from, no husband, no
children, and her family didn't seem to care one way
or the other.

Odd, that. Lydia was Yupik, at least part, and the
Yupik had some of the strongest cultural ties to family
that Liam had ever seen. The Three Musketeers could

take lessons; it really was all for one and one for all on the Yukon-Kuskokwim River delta. Still, there were dysfunctional families of every race, color and creed. And the Tompkinses weren't dysfunctional, exactly, just not that close. It wasn't a sin, it wasn't all that unusual, and it certainly wasn't a crime.

He looked at Lydia's chair, and remembered what Clarence had said over the chessboard. *That girl had boys buzzing around like mosquitoes, wanting to suck that juicy little thing dry.*

He tried to imagine a teenage Clarence, and failed. He tried to imagine a teenage Lydia, and was more successful. Stan Tompkins Sr. must have been one hell of a guy to come out ahead of the bunch chasing Lydia. She was seventy-four when she had died, which meant she would have been a teenager during World War II. He doodled some numbers. She would have been born in 1926. A kindergartner in 1931, sweet sixteen in 1941, able to vote in 1946.

"Liam?" He looked up and saw Wy yawning in the doorway. "I must have dozed off," she said. "What are you doing?"

"Oh, hell, Wy, I'm sorry," he said, shoving the grid to one side. "I started doodling and I lost track of time."

"It's okay." She slid into his lap and tucked her head beneath his chin. Her firm, soft weight felt very sweet. She looked down at the grid. "Oh, you're doing that square thing you do." She pulled it toward her. "Lydia was born in 1926? God. I wonder what the world was like then. About all I know is they couldn't use boats with engines to fish for salmon on Bristol Bay. Plus we were a territory, not a state."

He stared down at the grid, something tickling at the back of his brain, something he ought to be seeing.

Wy stirred. "She was born in Newenham, right?"

"Yeah. It's on her birth certificate."

"She has a birth certificate?"

"Why wouldn't she?"

"A lot of people her age who were born in the Bush don't have birth certificates. No hospitals and damn few doctors back then. It's hard for Native elders to get social security sometimes because they can't prove they were born in the U.S." Her finger traced the line to the box where he had written Lydia's milestone dates. "Sixteen in 1941. Wasn't that the year that C-47 augered into Carryall Mountain?"

He stared at the top of her head.

"I was wondering if you could have seen the crash from town," she said. "It isn't that far away, and if it was a clear night . . ."

"I need to get a new job," he said.

"What?" She blinked up at him, soft-eyed and sleepy.

"Filing at City Hall ought to be just about my speed."

"Liam—"

"I love you," he said, and kissed her hard.

She blinked. "Okay."

"No, I mean it, I love you, but it's just that right now I love you because you have the one working brain between us." All thoughts of sleep vanished and he dumped her unceremoniously off his lap and pulled a fresh sheet of paper to him. "Look." He drew a grid this time, and put a list of dates down one side. "Lydia was sixteen in 1941. On the night of December twentieth, 1941, a C-47 crashes into Carryall Mountain. Suppose it was clear enough between here and there to see the crash? What would you do if you saw something like that?"

She leaned against the desk, crossing her arms and hugging them to her. "I'd go look."

"You bet your ass you would. Maybe you went looking to aid survivors, maybe you went just to see what you could see, but you would go look, and so would anyone else who saw it happen."

"I'm sorry, what does this have to do with Lydia?"

"Wy. The wreck is found one day, and the next day Lydia is murdered in her own kitchen, with no signs of forcible entry, which means she most probably knew her attacker. And in Newenham, that could be someone she has known a long time. I was just talking to Clarence down to the bar and he has some very fond memories of Lydia in high school. So did Moses. I wonder who else did?"

"I am really, really tired," Wy said. "You're going to have to explain better than that."

"Okay, try this on for size. It's December twentieth, 1941. Nineteen forty-one, hell, I didn't even think of that! Pearl Harbor was attacked two weeks before. We were at war, and Alaska was way too close to Japan. They practically started building the Alaska Highway the next day."

"I still—"

"Think a minute!" He actually gave her a little shake. "The attack had been two weeks before, and it was so kick-ass that the military from Nome to San Diego was expecting an invasion at practically any moment. They would have alerted every American coastal community on the Pacific Ocean to be on the watch."

"So, if somebody saw the C-47 go into the mountain, they might have thought it was the beginning of an invasion?"

"Why not? The blood wasn't dry from Pearl. Midway hadn't happened yet, and Japan looked invincible. So say a guy was out with a girl—Clarence told me the big deal was to get hold of a truck and drive your girl and your friends and their girls to Icky and have an all-day party on the beach at One Lake. That's forty miles closer to Carryall Mountain and Bear Glacier."

"An all-day party on the beach at One Lake," she said, considering. "I hate to rain all over your parade, Liam, but I don't think so."

"Why not?"

"It was December."

"Oh. Oh. Well, hell. Okay, maybe not. Damn it." He couldn't stand it; he had to pace. He rose to his feet and began to quarter the office. "Okay, then they saw it from Newenham."

"Liam, I'm willing to stipulate that they saw the plane go in. They weren't that long out of Nome and they were probably pretty heavy with fuel, so it probably went off with one hell of a bang. I just don't know," she said pointedly, "what all this has to do with Lydia."

"If I'm right, it has everything to do with Lydia. Listen, Wy." He sat down again and pulled a third sheet of paper toward him. "Here is Lydia, sweet sixteen, out on a date with one of her many swains." He drew two boxes, one Lydia, one swain. "It's evening—what did they say; they think the plane went in around midnight. Maybe they're parking and making out."

"Did they make out in 1941?"

"Then *boom!* and fire on the mountain. They're curious, so they go take a look. The plane is a total loss, but something has been thrown clear."

"What?"

He looked at her. "Gold."

She snapped her fingers. "The coin!"

"What if there were more of them?" He drew another square and put all Lydia's kids inside it. "One thing that's been bothering me, all the Tompkinses have enough money not to work. I know the bay used to be a bonanza for salmon fishermen, but I don't see anyone else in Newenham with a lifestyle like theirs. Most of the old-timers, their houses are paid off and some of them their boats, but they're still out there hustling for anything with fins that swims into range. Lydia, yes, I could understand her being provided for, but the kids, too, and so well? Well, what if the money came from Lydia, not Stan Sr.? What if it came from what she and her date found at the crash site?"

"She could have gone up there alone."

"Then she'd still be alive." He sat back. "And then, sixty years later, the wreck resurfaces. I bring the arm to Bill's and everybody sees the coin."

Wy was still puzzled. "I still don't understand. Why was Lydia killed?"

He was sitting in Lydia's chair, and he thought of her again as he had seen her the evening he met her, feisty, strong, independent, with a bawdy eye and a fearless spirit. "Maybe she wanted to tell the truth, that they'd stolen the gold from the crash site. Maybe he didn't want her to."

"Who, Liam? Do you know who?"

He looked down at the sheet of paper, and traced over the outline of the box marked *swain*.

"Yes," he said.

EIGHTEEN

"I love younger men," Jo said, bouncing into Wy's house an hour later. "Give your friend Mr. Wiley my compliments, and tell him I said so."

"First thing on my list," Liam said.

Jo peered at Wy. "You look like you've been up all night."

"So do you," Wy said, and shoved a cup of coffee at her and another one at Liam.

Jo perched on the stool next to Liam's. "Your father is a piece of work," she told him.

"Tell me something I don't know," he said before he thought, and then scowled away any lingering trace of willingness to discuss his father with the press, or with anyone, for that mattter.

Jo sipped her coffee, looking at him over the rim of her mug. "He came here planning on retrieving that C-47."

Liam sent Wy a warning glance, and shrugged. "So? Like he said, the air force brings back its own. Nothing new or wrong in that." He kept his inevitable reflections to himself.

"This wasn't an ordinary crash," Jo said. "I just got off the phone with a friend in D.C. This wasn't an ordinary crew on board this flight, either."

"What do you mean?"

"The copilot's name was Aloysius March."

Liam and Wy exchanged glances. "That name supposed to mean something to us?"

"Aloysius March was Walter March's father."

"And Walter March is . . . ?"

Jo huffed out an impatient sigh. "How the hell am I supposed to make a living if my own friends won't read my own paper?" Snit over, she smiled, and it was a low-down, mean, dirty, nasty little snake of a smile. "Gen. Walter March is the nominee for chief of staff for the U.S. Air Force."

They absorbed that in startled silence. "So Dad's going after his boss's dad's body," Liam said. "Sucking up to the nth degree, one more step up on the career ladder, but so what?"

"He's using air force funds to do it."

"I'm shocked—shocked—to hear of misappropriation of funds going on in the U.S. armed forces," Liam said, very dry.

Wy agreed. "I don't see the big scandal here. Like he said, he's going after three of their own. I don't think that's a bad thing, frankly. I think it's kind of, I don't know, right. We're still looking for the bodies of American servicemen in Vietnam. We should be. How is this any different, other than being a different war?"

Jo added half-and-half to her coffee. "I don't think recovering the bodies of the honored dead is what this is about, Wy."

"Why not? Why does it have to be any more complicated than that? Honest to God, Jo, you see more conspiracies than John Birch."

"Maybe you're right, Wy, maybe I've been in the newspaper game too long, I can't see the simple truth when it's staring me in the face. But I don't think so. Not this time, anyway."

"Why not?"

"Because I asked my friend to pull the service records of the three crew members."

"And?"

"And he couldn't. They're listed as classified."

Moses' side of the bed was empty when Bill woke up. She found him down at the bar when she got there, back in the office growling at the computer. "If this keeps up, I'm going to hire you to keep the books," she told him.

"I'd rather spend the rest of my life listening to Puff Daddy," he said. "Look at this."

She came around the desk to look over his shoulder. "Oh, man. Are you back at that?"

"I think it's important."

"Think, or is something telling you so?"

He leaned back. "I'm telling you, babe, there's nothing going on here except my nose is itching."

"I can fix that," she said.

He dodged her hand. "Where's the coin?"

"I gave it to Liam."

"Damn it. I'd like to get another look at it."

It was an hour before opening and she had time to humor him. "Tell me why you think it's important."

He decided to give her a little history. "The U.S. didn't even make twenty-dollar gold pieces until the

California gold rush. Until then, 1849, the U.S. minted only one-dollar, two-fifty, five-dollar and ten-dollar gold coins."

"Two-fifty?"

"Yeah, I know. But we used to have a two-dollar bill, don't forget. The early nineteen hundreds, man, they were making some cool-looking money. The buffalo nickel, the Mercury dime, you know the guy with wings, and the dime was still silver back then. The quarter with Lady Liberty on it." He pulled a handful of change from his pocket and slammed it down on the desk in disgust. "Look at this crap. That could be Albert Lincoln who owns the Ford dealership, and Greg Washington who plays forward for the New York Knicks, and I can't even tell who the guy on the dime is. Plus, ain't none of them made of enough of any precious metal to actually be worth what the face value on the coin is. Always assuming you can read it without a microscope."

Moses was very indignant. Bill concealed her amusement. "But our coin was minted in 1921, didn't we figure? That's not even a hundred years old."

"Well, I haven't quite figured out how valuable it is," he admitted. "There's a lot of stuff I don't understand, like grading and luster and I don't know what else." He thought for a moment, and added, "I got tangled up on an auction site and accidentally bid five hundred dollars for one, though."

"You did what!"

He looked a little sheepish. "It's okay; somebody outbid me. It went for five forty-nine."

She whistled, and he nodded. "So I been thinking, Bill."

She matched his tone. "What you been thinking, Moses?"

"I been thinking there might have been more of those coins on that plane."

She sobered. "I don't like the sound of that."

"Me, either," he said grimly. "Imagine the treasure hunt a rumor like that would start."

"It's already started." She told him about the Gray gang. He swore. She looked at the monitor screen. "It's too bad Lydia isn't still alive."

"Why?"

"She knew about coins."

Moses stared at her.

"It's true. She had a collection of old American coins, old quarters and nickels and dimes and pennies, just pocket change really, that she'd been saving up since she was a kid. She subscribed to a magazine, *Quarters R Us* or something like that. I used to see it lying around the house when we were at her place for book club." She brightened. "In fact, I'd forgotten all about it, but I think she had some other, more valuable coins, too. Yeah, I remember she pulled out an album one time, it was really cool, had all these little pockets inside it for each individual coin." She smiled. "She was annoyed with me, because I was more interested in the album construction than I was in the coins." Her smile faded. "You know, now that I think of it, she might have . . ." Her voice trailed away.

Moses' face had gone very hard. "Might have what?"

"It's silly, it couldn't possibly . . ." She met his eyes. "I've got to be wrong about this, Moses."

He was inexorable. "Wrong about what?"

"Now that I think back, she might have had one of those coins in that album. Just like the one that was in the hand."

Wy had a pickup in Ekwok she couldn't get out of, so Jo accompanied Liam to the post. They arrived at the same time as Diana, who looked as drug-out as Liam felt. He brought her up-to-date. She listened, nodding, and when he finished said, "Makes sense to me. I just rousted Brewster Gibbons out of bed and hauled his butt down to the bank. Karen bought her town house for cash."

"How much?"

"A hundred and twenty thousand."

"Jesus. What'd she do, write a check?"

"She did, and this is the interesting part. She didn't have much left over."

"Her bank balance looks pretty good."

"Yeah, but that's the least amount it's ever been. Gibbons says she's been steadily depleting her trust fund."

"What else?"

"While I was at it, I checked on Lydia's finances. Her house is paid off, too, although that's not quite so surprising. I checked on the other kids. All of them have very healthy cash balances, and none of them have any outstanding debts, at least not with Brewster's bank. Jerry's balance is just as healthy, it's just that every check has to be cosigned by his mother."

Liam frowned at the figures she'd scribbled. "Healthy. I'd call that filthy rich, myself." He picked up the phone and dialed a number in Anchorage.

It rang five times before Jim picked it up. "Yeah."

"Jim, it's Liam."

"Like I didn't know." There was a protesting female murmur in the background. "Sorry, honey. I'll take this in the other room; I have a feeling I'm going to have to get on the computer."

"Thanks, Jim."

"Fuck you, Campbell. What do you want?"

"I need everything you can dig up on the Tompkins family in Newenham." He gave Jim the names. "I'm particularly interested in their financial affairs. If they owe any money, if there is any money coming in. Like that."

"Gee," Jim said without enthusiasm. "Is that all?"

"And I need it in thirty minutes." Liam hung up on the resulting explosion and looked at Diana. "Go down to the school. See if they've still got records for who was enrolled in high school in 1941. Make it for four years either way. Since the students are in their seventies, there probably won't be any surviving teachers, but ask anyway."

"Gone." She went.

Liam looked at Jo. "I meant to ask you. Where's Gary?"

She smiled. "I sent him home first thing this morning."

He leaned back and gave her a long, considering look, which she met with equanimity. "Did you, now."

"I did. That was a mean, rotten thing to do to you, Liam, and I'm sorry."

He cocked his head. "Once more, with feeling."

She laughed. "Look, Wy's the best friend I ever had. For a few months, she was even my sister-in-law. Friends watch out for their own."

He couldn't resist. "Like the air force."

"Even better than. The thing is, I got this idea you might be bad for her. You were, the first time around."

"No, I wasn't."

"No?"

"No. For Wy, the first time around I was a fucking disaster."

"Thank you for not making me say that," she said primly, and grinned.

"So I'm not a disaster this time?"

She met his eyes head-on. "No. Understand me, Liam, I can get along with the devil himself, if the devil is dating my best friend. Nothing gets in the way of the friendship, not for me. Loyalty is what I do best."

"It's my favorite thing about you."

She looked surprised, and suspicious, and maybe even a little flattered. "Wy's family. Wy loves you. That makes you family, too."

"A cop and a reporter," he said. "It'll never last."

She laughed again. "That's what they said about Chuck and Di."

The phone rang. "Okay, you prick," Jim said, "get a pencil." He dictated rapidly, without checking to see if Liam was keeping up. "That do you?"

"That does me just fine."

"Dunaway there?"

Liam was surprised. "How did you know?"

"I know everything. Put her on."

Liam handed Jo the phone. "Somebody wants to talk to you."

She took it. "Dunaway." She listened for a moment. Liam watched as her face flushed a deep, dark red.

"None of your goddamn business," she said, and slammed the phone down. Liam got his fingers out of the way just in time.

"What was all that about?"

"None of your goddamn business either," she snarled. "Just so you know, Campbell, that family business doesn't extend to your friends."

"Okay," he said, and refrained from any comments about younger men because it seemed safer. He made a mental note to call Jim back at his earliest opportunity.

"What do we do now?" she said, seeming to master her rage.

"I don't know about *we*," he said. "I'm going out to the base."

"Can I come?"

"No."

The base officer quarters was of a piece with the rest of Chinook Air Force Base, freshly painted and tidy, the sidewalks neatly shoveled and the storm windows fastened down. He found Charles in the same room he had stayed in that summer. The colonel was surprised to see him and, Liam thought, somewhat wary. "Come on in," he said.

Liam closed the door behind him. "What's with the crash site, Dad? What do you expect to find?"

"I expect to find the bodies of three men who died serving their country in time of war," Charles said.

"One of whom fathered the man currently nominated for the air force spot on the Joint Chiefs of Staff."

Charles looked startled and then rallied. "Who he happens to be related to doesn't lessen his sacrifice."

"No," Liam admitted. "But there's something else." He was suddenly sick of the dance they always did. "Ah, hell, Dad. Wild Bill Hickok died in 1876."

Charles was taken aback. "I— What?"

"The coin we found with the arm was minted in 1921."

"Oh," Charles said blankly. A sudden and unexpected grin spread across his face. "I never was a very good liar."

Liam sat down without invitation in the room's only chair. "Unless you're doing something illegal by recovering that plane and the bodies of the crew, and I can't see how you are, I don't care why. I just don't like being bullshitted. I can keep my mouth shut." After last summer, Charles had to know that was the absolute truth. "Tell me enough so that I'll want to and I'll go away. Or I'll buy you a beer, or take you caribou hunting, or whatever you want."

They stared at each other in silence. It was hard to tell which of them had been more surprised by Liam's words.

Finally Charles said, "You'd really take me caribou hunting?"

"Sure." Liam shrugged. "I've never been, but there's a hell of a herd northwest of here, the Mulchatna herd. Hundreds of thousands of them, the Fish and Game's practically begging people to go shoot some so they won't eat themselves out of house and home and wind up starving to death."

The years of armed truce weren't easy to shake. "I don't know, Liam, you might shoot me and bury the body, once you got me out there."

Liam got to his feet, disgusted.

Charles rose, too. "Don't go, Liam. It was a joke. A bad joke, I admit, but it was a joke. Sit down." He hesitated. "Please."

Liam couldn't remember his father ever having used that word with him before. He sat down again, partly because he wasn't sure his legs would carry him to the door.

Charles reached for a plain buff file marked *Restricted Access* in big red letters and held it up. "The official investigation into the crash."

"What happened?"

"It was too clear."

"What?"

Charles smiled. "I know, doesn't make a lot of sense, does it? But it was. Unlimited ceiling, fifty-mile visibility. It was too damn clear, and too cold, and the aurora was out in full force, hanging right down to the ground, if you can believe the eyewitnesses. All the colors they come in and all over the sky. There was no distress call from the crew, no indication that anything was wrong."

"What were they doing so low? And weren't they a little off course?"

Charles' laugh was short and unamused. "A little. Their flight plan was for Krasnoyarsk. Instead, they were on a heading for Dutch Harbor. Either their instrumentation was off or they were, or they were just blinded by the lights. A couple on the ground saw the fireball when they impacted, and then a plume high up on the mountain. They called a pilot who was living in Newenham at the time, some Scots name . . ." He thumbed through the file.

"DeCreft?" Liam said. "Bob DeCreft?"

Charles looked up. "That's right. How did you know?"

"One of the original Bush pilots. He'd lived here a long time. Go on."

"DeCreft was in the air within the hour. Said in his interview that he followed a creek up so he wouldn't get fuddled—his word—by the lights. Said he saw the impact site at the eleven-thousand-foot level, and then where the remains of the plane had fallen three thousand feet onto a glacier and into a crevasse."

Liam was silent for a moment. "I don't understand, Dad. Why are you so hot to pull this particular wreck out? Everything Wy said was true; it'll be difficult and damn dangerous. Not to mention which the weather around these parts is not at its most reliable at this time of year. Your people could be getting themselves into some serious trouble."

"I know that, Liam. I'm not doing this because I want to; I'm doing this because I've been ordered to."

"Is it because the father of the guy who's going to be your boss was one of the crew members?"

"No," Charles said. He shook his head. "If only it were that simple."

Trust builds trust. "Does it have something to do with the fact that the service records of the crew are classified?"

Charles regarded him with exasperation and, if Liam was not mistaken, maybe even some pride. "So you know that, do you?"

"I do."

Charles looked at the file, and set it to one side. Elbows on his knees, he linked his hands and stared at them. "The copilot's name was Lt. Aloysius March, and yes, he was General March's father. But there were two other members on board that flight. One was the pilot, a Capt. Terrance Roepke. The other was a navigator, a Sgt. Obadiah Etheridge."

"Where were they going?"

"Officially? Krasnoyarsk."

"And unofficially?"

"Oh, they were going to Krasnoyarsk, all right. After they had refueled, they would have continued on to Attu, and made a big circle back to Anchorage by way of Dutch Harbor."

"They were hunting."

Charles nodded. "For the Japanese fleet. It was right after—"

"Pearl Harbor!"

"Who's telling this story? Buckner and Eareckson and the rest of them were expecting an invasion at any moment. They wanted intelligence. This flight wasn't the only one of its kind."

"What makes this one special?"

Charles was silent for a long moment. Liam kept quiet, thinking that if he did so he might actually hear the truth.

"There was reason to believe," Charles said, very carefully, "that there was a spy on board."

"What kind of a spy? A Japanese spy?"

"A German."

This was starting to sound like the script for a movie. "I still don't get this mad rush to recover the wreckage. Let it lie, Dad, and the story will die with it."

"Orders. From General March himself." Charles smiled thinly. "We don't know which member of the crew was a traitor."

Understanding came at last. "And General March is afraid it is his father."

"Yes."

"Which would not be good for his confirmation hearing."

"No. And then there's that damn gold piece."

"Why does it bother you so much?"

"I'm worried there might be more of it," Charles said in a level voice. "And if there was more—"

"You're worried about what it was going to be used for," Liam said. "Smuggling? Spying? Sabotage?"

Charles nodded. "Any or all of the above."

"There was more gold, once," Liam said, and had the satisfaction of seeing his father look surprised.

"How do you know?"

Liam told him, and at the end said, "May I see the file?"

Charles hesitated for only a moment before handing it over.

Only one of the names of the two people who had witnessed the crash surprised him.

December 19, 1941

We go tomorrow. Its cold as hell. Peter showed me a poem by this guy Service which is about another guy named Mcgee who climbs into the furnace of a ship to get warm. Man if there was a ship with a furnace around here Id climb into it too.

We got the briefing on the route this morning. Supposed to be CAVU all the way. The Bering Strait is frozen over so it fucking well better be clear as a bell or were not going to know which way is up. The forecast calls for clear but this weather can turn completely around in twenty minutes or less you just never know. I asked Roepke what our mission was and he put his hands over his ears and looked under his bed. I don't think Hitler gives a shit where were going. But the emperor of Japan might so maybe hes right. They told us to pack enough for a week so I reckon we won't be gone long.

No letter from Helen. No letter from Mom. I dont know whats going on but its a real war now and I cant think about that. There might be something I can do though. Ive got to try anyway.

Peter gave me a present of a brown leather valise. Its old but nice and it looks smaller than it is. Ill have to recalculate the fuel load.

NINETEEN

Eric Mollberg's small, neat house perched on the extreme edge of the bank of the Nushugak River, where it looked as if it was of two minds, either to take flight or to topple down the cliff. It had a yard full of outbuildings, and a power line looped its way down the driveway between poles. A snow machine sat next to Eric's dirty white pickup, which Liam recognized on sight from having pulled it over half a dozen times since he'd come to Newenham. Next to the pickup was a small drifter on a trailer. The name of the drifter was the *Mary M.*

A red Nissan longbed with a white canopy was parked in back of the boat. "Shit," Liam said, and parked in back of Eric's truck.

"It's open," he heard Moses yell when he knocked, and he went in.

The kitchen had that thin layer of grime and that faint odor of fried everything associated with many men who live alone. That said, the dishes weren't piled too high in the sink and Liam wasn't afraid to take the seat opposite Eric, who sat nursing a mug in his gnarled hands. "Eric," he said.

"Liam," Eric Mollberg said without looking up.

Liam nodded to Moses. "What's up?"

"You still got that gold piece?"

"Turned it over to the air force."

"There was a bunch more where that came from."

"I was getting there."

"I figured. That's why I came out here."

They both turned to look at Eric, who seemed to shrink visibly in his chair. "I didn't mean to do it," he said, his voice quavering.

Liam stifled a sigh. The annals of criminal investigation were riddled with pleas of "I didn't mean to do it." If everyone who hadn't meant to do it hadn't actually done it, law-enforcement agencies all over the world could go to half-strength and no one would ever notice the difference. He got out his notebook, in which he rarely wrote a word but which worked remarkably well to fascinate and intimidate suspects. "Can you tell us about it, Eric?"

He was in love with her, with Lydia, madly, passionately, crazily in love. So were most of the junior and senior men at Newenham High School. Might have been because there were five guys for every one girl. Might have been because she was just so damned pretty. Lydia Akiachak was the belle of Newenham High School, and she had picked him. She'd picked him to take her to the Christmas dance at the high school, and after the dance she hadn't said no when he suggested driving out River Road to watch the northern lights. There was a place where they went to park, and somebody had been out to the end of it that morning and told him that the snow was packed down enough to make it there. He didn't care if they never made it back.

So there they were, and just about the time things were getting interesting they saw the fireball. They drove back into town and told the first pilot they found, Bob DeCreft, who was two days away from leaving after he'd joined up. Bob went up to take a look, and when he got back told them the wreckage was right on the top of Bear Glacier but that it was about to slide into a crevasse, and that there was nothing they could do. But Lydia, she was that kind of girl, she wanted to check for survivors, even though Bob told her there couldn't be any out of that wreck. What about parachutes? she said. What if there's somebody hung up on the edge of the mountain, just waiting for us to come get them?

So they went. Bob said they were nuts and he refused to go with them, but he loaned her his bibs and boots and they drove straight from the airstrip to Icky and then up the trail to the little airstrip the CCCers had put in the summer of '38, back when they were surveying the refuge. It wasn't a long hike after that, and what with all the lights it was bright as day out so they couldn't get lost. The glacier wasn't that hard to climb, maybe because the snow was piled so high along the sides and it was firm enough not to go through when they walked on it.

They got to the wreckage about five in the morning, by his watch. Some of it was still smoking. A lot of it had already slid into the crevasse, the edge melted by the heat of the pieces of the plane. There were some body parts on the snow, and a headless body sitting in the front part of the plane. The smell was awful. They were both horrified, and in a hurry to get away from it, when she stumbled over a charred leather bag. It was heavy, and she hurt her foot. It made him curious, so he opened it. And that was when they found the coins.

"There were hundreds of them," Eric said, a faraway look in his eyes. "Gold coins, sewn into individual pockets in long strips folded over on each other. It was like . . . treasure. We'd found it; it was ours."

So they'd hauled the coins down the glacier and back to Newenham. Eric was all for selling them for the weight of the gold; it would be easy enough in Alaska. Lydia knew something about coins, though, and she made him wait while she wrote letters and waited for replies. It took most of six months, by which time the Japanese had invaded Attu and Kiska, and Alaska was really and truly at war. He joined the army and left Lydia and the gold coins behind. When he got back, four years later, she had married Stanley Tompkins the month after Eric had left, and already had one kid.

"I always wondered about Betsy," Eric said. He gave Moses a covert look. "I made it my business to look up her birthday. The time was about right. I figured then, I owed it to Lydia to leave her and the coins alone. And then I met Mary, and I did good for myself and for her, and, well, I didn't think about those damn coins anymore."

You were just married and starting a family, Liam thought. The entire world was recovering from the war. Sure, you didn't think about the coins.

"The years went by, good years," Eric said. "And then Mary died. And my life was over."

Or that's what he'd thought, until Lydia came

knocking at his door three months after they'd put Mary into the ground. Stan Sr. had been dead four years by then, of course. She was lonely, she said. She knew he was, too. Seemed foolish to be lonely when they lived right down the road from each other, and had known each other for so long, and at one time so well.

For four months everything was wonderful. The overwhelming ache of loneliness receded, and Lydia astonished Eric by showing him that he was still inter ested in sex. They left Newenham separately and met in Anchorage for the Fourth of July holiday; she stowed away on the *Mary M.* and they motored down to Chichagof Cape and back one sunny July week; they went over to Egegik to his grandmother's fish camp and skinny-dipped in the lagoon like they were kids again. It was a halcyon four months.

And then he had to go and ruin things by proposing. She wouldn't marry him. She didn't want to marry again, not after Stan.

That was when he realized that Lydia really had loved Stan, that she had most probably never loved him. That was when he realized that Betsy probably was Stan's child, after all. That was when he realized that Lydia hadn't waited even a month after he'd joined up before she slept with another man.

He still loved her, but sneaking around, as fun as it had been in the beginning, didn't look attractive in the long term. Marriage or nothing, he said. Nothing, she said.

"That was when you went on the toot," Moses said. "We all thought it was some kind of delayed reaction from Mary dying."

Drunk seemed to be the easiest way to get through it, so Eric did his best to drink the town dry. Even that wasn't enough.

Then they found the wreck of the C-47. And the arm. And the gold coin. The memory of the night the plane had crashed and he and Lydia had hiked up the glacier returned full-force. He'd forgotten it, until he saw the coin.

He went to her house and told her. Maybe we should tell, she said. No, he said. He was a town councilman, a city father; he had the respect of everyone in Newenham. You did until you fell down a bottle, she said. He slapped her. She slapped him back, and called him names. He grabbed her and shook her, and she fought and pulled away and tripped and fell against the counter. He was just trying to calm her down, trying to talk some sense into her. And then she was dead.

"Why did she want to tell about the gold?" Liam said.

Eric looked at Moses. "You know what she was like. A good woman, a righteous woman. She said we stole that gold. She said she'd sold the coins to a collector Outside to finance Stan's first seiner. She said her family was rich because of that gold, and that her children were ruined because of it. I think she thought if we told that it would reverse things somehow. I don't know how. It wasn't like we could give it back. We never knew who it belonged to in the first place, and Lydia said it was illegal for people to own gold back then so we'd never be able to find out."

"What about Karen?" Moses said.

Eric hung his head. "She knew about the gold. She'd heard her mother talking to her father when she

was little. All she heard was that her mother and me
had found some gold when we were kids, and she decided there had to be some left, and that I knew where
it was. She wanted some, and she called me to meet
her at her mother's house."

"And you strangled her."

"She said such hateful things, things about her
mother. Things about how her mother slept around
with a hundred men and how I shouldn't think I was
anything special. And then she got into details. Things
about how when she was short of cash Lydia was too
busy spending money on her men to give her daughter any. How Lydia had written her a check for five
thousand and said that was the last of it. Then she
started in again on the men, and what she'd seen Lydia
and Stan Sr. doing when she was a kid. And there we
were, standing in the kitchen of her own mother, the
woman I loved."

The woman you murdered, Liam thought.

"I was trying to rip her tongue out, tell you the
truth. There was no bearing it. She had a mouth on her,
that girl." He clasped tough, stringy hands together on
the table. "She just wouldn't shut up. So I shut her
up."

The three men sat in silence. Outside, snow was
falling softly in big fat flakes. Snow had a quality of
hush like no other, Liam thought, a muting, calming
influence. Peace.

"How did you know we flew up to Anchorage last
night?"

"What?" Moses said.

Eric looked sheepish. "Oh, hell. I was in the bar
when Wy called Bill to come stay with her boy. I fig-

ured it'd be easy enough to take a shot at you on the
way home. I know the flight path for the approach into
the Mad Trapper; I live right under it. I took the skiff
across the river and . . ." He shrugged and dropped his
head.

Moses shot to his feet and began slapping Eric's
head, open-palmed slaps with the full force of his arm
behind them. "You old fuck! You were shooting at my
granddaughter!" He started slapping with both hands.
"Get on your feet! Get up! Get up, goddamn it, so I can
take a decent shot at you!"

Eric cringed away.

"Goddamn you, Cal, we've known each other since
high school! What the hell did you think you were
doing?"

"Moses. Moses. Moses!" Liam came around the
table and pulled Moses away. "Knock it off. Just calm
down, now."

Moses backed down, fuming.

Perfect peace, all right.

"You called him Cal," Liam said.

"It's his name," Moses snapped. "Calvin Eric. We
called him Silent Cal in school, when we were studying Coolidge."

The *SC* on Lydia's calendar. Silent Cal.

"Calvin Eric Mollberg, I'm arresting you for the
murders of Lydia Tompkins and Karen Tompkins. You
have the right to remain silent. You have the right to an
attorney. . . ."

TWENTY

"Sad," was Wy's verdict.

"Pitiful," Liam said. "You know what I hate?"

They were lying in Wy's bed, the infamous twin-size bed that was too short for Liam on both ends and too narrow for both of them to sleep in side by side. It wasn't a problem for either of them at the moment, but Wy had a feeling it was right around the corner. "What do you hate?"

"I hate stupidity. I hate incompetence. I hate ignorance, and ineptitude, and all those other words that begin with 'I' that denote idiocy. For crissake, Wy. The man's seventy-five years old, he's lived a mostly blameless life, he was a good husband, a good father, a goddamn pillar of his community. Now he gets to spend what's left of his life locked up with a bunch of drug dealers and child molesters and, of course, his fellow murderers. I mean, Jesus! Can you see him in a cell with Gheen?"

She tucked herself more securely into the curve of his body. "I don't think they're going to put anybody in with a serial killer, Liam." Although she had liked

Lydia a lot and it wouldn't have hurt her feelings if the Alaska Department of Corrections in their infinite wisdom had decided that Gheen and Eric Mollberg were destined as cellmates.

"And Lydia. Goddamn it. I liked her. Hell, I think I was halfway in love with her. I told you about her beaning Harvey with the jar of tomatoes, didn't I?"

"About five times. And they were sun-dried tomatoes."

"She was a great old gal. She flirted with me. Seventy-four and the juices were still running. And come to find out she's who she is because she's a grave robber."

Wy had known Lydia some, enough that Lydia had offered her a place in the Literary Ladies book club, but Wy's job kept her in the air so much she would have missed meetings the entire summer. She had declined, but every now and then she'd run into Lydia at the post office and they'd trade titles. "I liked her."

"Everybody liked her. A lot of people loved her. Some downright lusted after her, even after she was a grandmother, too. Doesn't mean what she did was right."

Wy had spent more time in the Bush than Liam had. "Someone would have come along and taken it."

"Human nature, I know, I—"

"No, Liam." Wy squinched around until she was facing him, her butt hanging precariously over the edge of the bed. "Nothing ever goes to waste in the Bush. She had a good use for it; she bought her husband a boat. That gold was like the Blazo cans they beat flat into shingles, and the fifty-five-gallon drums they turn into stoves. It was like when a SeaLand cargo ship hits a storm and washes everything overboard and it all floats up on shore. Finder's keepers. It's the law of the land."

"She was saying they should tell at the end. She must have known it was thieving when she did it if it came home to roost sixty years later."

"You think she'd been agonizing over it all these years, wallowing in her own guilt?"

Liam thought of some of the interviews he and Diana Prince had done. "No."

"She lived her life, right through up until the end. I think," Wy said, propping herself up on an elbow, "I think when she heard about the plane being found and the arm and the coin, that maybe she thought it was time, that was all. It wasn't an attack of conscience." She tapped his chest. "But Eric Mollberg heard it that way because he was feeling guilty. He was happy to shuffle off the burden of the coins to her in the first place, happy to join the army and go off to war. She was sixteen, Liam. She wasn't a criminal mastermind; she was just an opportunist, like everyone else who lives in the Alaskan Bush, like everyone needs to be to survive."

She smiled down at him, and in a lightning move he reversed their positions. "I'll make you a deal."

"State your terms."

"I won't take the job in Anchorage if you get us a bigger bed."

She flushed a faint, rosy pink. "Do you mean it, Liam?"

"I emphasize the one word in that sentence that means the most: bigger."

"I don't want you to stay in Newenham for me,

Liam, or for Tim. I want you to stay here because you want to stay here."

"Not king-size, that'd be too big, I'd never find you."

"I mean it, Liam. I don't want to live my life having to be grateful to you because you stayed with me the second time around."

"A double isn't big enough. My feet would be bound to stick out over the edge, and I hate that."

"I don't want you to turn down a job you really wanted just because I don't want to leave Newenham."

"A queen," he said, kneeing her legs apart and coming into her. "Now that would be juuuust right." He kissed her thoroughly.

She looked up at him, tears in her eyes. "Are you sure? Are you very, very sure?"

"I am very, very sure."

Her nose ran when she cried. It was very, very unattractive, and he waited while she fumbled a Kleenex off the nightstand and blew. It was very, very unromantic.

"Liam?"

"What?"

"Will you marry me?"

His eyes widened. He smiled, a long, slow, sweet smile.

"I thought you'd never ask."

She called Gary the next day before her first flight. "Gary? It's Wy."

His voice warmed. "Hey, girl."

"Jo sent you home, huh?"

"Yeah, she said it would be best." He paused. "And it was. Wasn't it?"

"It was." She took a deep breath and let it out slowly. "You're part of my college days, Gary. You're part of my youth. I'll always care. I'll see you at—"

"Don't," he said, and hung up.

" —Thanksgiving at your folks' house," she said to a dial tone. She replaced the phone gently in its cradle. She'd hurt him, and she knew it, but her future was here.

With Liam, and Tim, and Bill, and Moses. She smiled.

Moses was sitting on a stool at Bill's. Bill was nowhere to be found. "Arraigning Eric," Moses said.

"I'm sorry, uncle," she said. "I know he was a friend of yours."

"This one I never saw coming," he said, and tossed off the rest of his beer. "Who says there's no god?"

"Come to dinner tonight. Bring Bill."

"I'm sorry," he said suddenly.

"Why? What for?"

"For being your grandfather. For making you who you are. I'm sorry as hell. A man like me has no business scattering his seed around."

She was hurt, though she tried not to show it. "Come to dinner tonight. You and Bill. A family dinner."

His face was creased with weariness, and for the first time in her eyes he was showing his age. His smile, when it came, was lacking its usual malice. "You sure you don't want to keep your distance?"

"I'm sure." She sounded surer than she felt, but he

was her grandfather, he'd owned up to it at last, and she wasn't going to let him draw back. She might not have that much time left to learn from him.

"I'm good for a while yet," he said, and laughed his rich, knowing laugh when he saw the expression on her face.

They went back up to the crash site two days later, after the snow stopped falling, to watch Charles' crew pick at the remains. There was an open fracture of the tibia before the morning was out, and in the first fifteen minutes after lunch a dislocated shoulder and a near miss with a calving chunk of ice. The crew chief flatly refused to put his men back to work after that. His men were in complete agreement.

"I could probably court-martial the lot of you," Charles said.

"You probably could, sir," the man agreed. "But at least we'd all still be alive while we were locked up in the brig."

Charles sighed. "Pack up your gear and head back to base."

Liam, listening in the background, stepped forward when the men moved off, carrying a stretcher. "So we'll never know who the spy was, or if there even was one. Or who was carrying the gold, or why."

"Short of a written confession discovered under a rock up on that glacier, miraculously intact after all these years, no."

"The general won't be pleased."

Charles removed the aviator's cap that looked so well on his head and smoothed down his hair with the same hand. "Ah, hell. Fuck him if he can't take a joke."

They laughed together.

Wy, picking her way over a fractured slab of ice, which was now covered with a foot of snow, heard the sound and smiled to herself. Campbell *pere et fils* seemed to be getting along better. Good.

Something prickled at the base of her neck and she shivered. The temperature was dropping, or so it seemed. Her feet carried her forward, a little too close to the face of the glacier for Liam's comfort. "Wy, don't get so close to that damn thing!"

She didn't hear him, the prickling at the base of her neck driving her on. She waded through snow to another slab of ice and peered into a dark blue hollow.

"Wy!" Liam was coming up behind her. "Wy, come on, get back."

He stopped beside her. "What are you looking at?" When she didn't reply, he bent over and looked. "What's that?"

He reached inside the hollow. It was narrow and very deep, and he had to stretch to find anything. It was a tight fit, too tight. He stood up and pulled his arm out of his parka and reached inside the hollow again. This time his hands closed over it, a book, short and wide, maroon in color and embossed with very faint gold letters. The flash of the letters was what he had seen, winking up at him from inside the hollow.

" 'The Standard Pilot Logbook,' " he read out loud.

He opened it up carefully, afraid it would fall apart in his hands. The pages were damp but the writing on them was still legible. "Sgt. Obadiah Etheridge, pilot navigator, U.S. Army Air Corps," he read, followed by a serial number and an address in Birmingham, Alabama.

He turned the page.

Thanksgiving, 1941

Turkey and stuffing in the mess. It was awful. The cook runs a laundry in Memphis Tennessee in civilian life. He says he told them that when he signed up and doesnt know how he got assigned to be a cook. Typical army situation normal all fucked up.

"That's one of our guys," Charles said, coming to stand at Liam's shoulder. He looked at Wy, standing mute before them. Her face looked bleached of color, and her expression was strained.

So was Liam's. "How the hell did you know it was there?"

December 20, 1941

Im writing this in the air. We took off in the dark but then its dark all the damn time up here. It was so cold the fuel wouldnt ignite at first and for awhile I dint think we were going to make it up. I saw Roepke come out of the old mans office before we took off. March was watching too. Wonder what lluate ahout he said to me. I dont care I just want to do the job and get back.

Captain Ross had to have his lower lip cut away because of frostbite.

I wonder if I could transfer to a base closer to home. If I told the old man about Helen losing the baby maybe hed okay it. Maybe not, because theyre expecting the Japs to invade any minute now and theyre bringing more men in all the time. Everybodys coming north nobodys going south. I have to do my duty. We got us a real war now.

Its okay though, after this trip Ill have some more money to send her and shell be okay for awhile.

I hope shes okay. Helen, I love you. I wish you were here. The northern lights are all over the sky all different colors red and white and green you wouldnt believe how beautiful.

Have to take a bearing now.

COMING IN OCTOBER 2003
FROM SIGNET MYSTERY

SWIMMING WITH THE DEAD
An Underwater Investigation
by Kathy Brandt   0-451-21020-4

Summoned to the sun-drenched beaches of the British
Virgin Islands, Hannah Sampson is fully prepared to
face unknowable dangers beneath the crystal-clear
water of idyllic paradise—But the possibility of murder
runs deeper and darker than the sea itself.

WHO LET THAT KILLER IN THE HOUSE?
by Patricia Sprinkle   0-451-21019-0

Georgia magistrate MacLaren Yarbrough is back in a
brand-new Thoroughly Southern Mystery...A black cloud
covers the town of Hopemore, Georgia, when a favorite
teacher is found dead. But if this is murder, darkness
may be lurking in places where even sharp-eyed
MacLaren would never think to look.

**Available wherever books are sold, or
to order call: 1-800-788-6262**